About Roland Cheek Western Sagas

Stan Lynde, much loved Western writer and creator of the cartoon strip Rick O'Shay says of Roland's Echoes of Vengeance: *"Cheek paints his young protagonist's odyssey with a deft hand, portraying the values of courage, principle, and friendship on a canvas as broad as America itself."*

Fine Western author Richard Wheeler has this to say of Roland's Western writing: *"Like Louis L'Amour, Roland Cheek knows how to start a story at a gallop and hold the reader to the last page. He writes richly and authentically about the Old West, drawing from an encyclopedic knowledge of his subject."*

The Billing's Gazette says of Bloody Merchant's War: *"... Cheek takes the struggle beyond the usual disputes over land, animals and political power, beyond the race and divisions that leave [Jethro] Spring caught between the Native American blood of his mother and the so-called civilized world of his white father. While all these elements drive action in the novel, what sets the book apart is the struggle for men's souls."*

Roundup Magazine, publication of the Western Writers Association, had a similar take on the same book: *"A fascinating look at the Lincoln County War from another perspective, with highly charged dialog that will shock you like a live wire, and genuinely living characters. There's nothing two dimensional about the folks in this book."*

The Tulsa World has this to say of Lincoln County Crucible, the conclusion of Roland's two Lincoln County sagas: *"Roland Cheek has used the history of the

Lincoln County War and gives it a fresh twist. The dialogue is extremely well-done and the action scenes are alive with excitement."

Now comes Gunnar's Mine, fourth book in Roland Cheek's sweeping *Valediction for Revenge* Western series featuring the adventures of wanted murderer, Jethro Spring, outcast progeny of a Blackfeet mother and mountain man father. Gunnar's Mine takes place in southwestern Colorado, near Telluride. It's a story pitting lonely independent miners in a life-and-death struggle with one of America's greatest (and greediest) mining corporations. Again, Jethro Spring is caught between right and might.

Non-fiction Books by Roland Cheek

Learning to Talk Bear

Phantom Ghost of Harriet Lou

Dance on the Wild Side

My Best Work is Done at the Office

Chocolate Legs

Montana's Bob Marshall Wilderness

GUNNAR'S MINE

GUNNAR'S MINE

ROLAND CHEEK

a Skyline Publishing Book

Copyright 2003 by Roland Cheek

All rights reserved. No part of this book may be reproduced or transmitted in any form or by any means, electronic or mechanical, including photocopying, recording or by any information storage and retrieval system—except by a reviewer who may quote brief passages in a review to be printed in a magazine or newspaper—without permission in writing from the Publisher.

Cover design by Laura Donavan
Text designed and formatted by Michael Dougherty
Edited by Narelle Burton
Copy edited by Jennifer Williams

Publisher's Cataloging in Publication

Cheek, Roland.
    Gunnar's mine / Roland Cheek: author ; Narell Burton, Jennifer Williams: editors. — 1st ed.
    p. cm. — (Valediction for revenge ; 4)
    ISBN: 0-918981-11-5

    1. Frontier and pioneer life—West (U.S.)—Fiction.
    2. Placer mining—West (U.S.) 3. Hardrock mining—West (U.S.)
    4. Southwestern Colorado—Fiction. 5. Western stories.
    I. Title.

    2003

ISBN: 0-918981-11-5
LCCN: 2003104368

Published by   Skyline Publishing
                       P.O. Box 1118
                       Columbia Falls, Montana 59912

Printed in Canada

Dedication

To Larry and Alice, Lyle and Phyllis. Forty years of steadfast friendship must be worth more than they've thus far received from our winsome smiles and distinct pleasure of being in their company.

Chapter One

"For a good man ay look, ya?"

The hum of conversation died in the rough-hewn room. Jethro Spring spun on his stool made of a pine block, not realizing he was the one being addressed. His gaze almost passed over the kid with the oversized mackinaw coat and baggy trousers that he'd watched sidle into the eatery a few moments before. Only this kid wasn't a kid at all—not with such a deep voice, Swedish accent, and rutted face. Even sitting on the pine block, Jethro's gray eyes were still at a level with the pale, watery orbs of the little man addressing him. "I'm sorry," Jethro said. "Were you talking to me?"

"The horses outside. Dey are yours?"

"The sorrel mare and the gray with the top pack? They're mine. Why?"

"Dey are cared for good. To treat animals so is not always done in this place. Such a man is one ay want for work. Yew will do so, ya?"

Jethro smiled. The little runt had a black and white dog sitting at attention at his feet—maybe some shepherd in it. The mutt's ears were at half-mast, with orange-brown eyes riveted on her master. But when Jethro twisted to get his bowl of soup and swung back, the dog read the move as a threat and leaped to her feet, ruff standing aloft, teeth bared.

The little man let an arm fall, palm extended and the dog fell back onto her haunches, staring up attentively. "Yew will work?" the dog's master asked again.

Jethro sensed that every eye and ear in the log building strained their way. "There are five other men in here. Why me?"

"For me, ay would not let dem work. It is yew ay want."

A ripple of muted laughter swept the other men crowded at the plank counter. Jethro began spooning soup. Between spoonfuls, he said, "Hell, little man, I'm an Indian. You want to hire an Indian?"

Pinched lips showed the Swede's annoyance. "Is Indians not able? It is work yew need. Ay have work. Is this not so?"

Jethro finished his soup and laid the bowl on the plank at his back. "I just rode in here fifteen minutes ago, yet you seem to know a lot about me. That's plumb amazing if true."

"Is true. Is night, soon will be. Is cold. If money yew had, yew would stable your horses. If money yew had, yew would have more than soup, ya? Yew are hungry. Your face shows yew are hungry for long time. Snow will soon come. Your horses will then be hungry."

Jethro's was a thin smile. The Swede continued, "The shoes of your horses are no goot. You come from above, over the mountains and you have far to go. You must soon work. You will do so for Gunnar, ya?"

Jethro dropped his hand to the dog, who licked her

Gunnar's Mine

lips and avoided the hand, continuing to stare adoringly at her master. "What the hell," he said at last. "If you treat your hired help as well as you must treat this dog, I could probably do worse." Jethro stuck out a hand and developed a new alias on the spot. "I'm Jason Frost. And you're who?"

The little Swede took the hand with one that was calloused and hard. "Ay am Gunnar. Einarssen, too." The Swede signaled the cook. "Bring dis mans some meat, Walter. One who work's with Gunnar, he must eat like horse."

One of the other patrons laughed. "Hell! He'll *be* meat if he works for the runt."

"The horses, ay will take to stable," Gunnar told Jethro. "While yew eat, ay will do this. Then we go to cabin."

Jethro slid from his pine block. "No pard. I take care of my own horses. You got your rules; I got mine. I'll eat when I get back." He paused. "That is, I'll do it if you'll take care of the stable bill."

The Swede nodded. "Next door is stable. Walter is owner."

An alpenglow washed summits of the eastern hills as Jethro Spring untied the sorrel mare and his gray packhorse from the hitchrack. He kicked at a clod, knowing he needed the work—no doubt about that. But what kind? Must be a mine. Hell, he knew nothing about mining. Closest he'd ever been to a pick and shovel was building roadbeds for rail lines. Well, he wasn't in any position to be choosy. This looked like as good a place as any, perhaps better than most, to shelter for a few days, or weeks, or even months. Especially for a man with 'JETHRO SPRING—WANTED, DEAD OR ALIVE' posters out on him.

Inside the stable he stripped the pack and saddles from his horses, wondering why the little Swede chose *him*. Five other men were inside and the Swede came straight to *him*. What was it the little man said? That they wouldn't work "for me." And "I wouldn't let them—it is *you* I want." Then one of the others at the counter had said, "He'll be meat if he works for the runt." What did that mean?

He rubbed down each of the two horses, first the sorrel mare, then Baldy, the gray. Then he took them to stalls and forked hay into their mangers. He decided he'd find out soon enough what the Swede meant, and headed back to the log-and-wattle eatery.

The other men were gone when Jethro entered. A long-barreled Colt lay upon the counter near the little man's hand. The new workman threw saddlebags and bedroll into a corner.

"You had to fight them other guys off with a gun, Gunnar? That why you're called 'Gunnar'?"

The watery blue eyes turned on him. "They don't scare Gunnar." There was no smile.

"Did they try?"

The little man turned to his steak. An even larger steak was set before Jethro. A few minutes later, the Swede said, "Ay have mine. Nordic Summer is name. Is like beautiful woman. Yew will see."

The mine might be like a beautiful woman, but wading the San Miguel to get to it was a tad annoying, and as far as Jethro could make out in the flickering candle-light, Gunnar's tiny cabin failed the luxury test. There was one bunk, a table consisting of two warped planks laid across a pole frame, two small-diameter pine blocks for chairs, and a cookstove. Empty dynamite boxes standing on end served as cupboards.

Gunnar kicked a few odds and ends from a corner and said, "To sleep, yew will do so here. If stay yew do, we will build bed."

Jethro picked up a straw broom and swept out his

corner as best he could in the uncertain light. The black and white dog crawled under Gunnar's bunk and soon began snoring. It seemed to the younger man that he'd just fallen asleep when pans began rattling in the cabin. When he sat up, Gunnar said, "Soon will be day. We will not waste it."

The little man, holding a pan, paused on the way from stove to table to watch as Jethro buckled on his gunbelt. He opened his mouth to say something, then set the pan to the table and turned back to the stove. Jethro took a dipper of water from a galvanized bucket perched on the stove. Outside, not knowing where—or if—there was a wash basin, he dribbled water over his hands, splashed some on his face, and brushed his teeth with a forefinger. Back inside, he took a pine block and dug into flapjacks and sidemeat.

Later, he pulled a dishpan from the wall, filled it with hot water, and pared soap flakes into it. Gunnar crowded to the stove. "We do our own, each of us," he said.

Jethro shrugged. "Does that mean we each cook our own? After I get squared away, that is."

Gunnar ignored him to wash his plate, cup, and pans. Then the little man pulled on a mackinaw coat. "If ready yew are, den yew should follow." Jethro jerked a sheepskin-lined canvas coat from his bedroll and hurried behind the dog. He'd almost finished buttoning the coat by the time they reached the mine tunnel.

Daylight filtered weakly into their valley as Jethro paused to stare about. The shaft, roughly four feet in height and width, was cut into an imposing, sloping rock wall of reddish basalt that Jethro remembered from his days laying steel, almost directly east from here, across the summit of the Rockies, through the Arkansas River's Royal Gorge. The little Swede, bent over, had continued into the mouth without pause as Jethro eyed his surroundings in the growing light. Beyond the redrock wall were mineralized outcrops of grayish-green and brownish-red intrusions in southeast to northwest lines.

Gunnar's face appeared at the tunnel mouth. "Yew see Nordic Summer, ya? She is thing of beauty, yew betcha."

Jethro grinned and waved the other back. So low was the tunnel ceiling, he had to drop to his hands and knees in order to crawl forward. The tunnel floor was mostly sand and small gravel, slanting downward at an almost imperceptible angle. Up ahead, a rhythmic banging began. When he arrived at the headwall, the dog growled at his approach and Gunnar murmured something in Swedish. At the command, the dog curled into a ball and thrust her nose to her tail.

The Swede had a drill bit in his hand and was 'single-jacking'; driving the bit into the wall with a short-handled, four-pound sledge. "Is called a" (bang!) "single-jack," he grunted. "Yew must twist" (bang!) "after yew strike."

"Gunnar," Jethro said, "I've used a single-jack. But there's not enough room for us both to work in here. Even if I knew where you wanted me to drill, and even if there was another drill and sledge, there's not enough room. I'm not sure ..."

"This one yew have. Ay will work outside." The little man handed Jethro the drill and sledge, then crowded past to allow his workman room at the tunnel's headwall.

The younger man crept forward, took a sitting position, set the drill in the depression left by the Swede and, in the dim light, took a practice swing, two, three. Then he delivered a heavier blow, twisted the drill, then another.

"A drill yew have used before," the Swede murmured from behind. "Yew have worked the mines, ya?"

Gunnar's Mine

"Nope," his workman grunted. "But I've drilled a little rock."

A few moments and a dozen blows later, Jethro paused to catch his breath and ask, "Where's the spoon?"

In reply, Gunnar handed him a long rod with a tiny dipping spoon on the end. Jethro took it and scooped the rock dust from his hole. While he did so, Gunnar crowded forward and with a forefinger, spotted places for four other drill holes in the tunnel wall. As he turned away, the stooped older man's watery eyes passed inches from the seated younger one's. Jethro thought something passed between them in that brief moment and wondered what it was.

When Gunnar retreated a few feet, he stopped and squatted on his heels, wrapping arms around knees, again watching his workman swing the sledge. "The powder. Yew work?"

Jethro paused and shook his head. "Not if you're using black. I've seen some dynamite handled—even done a little myself." He swung again and added, "But I'm not comfortable with it and probably not safe enough with it." More swings, and when he looked around to see how the little Swede accepted his admission, his boss was gone.

The morning slipped by. He finished one hole to such depth as he could spoon rock dust and began another. He was in the second hole to several inches when the light dimmed at the tunnel entrance and Gunnar and his dog appeared. "Ay will swing the hammer. Yew will eat. At cabin is meat and potato."

Outside, Jethro glanced at the clear, blue sky and breathed deeply. A robber jay squawked from a scrub juniper and a pine squirrel scurried after cones he'd recently cut from surrounding trees. The man took another deep breath, sighed, and smiled. After a few moments he strode to the murmuring creek, drank his fill and washed rock dust from his arms and face. Then he turned toward the cabin and stopped abruptly. Its door was open.

Jethro drew his revolver and slipped forward, moccasin-soled boots barely whispering on the path. With only the barest pause, he leaped into the cabin and darted to one side, out of the beam of doorway light. A man looked up in surprise, a fork filled with slices of Jethro's steak halfway to his mouth. The stranger wore a rough-cut, broadcloth suit and a wide-brimmed, flat-crowned brown hat. The coat was buttoned to the top, but an open-necked, white shirt peeked from the throat. He wore wire-rimmed glasses.

Seconds passed. The only movement was the thumb on the revolver hammer, the only sound the "click" as it was eared back. Then the fork and steak and hand and arm ratcheted to the tabletop and the stranger said, "Who the hell are you?"

Jethro slid three feet further right, into deeper shadow between the open door and the cabin's single muslin-covered window. "For starters," he replied, "you're eating my dinner."

The stranger never blinked. "That so? I thought it was the Swede's." He laid the fork and steak on the plate and dusted his hands, then started to push back from the table.

The roar of Jethro's .45 was deafening in the tight space. Splinters flew from the tabletop and the stranger jerked both hands above his shoulders.

"Explain," the gray-eyed man said, "and make it quick."

"I'm a friend of Einarssen's. I stopped by to see him. I thought he'd fixed his dinner and stepped out. I thought he'd laugh when he came back and found me eating it. Touchy bastard aren't you?"

"Name?"

"Whittle. I own a claim down to Placerville. Can I put my hands down?"

"Get up first."

The stranger—Whittle—scooted back and stood. The right flap on his thigh-length, broadcloth coat thrust out from his side.

"Lay your gun on the table, but do it careful."

The man did as instructed.

"Any more?"

"No. I ain't no gunhand."

"Now get out of here. You can come back tonight and get your gun. Do it after Gunnar comes back. That's the same time you and him can laugh off your eating my food. That's also the same time you can find out if I'll laugh with you."

Whittle stalked slowly to the door, his face blank. But all the while, the man stared through the wire-rimmed glasses straight-on into Jethro Spring's flat, gray eyes.

Chapter Two

"You know a man named Whittle?" Jethro asked as he took the drill and sledge from Gunnar.

"Ay know him."

"Says he's a friend of yours."

"A friend he was. Now, no. Why yew ask?"

"He stopped in to see you." Jethro began swinging the sledge. "I told him to come back" (bang!) "when you're home." (bang!)

As the stooped-over Gunnar and the dog shuffled toward the light at tunnel's end, the younger man continued, "He was" (bang!) "in your cabin, sitting at your" (bang!) "table, eating my dinner" (bang!) "and it pissed me off."

If Gunnar or the dog heard, they made no comment.

Gunnar's Mine

The dog came first when the two returned, trotting up the tunnel to the last bend, then turning back after analyzing the work's progress. Gunnar soon appeared, bent and obviously weary. "Is too dark for work. Let's go to the cabin, ya?"

"I'm ready." The younger man leaned the sledge, spoon, and drill bit against the tunnel wall and began crawling out behind his boss. As the men exited the Nordic Summer, the same alpenglow washed the same peaks as it did the evening before.

"Gunnar," Jethro said as they made their way down the trail, "what is it you're looking for here?"

"Gold."

"Okay. I see a big rubble heap outside the tunnel, but why aren't you crushing it and panning it?"

"No gold is there."

The men stopped at the creek and slipped from their shirts and trousers, wading into the icy water. The dog, inseparable from her master, waded after Gunnar. Jethro asked, "What's your claim size? Does it take in the black and brown outcrops on the ridge above?"

"Ya."

Soon the men stood on the bank allowing themselves to drip-dry in the gathering gloom. As they were slipping into their trousers, the dog shook herself, spraying water droplets over Jethro. He grinned and asked, "Why aren't you punching into those dikes? There must be minerals there. Why cut a tunnel into hardrock where there's no minerals?"

Gunnar fastened the second strap on his overalls and belted his middle with a rope. "We feed the stock, then eat at Walter's, ya?"

At the cabin, Gunnar ran his fingers over the splintered hole made when Jethro fired his gun into the table planks. "Why yew do this t'ing?"

"I was hungry and I wanted to get the bastard's attention."

A fleeting smile—the first Jethro had seen from the little man—swept quickly over Gunnar's face. "Den what?"

"He got real attentive."

"Who was more—how yew say it—pissed, what?"

Jethro grinned. "Can't say. But I had his gun and mine, too."

Andrew Whittle came for his revolver the following morning while Gunnar hammered together a bunk for Jethro, and Jethro hammered the remaining "shot holes" in the tunnel headwall. The younger man never discovered what was said between the two, but the revolver was gone and a blank quit-claim deed covered the bullet hole in the table when he returned to the cabin for his noon meal.

Meanwhile Gunnar packed the holes with dynamite, fusing them to blow simultaneously. The little man was ambling down the trail to the cabin when he met Jethro returning to the tunnel. "We work no more dis day. Ay won't go in tunnel same day is blasted."

The explosion came while they were at the stream. Jethro whirled in time to see a puff of dust blow from the mine mouth. The Swede turned with him, but instead of the tunnel, he studied the mountainside above. Finally the little man fumbled for a pipe, stuffed it with tobacco, tamped it, and struck a match. "Tomorrow. We go in and see if all holes blow clean. Den one will drill more holes, while other, the rock he will move."

At the cabin, Gunnar set a half-empty bottle of whiskey on the table. Jethro brought two cups and pulled the cork with his teeth. Gunnar, he noted, poured very little for himself.

"What ay would like," the elder man said, "is to drill wall each day. Den as we leave, set fuses."

"A foot a day," the younger man mused. "That's ambitious, isn't it?"

Gunnar puffed on his pipe. "Ay don't know what yew say."

"Can we do it? A foot each day?"

Gunnar shook his head. "Will need drill bits made sharp. Ay will go to Telluride for this."

"How many drills do you have, Gunnar?"

"Two is what." Then the little Swede's face went passive. "Four is what ay had. Two were needed by somebody else."

"Stolen? Do you mean they were stolen?"

When the little Swede said nothing, Jethro murmured, "They must have been stolen by a miner."

"Or to stop a miner."

Jethro turned his gaze to the ceiling. "Your drills need sharpening now, don't they Gunnar?"

"Ya. Maybe one day. Maybe two. Maybe t'ree."

"And you've got to go clear to Telluride to find a blacksmith to do it?"

"Ya."

"Why not lay in a bigger supply of drills?"

Gunnar knocked the dottle from his pipe, then thrust the pipe inside a mackinaw pocket. "No money," he said as he rose and headed for the stove.

"How about I fix supper?" Jethro said. "You can tell me what you plan while I do it."

Gunnar wadded up the blank quit-claim deed and used it for fire starter. "Beans is good," he said. "Ay have big pan soaking."

"I'm real good on bannock bread, too. And fitter'n a fiddle if there's oatmeal to mix with the flour."

Gunnar turned, a smile cracking his rutted face. "Ay have an onion, maybe, ya?"

Jethro clapped his hands and shouted, "Beans and onions and bannock bread! Who could want more?"

Later, while the pinto beans boiled, the younger man pumped the other about how he came to the San Miguel....

The little Swede, already nearing middle-age, stepped from the boat in New York City and promptly bolted West. With no fixed destination in mind, he wound up at Promontory, Utah in 1869 and while the first transcontinental railroad was being spiked together, Gunnar walked into the Wasatch Range before making his way back to Colorado's Front Range. Along the way, the little man picked up a few rudiments of placer mining.

Patience, he had, but patience might have been his only asset. Eventually, years later, Gunnar Einarssen found himself at the 'grand junction' of the Gunnison and Colorado Rivers. While there, he heard of a new strike in a place called Placerville, on the San Miguel River. Though the seasons approached winter and the more direct route across the Uncompahgre Plateau would be dangerous for a foot traveler, the little man still determined to try his luck there. So Gunnar chose a second suicide route, descending the Colorado on a makeshift raft to the mouth of the Dolores River. Providence perched on his shoulder, for the little man made it without more mishap than several soakings of his meager belongings. At the Dolores, he followed that

Gunnar's Mine

river upstream to its fork with the San Miguel.

Usually hungry, sometimes thirsty, but always determined, Gunnar Einarssen arrived at Placerville in late March of 1880, at a time when most of the gold-bearing gravels were claimed and largely panned out. Then news hit of a discovery only a few miles upstream in a fold of spectacular mountains. Placerville was abandoned in the stampede.

Gunnar didn't think much of the tellurium, sulphur, and selenium compounds containing telluride gold and, having no hardrock experience, headed back down the San Miguel. He camped across the river from the the mouth of Fall Creek and just before turning in one evening, tried a pan of gravel. Only a couple of flecks were left after what had obviously been extensive past panning and sluicing. So the Swede shrugged and lay down under a tree to consider his fate.

The following morning, carrying a shovel and pan, Gunnar waded the river and hiked a short way up Fall Creek to do additional exploratory work. On the way he was attracted by what he thought an ancient streambed coming in from beneath the basalt rock rising to the south and west. Puzzled, the little man dug out a crack in the dry streambed and washed a pan of gravel in the nearby rushing creek. The pan's bottom winked yellow after he'd flushed away the topsand and picked out the pebbles.

The little man smoothed over evidence of his dig and followed the ancient streambed up to the basalt cliff. There he filled another pan with gravel and sand and carried it back to the rushing little stream. It, too, winked yellow.

Gunnar filed a standard 50 X 400-foot placer claim on Fall Creek, then followed with the more extensive 300 X 1,500-foot hardrock claim on the basalt hillside over the ancient streambed. Cannily, the Swede claimed 'discovery' rights on the hardrock district and was awarded an additional 300 x 1,500 feet. The placer gold from the ancient streambed maintained Einarssen's placer claim and the assessment work he did on his tunnel met the hardrock requirements.

Towards the end of Gunnar's tale, it finally became apparent to Jethro that his employer's objective was to track the ancient streambed, hoping to strike the source of gold somewhere beneath the overlaying igneous rock. "But Gunnar," the younger man asked when the thought struck, "how can you be sure you're following the old stream upstream? The tunnel is sloping down."

Again came the fleeting smile. The little man broke off a piece of bannock and, sopping his beans with it, said, "Someday ay show yew how stream washes gravel and it lays it one way. Why tunnel goes down now can only be one t'ing—the ground pushed up, maybe when volcano sends stuff over. But is true. Down streamed from here is up from where gold came from."

After he and Gunnar washed their dishes, Jethro carried a fresh bucket of water from the stream. Later he straddled a pine block and leaned back against the cabin wall, musing aloud, "Placer gold is fine, usually pretty much dust. It can be carried for miles down a stream. How far do you intend to follow the old streambed? Hell! Tunneling a foot a day, it can be farther to the source than either of us have time to live."

In reply, Gunnar rummaged behind his bunk, then threw a tobacco sack to the younger man. The sack was weighted with what Jethro knew without looking was gold—obviously in nugget form. What he didn't expect, until he poured them into his palm, was the size and angular shape of the nuggets.

"From old stream," Gunnar said. "Not washed far, yew t'ink? Break from quartz vein, ay t'ink. Ahead is vein. Rich, we will be, you betcha."

Gunnar's Mine

The entire afternoon had been fascinating for Jethro. And when he slipped into the soogan that lay atop his new bunk, the young man's thoughts were filled with Gunnar's dream.

———•••———

Gunnar was so eager to explore rock exposed by yesterday's blast that it was still dark when he and his workman entered the tunnel with candles. The little man and his black and white dog hurried forward, while the taller Jethro had to crawl after them, sliding a shovel and coal bucket ahead. When he arrived at the headwall, Gunnar had already examined the rubble and was turning from the wall in disappointment. He took Jethro's shovel and coal bucket, saying, "Yew drive. Ay will carry rock." When Jethro held the shovel for a moment longer than necessary, the Swede added, "To crawl, ay don't."

So Jethro spent the morning punching holes in the tunnel headwall while Gunnar carted rubble. Then, just before noon, Gunnar brought in four, large, canvas bags and had Jethro hold them one by one for him as he shoveled gravel from the exposed ancient creek bed into the sacks. After he'd loaded a sack with as much gravel as he could carry, he set it aside and began filling another. When all the sacks were loaded, the little man, struggling with one, disappeared down the tunnel, saying "Yew bring one, too."

After they had the sacks outside, Gunnar said, "Yew go to eat. Beans there still is. And bread. Ay will drill."

Jethro shook his head. "You haven't eaten either. When do you eat?"

"No time," the little man said, waving a hand. "Go."

Jethro draped an arm over the little man's shoulders. "We'll eat together, Gunnar. If we don't blow that hole today, we will tomorrow. Life is too short for us not to see a little of it as it runs by."

They ate silently, Gunnar hurrying as if begrudging every lost mine-moment; Jethro hurrying out of deference to his little boss. Then Gunnar paused while focusing his watery eyes on Jethro. "Yew not ask how much ay pay. Why?"

"That's not important to me."

"Is not smart."

"Maybe not, but it's Jethro-ish." He knew he'd erred the moment it popped out and he dipped his face to his plate.

"Ay do not know 'jethro-ish'. What is?"

The younger man kept his face down. "Aw, it's just a saying, Gunnar. Means I don't really care how much I earn. Long as me'n the horses live, that's enough."

He raised his eyes and his friend shrewdly said, "Yew mean Jason-ish, ya?"

Jethro carried his plate to the water bucket. "Let's get a move on. That drill's a-wastin'."

While Jethro returned to driving the drill, Gunnar busied himself outside. Periodically he carried a sack of wet gravel and sand back inside, spreading it over the area where it originated. "Find anything" (bang!) "worthwhile?" Jethro asked.

Both the Swede and his dog ignored the question to scurry back outside. When Gunnar returned with the last sack, he watched Jethro for a few minutes, then said, "Next time we make tunnel bigger. For more room so yew can stand and swing. Drive faster."

Jethro handed the sledge to him and crawled for daylight. The dog came with him. Outside, the dog still wouldn't allow Jethro to touch her, but she did sit in the tunnel mouth all the while Jethro stretched nearby, and gazed up through pine needles and bare aspen limbs to watch fleecy clouds scudding overhead.

Sounds of distant banging traveled the 200-foot

Gunnar's Mine

length of the tunnel. When the dark-faced man pushed to his feet, the dog trotted down the tunnel.

"What is her name?" Jethro asked, waving at the dog as he took the sledge.

"Odina," came the reply. The dog wagged her tail and licked Gunnar's boot.

"Odina," Jethro said. The dog ignored him.

Gunnar wanted six holes drilled for the next blow. Only four were done by day's end. The little Swede did have supper nearing completion, however, so after Jethro had bathed and walked down to feed his horses, the boss and his workman crowded to the table.

"The bits, ay must take to Telluride," Gunnar announced.

"How will you take them?"

"Walk. Is way ay always do."

"That will take you two days, even if you can get a blacksmith right on 'em. Ride my gray horse and it'll only take one."

Gunnar stared at the wall behind Jethro and said nothing.

Finally the younger man cleared his throat and said, "Gunnar, the drills are dull because you haven't the money to pay for sharpening them, right?"

There was no reply. "Yet you have at least some gold, I know. Why don't you use the gold I saw to buy what you need for you and the mine?"

There was no reply.

Jethro pushed from the table, saying gruffly, "Well, I'm not sure what's going on. Maybe, on the other hand, I ain't supposed to. Hell with it, I'm going for a walk."

Without breaking his focus on the wall, Gunnar began speaking: "If dey see the gold, dey will know. No longer will ay be 'the crazy Svede' digging in a mountain."

Jethro settled back to his pine block.

"Just the placer dust, enough to survive, is what ay use. And ay hide the rest. 'Crazy Svede' is what ay want them to t'ink."

Jethro thought about what he'd been told. Then a puzzled frown came over the younger man's features. "I still don't get it. Why would someone steal your drill bits in order to keep you from mining if they don't already know?"

So Gunnar told the rest of his tale.

After the hardrock breakthrough at Telluride, disappointed miners who'd worked the gravel at Placerville remembered the odd-colored outcrops in the hillsides above their placer diggings. They returned to file hardrock claims and began digging into those hillsides in earnest. Some of the quartz ledges rising prominently to the surface proved promising, but the ore was terribly refractory and costly to reduce. The ore, however, did show sufficient promise to attract the attention of outside investment capital. Recently, a major mining company had moved into the area via staking claims, and by buying claims already held by others.

Thus far, most of the activity had centered on the hillsides east of Placerville. Only lately had there been focus across the river, on the Fall Creek area. Only lately had outside attention turned to the outcrops of green and blue copper carbonates, turning rusty brown from iron discolorations, and black stains of zinc that Jethro had found interesting. Claims surrounding the Nordic Summer had been filed, but as yet little activity had taken place.

"Dey offer to buy," Gunnar concluded. "Dey do dis and dey don't even know about the gold."

The dog stuck her nose on Gunnar's thigh and the man idly scratched an ear. Jethro propped his chin in his hands and stared morosely at the bullet hole in the

Gunnar's Mine

tabletop. Directly, the dark-faced man said, "And you're afraid to convert gold to cash for fear everybody will be on to you?"

Gunnar nodded. "Dey know me to be poor and crazy. Is best way."

"Yet you have to have enough money to get the things you need—like an ore truck and rails out of the tunnel. Like drill bits and sledge handles and shovels." He looked around and added, "Candles. God we're almost out of candles. And another water bucket. Probably blasting powder, too. Caps and fuses. Winter clothes."

Gunnar softly added, "Money to pay the man ay hire."

"You've got it, and can't convert it."

Again, Gunnar shook his head.

Then Jethro said, "But I can."

Chapter Three

Gunnar walked to the wall where his mackinaw coat hung, pulled out his pipe and tobacco, came back to the table and filled the pipe. Then he struck a match, touched it to the tobacco and blew out a satisfying cloud. Finally he stared at Jethro and said, "Say what yew t'ink."

Jethro shook his head and said, "Maybe I wouldn't trust me, either. Then again, almost nobody knows I'm here. What is it—Whittle? Walter? Those other four or five guys in Walter's place the night you hired me? Hell, I can ride out of here and nobody'll know I've been here, or gone. Winter's not come, so I can still get over the Uncompahgre to Montrose or Gunnison or Grand Junction. Grand Junction would be better because it's bigger and farther away.

"I can sell the gold, buy the equipment and supplies we need and get back here, still without anyone knowing. Take a week; maybe ten days. If I can find anyone

Gunnar's Mine

downriver to winter my ponies, I can turn right around and take'em there without anyone knowing I've been in and out. I can do it, Gunnar. I know I can."

The Swede studied him for a full five minutes, blinking only once in the interim.

At last, Jethro said, "Give me no more gold than you'll need to get by. Hell, I wouldn't risk everything on me, either."

Gunnar blew out the candle and said, "Ay will take one of the drills for to sharpen tomorrow. The other holes, yew can drill."

Gunnar left on Baldy at daylight, the little black and white dog trotting behind. After seeing them off, Jethro returned to the cabin, drank another cup of coffee and headed for the mine. He emerged in late afternoon, went directly to the cabin and sawed and split several blocks of aspen wood. Then he sauntered down to the creek to bathe. It was nearing dark and overcast when Jethro Spring returned to the cabin after feeding his sorrel mare. At last he cooked some potatoes and heated the remaining beans, ate and went to bed.

It was well after midnight when Gunnar and the dog returned. The little man lit a candle, and said, "If leave yew are to do, den while others sleep is time."

Jethro slid from his soogan and into his trousers. Several full Bull Durham sacks were scattered on the table. "The gray horse ay left eating hay and oats," Gunnar told him. "The mare ay gave oats, too. Extra food for yew is in packbags for gray."

The Swede handed a letter to Jethro. "Is in Svedish. Is for Vidkun Bloomquist. He farms below Redvale. Him ay want to winter your horses."

"When?"

"When yew get back."

"How much gold is on the table, little man?"

Gunnar shrugged. "Find one to trust who weighs it,

that is all ay ask."

Jethro said no more. Ten minutes and he was gone, bedroll over one shoulder, saddlebags over the other. Not even a dog yapped as he passed through Placerville. Trusting no one, he left the road, skirting along the base of the Uncompahgres until, sometime around noon, he came to the first big bend of the San Miguel. There he turned northeast, reaching up and into the foothills until he found a freshwater spring and enough grass for his ponies.

Off-saddling and hobbling Baldy, then tying the mare, he carried a telescope and his Winchester to a high knob and spent a couple of hours watching his backtrail. Finally convinced no one trailed him, Jethro returned to his horses, bringing in Baldy and turning the mare loose in hobbles. Then he rolled into his blankets as a thin snow began falling.

At daylight, Jethro caught the mare and loosed the gray. Knowing he carried enough gold to make him a target for every bandit in southwestern Colorado, he again carried the telescope to the knob to study the land below. At last he slipped the telescope closed and smiled. No one followed, nor had he started a fire to attract unwanted attention. If anyone had him in rifle sights, it would be pure bad luck ... his.

On the other hand, the dusting of snow that had fallen during the night would make it easy for him to read of any recent passage of horses and men.

He wanted coffee but settled instead for spring water. Gunnar had supplied him with a loaf of bread and he tore off a crust, chewing it methodically as he brushed the sorrel mare and saddled her. Then he brought in Baldy, brushed and saddled him, and hung the panniers to the crossbucks. At last, his bedroll went on top and was lashed down with a one-man diamond.

Jethro spent the better part of the morning winding

Gunnar's Mine

up the mountain to the tableland's crest. Warmer temperatures burned the newly fallen snow from the lower reaches, but hadn't yet reached the higher plateau.

He'd heard of the Uncompahgre for years, usually spoken of in a hushed voice, as if it was sacred to the speaker, but he'd never actually talked with anyone who'd been there. After reaching the huge, more-or-less-flat tableland that crowned the mountains, he suspected visitors to the region weren't all that common.

For one thing, it was nearly devoid of water. The snow, of course, solved that problem—at least for the short term. And the short term was all Jethro intended to be there while crossing the plateau and exiting to the northeast. Trouble was, from the beginning of his climb to 9,000-foot Colombine Pass, he was still thirty miles from exiting the plateau through Carson Hole.

His horses were fresh, though, even Baldy. They'd had a good rest the night before and half their climb was behind them before they'd even started the day. True, Baldy had traveled to Telluride and back—a round trip of about twenty-five miles—before yesterday had begun. But soaking wet, Gunnar couldn't weigh much more than a hundred pounds, so that trip to Telluride amounted to little more than exercise for the horse. What's more, Baldy was lightly laden now, and both horses were in top form. From the pass, it was only a short distance on up to the plateau. Jethro put the two horses into a steady, ground-eating trot.

Jethro Spring had been in few places more appealing. Most attractive under the circumstances was the fact that he didn't see another horse print all day. Secondly, the sheer raw beauty of high-altitude pinons and junipers and bull pines, all hiding jays and coyotes, mule deer and elk, eagles and jackrabbits beggared the man's imagination.

True, one might be taking chances with the weather

by traveling such a high, wild place on the first day of November, but hell, there wasn't even so much as a lone cloud coming from the southwest. Add to it the feel of a good horse working beneath his legs, combined with the smell of clean juniper on the flats and bare aspens in the draws was enough to drive a man a little soupy—had he had a little something in his saddlebags to nip on. He heard the cry of hunting hawks and the addled yapping of half-grown coyote pups near their dens. Squirrels scolded from the trees.

It was mid-afternoon when Jethro paused to dig out the bread, tear off another chunk, and stuff it into his mouth while a rising bitter wind tore at his sheepskin-lined coat and the horses' manes and tails. When night began to fall, the little cavalcade began their descent into Carson Hole. As they did, they were sheltered from the wind. A wolf howled in the distance. At that moment, there was no place Jethro would rather have been in the entire world.

With their saddles pulled, the man grained the ponies and put both out to graze while he chewed more bread and drank more water. When night fell altogether, he brought the mare to camp and left the gray to graze all night.

As daylight broke, Jethro brought in Baldy and turned out Tanglefoot. Unable to stand his own stomach pangs any longer, he built a fire, fried all his sidemeat, and boiled a couple of pots of coffee. Then, with the bread and sidemeat gone, and with cup after cup of scalding coffee as chasers, Jethro felt he could conquer the world.

He thought he might have to, too, when, as he saddled his horses, two cowboys appeared on the skyline. In silent warning, he slipped out the Winchester and held it across his chest. The cowboys reined to a halt, then circled around the touchy stranger to continue climbing

Gunnar's Mine

onto the plateau.

It was two hand spans until sundown when Jethro and his ponies forded the Gunnison above Grand Junction and one hand-span until sundown when he stabled the horses for the night. The man then carried his bedroll and saddlebags to a nearby hotel. There, he locked his room's door and leaned a chair against the knob.

The following morning, Jethro weighed his gold in two places and came up with an average weight of eighty-two troy ounces per Bull Durham sack. Since Gunnar had given him twelve sacks containing nearly pure gold, and with gold of such quality currently trading at $13 per ounce, Jethro walked from the bank with a total of $12,984 dollars buttoned into his coat pockets.

Within minutes, Jethro completed his shopping and rode from town, choosing a route east, up the Colorado River Canyon. An hour from town, he circled south, then west, skirting far around Grand Junction and fording the Gunnison upstream from the trading post of Whitewater.

Jethro traveled all night, circling north of the Uncompahgre, and crossing the low divide between the Dolores and Gunnison Rivers, finally plodding into a Dolores River covert at daylight. He hid the daylight hours in the covert, feeding his animals the last of their grain. Then he crossed the Dolores River at twilight and set a fast pace up the valley to the San Miguel, thence up it to the vicinity of Redvale, which he reached at daybreak. As chance had it, he stopped at Vidkun Bloomquist's farm to ask directions to the Bloomquist place.

Bloomquist read his friend Gunnar's letter, then threw hay to Jethro's weary horses and offered the dark-faced man a place to sleep. Jethro slept but a couple of hours, then borrowed two of Bloomquist's draft horses and continued on, passing Placerville shortly after nightfall and riding to Gunnar's cabin even before the little man had turned in for the night.

Gunnar helped Jethro unload his packhorse and within only minutes the younger man was again on his way to return the borrowed horses, reaching the Bloomquist farm before daylight. This time he accepted Bloomquist's offer of a bed. Not only did the gray-eyed traveler take to the bed, he stayed in it for fourteen hours.

Then he ate a huge meal and at sundown, trotted off toward Fall Creek without a horse beneath him.

It took Jethro six hours to drop into the San Miguel canyon and cover the twenty-eight miles from the Redvale farm of Vidkun Bloomquist to Gunnar Einarssen's cabin. During the passage, Jethro Spring had ample time to dwell on the thousands of miles of roadwork he'd done during the years he was known as the rising middleweight prizefighter, Kid Barry. He also had ample time to shake his head in dismay over how far out of shape he'd become since those memorable years.

Odina snarled, then barked when Jethro sat up at the headwall of the tunnel and flashed Gunnar a wry grin. "It's about time you got here," he said. "We'll never get to that vein if you sleep the day through."

Chapter Four

It was three weeks after Jethro's return from Grand Junction that Gunnar laid the nugget by the young man's bowl of stew. The nugget was long and angular, larger on one end than the other, feathering down to paper thinness on one edge. It was unusually burnished, as if the Swede had carried it in his pocket for some time.

Jethro picked it up, turning it over and over. "Nice, Gunnar. Got to be worth enough to buy steerage to Stockholm."

"Is yours."

"What?"

"Paid, yew have not. Now, yes."

Jethro picked up the nugget. He was guessing, of course, but it *had* to be at least two pounds. Twelve troy ounces to a pound; twenty-four ounces at $13 per ounce. "Hell, this nugget has to be worth three hundred dollars."

Gunnar turned from the stove. "Is more dan yew are worth, ya?"

Jethro grinned and said, "I won't be able to spend it, either—not without somebody finding out it came from here."

Gunnar nodded. "Dat is how I keep yew. Yew are too poor to leave."

Day turned to night; night to day. One after another, endlessly. Except for Sundays. A Sunday had no beginning and was without a defined end. The men climbed from their bunks when they wished, ate what they wished, when they wished. Sometimes they played cards, sometimes split or sawed wood. Or sometimes Jethro read whatever might be available—old newspapers used for wrapping purchased goods, tattered books on loan from Walter or another Placerville miner, pulp magazines with missing pages.

Occasionally Jethro read aloud, while Gunnar, who read only Swedish, listened and smoked his pipe and drank coffee.

Once, after Jethro finished reading for the evening, he saw tears coursing down the little Swede's rutted face. When he peered more closely, Gunnar said, "Ay t'ink dat little boy, he worse off dan we got. What you t'ink?"

The younger man smiled and patted the Dickens book. "I think Oliver had to be tougher than either of us, old man."

Christmas was another off-day. Jethro was up first in the frigid cabin, building a fire, putting on a bucket of water and a pot of coffee.

When Gunnar kicked from his bedroll, he found a bottle of Pike's Magnolia and a can of Sir Walter Raleigh waiting for him. The little man stomped to the table in bare feet and longhandled underwear to pick up and study the whiskey and tobacco. "Yew go nowhere and have no money. Dese come from only one place."

Jethro grinned. "Yeah, little man, I held out on you. I got'em in Grand Junction and stashed'em in Walter's stable. Who knows? Maybe there'll come a day when I'll come into enough cash money to pay you back for the loan you gave me then."

Gunnar stomped to his mackinaw, retrieved his pipe and loaded it with Sir Walter. Then he lit the pipe, backed to the stove, blew out a cloud of smoke and said, "Ay t'ink yew take some watching."

Jethro pulled out a worn notebook, thumbed through its grimy pages, marked one with a finger, and said, "The word is 'vigilant'. You're going to have to be real vigilant to … uh…" Again the younger man thumbed through the notebook until he found the word he wanted … "'apprehend' me."

Gunnar puffed again, then said, "If yew won't turn flatcakes, why yew don't let me?"

They'd finished breakfast and were in relaxed conversation about the little Swede's dreams when the dog raised her head and growled. The growl was followed by a rap on the cabin door. Gunnar lifted the latch and swung the door wide. "You are cold?" he asked.

"My oath," the newcomer said, crowding inside. "That I am. It's not bloody summer out here, you know."

Gunnar nodded as the man shrugged from a heavy oilskin coat. Then the newcomer spotted Gunnar's Christmas whiskey and Jethro Spring in the same instant. "I heard you had a mate up here, Gunnar," the man said, holding out a hand. "Me name's Billy Benbrooke."

"Jason Frost," Jethro replied, taking the hand and

noting the ready smile. "That's not a Swedish accent, is it?"

Billy Benbrooke retrieved his hand and used it to pick up the bottle of whiskey for closer scrutiny. "Aussie, mate. I might be a little weedy and rough around the edges, but I'm from otherwise good convict stock." Then he spat, "Bloody hell! The cork hasn't even been out for a run. Don't you bastards know it's Christmas?"

Gunnar brought an empty condensed milk can as a cup for their visitor.

Benbrooke laughed aloud as he pulled the cork. "Of all the places I plan to beat my stockwhip on today, I just might fancy this one best of all."

Jethro carried in another pine block for a chair, then went out for an armload of wood. When he returned, Gunnar was saying, "... mont', or maybe more. He left blank quit-claim dat ay used to start fire."

Benbrooke took a pull from his cup and said, "Well, they took me drills the night before last. Then somebody stuffed a packrat nest in m'stovepipe and, mate, I almost lost m'cabin. And judgin' by the smell, t'would be best if I had. Baby rats was in the nest."

Jethro poured himself a dash of whiskey and leaned against the log wall, listening.

"Davis and Snowcroft left this week. Davis got $200 for his claim and it's whispered about that Snowcroft got $250."

Gunnar shuffled to the stove for a cup of coffee. When he returned to the table, Benbrooke said, "And you know about Jones—that he couldn't cut muster after they broke his leg."

Gunnar slapped the table. "And yew will run?"

Benbrooke lifted his cup, pulled a big draft and said, "There's a difference between running and being run out, mate. I didn't span an ocean to die over a pile of rock I can't make heads nor tails of, anyway."

Gunnar's Mine

"Yew t'ink 'die' is right word?" Gunnar asked. "Yew t'ink dey kill yew if yew don't sell?"

"That's exactly what I think. They want it all, Gunnar. They want it all and they got a fair whack already." Then the newcomer laughed and reached for the bottle. "I've a badge of gameness, but I'm fond for staying alive, too, especially when the dingoes start eyein' off m'paddock."

"Who's 'they'?" Jethro asked.

Benbrooke and Gunnar both turned to look at him. Then the Australian chuckled and said, "Bless me. You haven't told him about Whittle and his outfit, have you?"

It was Gunnar's turn to chuckle. "Whittle, he knows."

Jethro asked, "Who does Whittle work for?"

Benbrooke glanced at Gunnar and the Swede said, "Yew tell."

Benbrooke shrugged. "That's the bloody trouble—nobody knows really. The transfers of deeds I've seen says it's the Colorado Basin Holding Company, but that's just it, a holding company. Whoever is in charge has an impatient tread, and they've money to burn."

"So this Whittle works for them?" Jethro asked.

Gunnar waved to cut off the Australian, saying, "Among us, Andrew Whittle was a friend. Den he sold to the company. Now one of dem, he is."

Billy Benbrooke nodded. "There's none as trusts him now."

"But," Jethro said, "two hundred, three hundred—that doesn't seem like much for good mining claims."

Benbrooke laughed again, reaching for the bottle. "It wouldn't be if anybody could find a key to the ore. There's minerals there; everybody knows. Enough to keep one's blood fairly up. But it takes big money to prove it, mate. Even then it might be too rough for such as you and me."

The little Swede took the bottle, reset the cork, and pitched it atop his bunk. "Ay have coffee," he said as Billy drained his cup.

"Gunnar," Jethro asked, "have these people threatened you?"

The little man stared at the bullet hole in his tabletop and said, "No. Not like Billy says."

"Like how, Gunnar?"

Benbrook interrupted. "Like they think he's hard and wiry and won't say die. They'll get rid of the weaklings first." Then the Australian added the punch line. "Besides, they know he's crazy and there's little sport in bringing a lunatic to heel."

The coffee wasn't to Billy Benbrooke's liking and soon the Australian made ready to leave. As he stepped through the doorway, the man took out a small piece of pine wood from the pocket of his oil-skin and handed it to Gunnar. "Merry Christmas, mate." The block had a carved aboriginal head in one side, a koala face on the other.

Gunnar took the carving and, stone-dead pipe dangling to his chin, strode to the corner where their spare drill bits leaned and brought a sharpened one to the Australian. "Merry Christmas to yew, too."

After Benbrooke disappeared into the lazily drifting snow, Jethro threw another log on the fire and said to his friend, "Okay, I want to know what's going on here. Is it just Whittle who's threatened you, or do they have others? Tell me exactly how the bastard threatened you and how you responded. Tell me what makes those mineralized outcrops different from other places. Tell me how a big company might work to tie up an entire mining district. Tell me how much risk you're in; how you figure to protect yourself, how you plan to fight 'em off. And then tell me if there's any other claim-holders left

Gunnar's Mine

with guts enough to stick it out with you."

Gunnar scratched the dog's ears throughout his workman's lengthy inquiries. When the younger man finished, the Swede repacked his pipe and puffed mildly for a few moments. At last, he sighed and said, "Is true, what Billy says. Dey want ever't'ing."

"Billy also says the ore is all mixed up and nobody knows how to reduce it."

Gunnar shook his head. "Ay don't know about dat. Ay don't know of hardrock mine. Ay only know of placer gold and the only way ay am here is to follow placer lead."

"And that's the only reason we're drilling a tunnel?"

"Ya."

"Then, little man, how come you filed hardrock claims?"

Gunnar held out his cup which Jethro filled with coffee. "Dose claims are big. Bigger dan placer claims. Ay don't know how far up placer lead is to gold vein. Maybe someday ay get dere and somebody else already dere."

Jethro's brow wrinkled in concentration. At last, he nodded and said, "Nobody knows you're after a pure vein somewhere inside that mountain. So far, they're looking at the mixed up ore in the outcrops, right?"

"Ya."

"But you have a lot of mineral outcrops on your claim?"

"Ya. But ay not work dere, and dey know is so."

"How would they know you're not working in gold bearing rock?"

"Because samples dey take from rubble."

Jethro laughed. "They're sneaking up here to take samples of the stuff you're blowing away from the top of your placer lead?"

"Ya. Ay let dem."

Jethro's head was bobbing like a cork. "And they think you're not smart enough to work where the real minerals lie."

Gunnar flashed a knowing smile and began caressing his dog's back.

Then Jethro frowned. "So they really do think you're crazy and can afford to leave you alone. But...."

"Ya?"

"What if the real wealth of this mine and all the rest really is in the ore found in those outcrops? What if whoever is behind consolidating this district knows something you don't?

What if the doubled 'right-of-discovery' claim you have is twice as valuable to them?"

Gunnar shoved from his block and turned towards the door. He jerked it open, and said, "Ay will not sell—to dem or nobody. All my life ay have not'ing. Now ay have the Nordic Summer. Ay want not'ing else. And no vun—you hear?—no vun will take it from me!"

Jethro held out a hand, keeping the little man in the room. "Okay, Gunnar. If that's clear, then maybe we better start figuring how to keep it."

So the two talked the morning through, and into the afternoon. Gunnar told the younger man how Andrew Whittle had offered to buy his claims. He said he really didn't believe Whittle had stolen the drill bits, nor pilfered the rubble samples. But he believed the man was responsible for directing others to do so.

When Jethro asked who might be working on Whittle's orders, Gunnar explained how the Colorado Basin Holding Company was doing exploratory work on Whittle's old claim; how they had a dozen men pushing an adit inside the mountain; how they had shipped several wagon loads of ore to the outside world to be reduced and assayed. The little Swede thought it possible one or more of the holding company's miners might be available for shady work.

Jethro nodded, saying, "They could steal you blind right now."

The little Swede was in the process of packing more Christmas tobacco into his crooked-stemmed pipe. "Ay catch dem, dey better look out."

"What would you do?"

"Ay beat dem wit' a shovel."

"What if they had a gun?"

"Ay not afraid."

Jethro's gray eyes burned into the little Swede's pale orbs. Then the younger man shook his head and said, "I believe you." He looked around the little cabin, as if seeing it for the first time. "I believe you have enough guts to do just as you say—and that's the problem." He pointed to the spare drill bits leaning in the corner. "Was that where your other spares were when they were stolen?"

Gunnar's silence was an admission.

"What if they burned your cabin, man?" The Swede exhaled a big cloud of smoke with a thoughtful frown. "Where do you keep your dynamite, Gunnar?"

"Under bed."

"Jesus Christ! And the caps—are they there, too?"

"Ay not crazy. Behind cups, in cupboard, dey are."

Jethro slapped his forehead. "I'll never touch that cupboard again."

"Why? From dynamite boxes is made."

They talked of other valuables left each day in the cabin—their cooking outfit, Jethro's Winchester, saddlebags, and telescope. Suddenly, the younger man asked, "Where do you keep your gold, little man?"

"Under pillow."

"Gunnar, don't you see? We've got to find—or make—a safe place for these things."

Gunnar nodded, then asked, "How?"

Jethro stared thoughtfully at the floor. At last, Gunnar, almost to himself, mused, "A side tunnel we could make. Den build door and lock."

"Good. Let's do it."

Most of the snow had burned off the south- and west-facing hillsides by mid-February. Arthur Dantley left Placerville shortly after Lincoln's birthday and Persimmon Hyskop after the Ides of March. The holding company had two more claims. By then, claims had been filed on all the available ground on both sides of the San Miguel, from Fall Creek to Placerville. Only four independent claimholders were left.

It was during the Ides of March when something strange on one of the mineralized outcrops on Gunnar's claim caught Jethro's eye. He climbed the mountainside to investigate. What he found was fresh digging, poorly smoothed over and only partially covered with brush. Investigation revealed that samples from others of Gunnar's outcrops had been similarly taken.

"Did you know about it, Gunnar?" he asked at supper. The two men were at Walter's place, tying into steaks and potatoes.

The little Swede shook his head. "No. At night is when dey come, maybe ya?"

That night Jethro slept near one of the mountainside's untouched outcrops. No one came. But four nights later, during a full moon, they did.

There were two of them. They carried picks and shovels and small canvas bags in which to carry their pillage. Jethro let them load their sacks. He watched them smooth over and lay brush over the signs of their pilfering. Then he followed them down the mountain. At the bottom, Jethro clubbed one of the trespassers behind the ear with his revolver barrel and said to the other, "Okay, friend, let's talk."

He did—long and volubly.

Jethro left the two thieves at daylight, the second dragging the first down to the creek to freshen up. When he intercepted Gunnar on his way to the mine, Jethro said, "Whittle sent them. He wants samples from every outcrop on your claim. They've been working at it since the weather broke at the end of January."

"Ha!" the Swede said, "Dey t'ink dey will stop me, the work, ya?"

"Gunnar, this is more serious than that. They're trying to find out whether you're worth driving out."

"Ay won't go."

"Dammit! You will if you're in a hearse!"

It turned into a struggle of wills—Jethro blocking the trail to the mine tunnel, Gunnar, hands on hips, staring up at his hired man. Finally Jethro stepped aside. "I won't be to work today, little man."

"Den for the day, ay won't pay yew."

Walter Hopkins wiped his hands on his apron and asked, "What can I get you, Jason?"

Jethro leaned his Winchester against the log wall, near the door. "You can start with information about Placerville, Walter."

"What do you want to know?"

"Who owns Colorado Basin Holding Company?"

"Search me."

"Who does Andrew Whittle work for?"

"Search me."

"How many claims around Placerville and here are still owned by someone other than Colorado Basin Holding Company?"

"Four that I know of, counting Gunnar's."

"What's the layout of the Placerville district? Draw me a map."

Walter Hopkins eyed the man he knew as Jason Frost. "I ain't in this," he muttured.

"I understand. Whatever you say will be left here."

Hopkins drew a crude map, showing the single street through the old gold camp, the mining claims to the east, the river to the west, and the road between town and river.

"Which claim belongs to Billy Benbrooke?" the gray-eyed man asked, shoving the paper back to the owner of the eating house. Hopkins drew an "X" through one claim, then added an "X" to two others.

As Jethro strode through the doorway of the crude log-and-wattle building, Hopkins called, "The Australian won't last. Gutierrez is your best bet."

CHAPTER FIVE

So it's Lincoln County all over again, Jethro Spring thought as he paced the Telluride freight road between Fall Creek and Placerville. Only this time, it's a little runt of a Swede and an Australian, and maybe two or three others against another faceless, big money outfit. It's still greed, plain and simple, and a willingness to run over the little guy to get it all.

Anger simmered in his gut as he strode along. He had no idea what he was going to do when he arrived at Placerville, beyond showing his face to demonstrate that he and Gunnar weren't cowed. But what would that accomplish? By the time he arrived, the two men he'd caught pilfering ore samples from Gunnar's claim would have reported their fracas with Jethro to Whittle. So that meant Whittle was on his list of people to see.

He laughed. Whittle was on his list from the moment he decided to go to Placerville; before, even.

Then the dark-faced man sobered. Where the road

dipped near the San Miguel, he ambled to the river to rinse face and hands, then sit on the riverbank in the sunshine amid the greening grass and first buttercups to take stock of his situation.

Here he was, wanted for murder, with a price on his head, heading into the middle of a dispute that would mean nothing but trouble for him. That the little Swede was unaware he was plunging into his own abyss, Jethro hadn't the slightest doubt. True, Gunnar was courageous and, like the Australian said, hard and wiry. But those were weak cards to play in the game Einarssen faced.

What could he, Jethro Spring, alone and unaided, do to protect the obstinate little Swede when he couldn't protect John Tunstall down in New Mexico? In those days he had men like Doc Scurlock, Billy the Kid, and the Coe cousins standing alongside. Gunnar, through his stubbornness, made protecting him as difficult as looking out for Tunstall, while the English rancher followed his 'sense of duty' in opposition to the Santa Fe Ring and its evil power.

Jethro plucked a dead grass stem and began methodically breaking it into tiny bits as he considered his options. He could ride out of the country, but wouldn't that smack of 'running out', as Billy Benbrooke had said? At least the Australian had the decency not to run away—not yet, anyway. *On the other hand,* Jethro reminded himself, *I own no claim, have no interest in gophering inside mine tunnels the rest of my life. So why should I stay?*

He threw away the grass bits piled in his palm and broke off another dead stem while considering his and Gunnar's assets. That Gunnar was considered crazy was one; that meant they won't take him seriously. It also meant they might underestimate the man if they decided to move against him.

Gunnar's Mine

Another asset Gunnar had without knowing it was Jethro Spring's fighting ability. At one time, known as 'Kid Barry', he was one of the better known middleweight prizefighters in the land. In addition, he'd been trained in the art of Oriental fighting and....

A deep scowl overtook Jethro upon thought of Ling San Ho, his Chinese friend and tutor, and how the man was killed in a race riot at end-of-track on the Arkansas River. He crushed the grass stem, then sighed and plucked another.

But probably the most important asset Gunnar and he had was his proficiency with a gun. A mouth corner lifted. Even Billy the Kid, at the top of his game, joked about his hesitation to test guns against Jethro Spring, then known as Jack Winter. Lincoln County, New Mexico, was filled with desperate gunslicks and outlaws, as well as equally capable farmers and cowboys trained on Indian skirmishes and rustler raids. In that place and time, Jethro had been merely one gunhand among many. Here in this remote corner of Colorado mining country, however, he suspected his skills were notable enough to stand out. An attack from ambush was another thing. The only way Jethro knew to respond to ambush was to respond to the *threat* of ambush, *before* it happened ... and that was what he planned to attend to right away.

A freight wagon from Telluride rolled past and Jethro waved to the driver. It was common knowledge that a railroad was headed out of Grand Junction, destined for the San Miguel and Telluride. It was upon the rail line's reaching Placerville that whoever was behind the attempted control of the district would want to begin operations. That meant, with the arrival of the rails, they'd want all claims in the area in their hands.

How long did Gunnar have before striking a vein rich enough to hire armed guards and buy the kind of equipment necessary to take the gold out? The line would have to come around the northwest end of the Uncompahgre to the Dolores River, then upstream to the San Miguel. Telluride needs the railroad now, so they'll work hard to build it. Still, I hear they have yet to cross the Gunnison, and they'll still be a ways from here when winter sets in. *Maybe a year, Gunnar. At the outside. If I can hold off the dogs until then.*

He threw away the last of his grass stem and rubbed his hands free of dust. A half-hour later, he pushed through the batwing doors of a dingy, low-ceilinged saloon with a high false-front grandly displaying the sign, SAN MIGUELL EMPORIUM.

The bartender eyed him as he stepped inside. The thought flashed through Jethro's mind that this might be a vaudeville performance and the man was an actor straight from stage casting ... coal black hair parted in the middle, black shaggy moustache, sleeve garters, a grimy white cloth tied around a beer-barrel belly. The man, chewing on a dead cigar, waddled slowly from the far end of the bar, wiping at imaginary wet spots along the way.

Two cowboys had been talking jovially with the bartender and remained, elbows to the bar, leaning indolently where they were. Three miners and what Jethro took to be a townsman, played poker at a corner table. He recognized none of them.

The bartender was in front of him now, saying nothing, staring steadily, unblinkingly over Jethro's shoulder. The newcomer said, "Anybody ever tell you you spelled Miguel wrong on your sign?"

"Lots of people, once. Nobody ever said it twice." There was still no change of expression, no point to the off-the-shoulder stare.

Jethro grinned. "It's got two *ells*. One is all it's supposed to have."

Gunnar's Mine

It took a full five seconds for the man's dark eyes to ratchet from beyond Jethro's shoulder to lock onto the gray orbs across from him. Then it took an additional five seconds for the man to take the cigar from his mouth and ask, "You want something?"

"A beer." Then the newcomer grinned again, and added, "I'd also like to see you change that sign some day."

The bartender lifted a bung starter from beneath the bar and laid it on the polished surface—a clear and present warning. Then he drew a beer and slid it down the bar. Finally he held out a hand, palm up.

Jethro dropped a silver dollar into the palm and the bartender laid the dollar on the back bar before turning to walk back to the cowboys.

"Change," Jethro said.

The bartender ignored him. Meanwhile the cowboys had turned to face the newcomer, staring hard his way.

He walked down the bar, carrying the bung starter. The cowboys backed up a step at his approach, but the bartender dropped his hands below the bar. Jethro said, "I wouldn't. Fact is, if I was you, I'd lay my hands on top, in plain sight."

The card game stopped and a chair scraped. A riveting glance from Jethro kept the players in their seats. Just to make sure, Jethro said, "Don't none of you play in a game when you don't know who holds the cards."

All laid their hands on the table top. Jethro's eyes locked on the bartender. He handed the man the bungstarter and said, "You overlooked my change. I'm not overlooking your oversight."

The bartender started to lower his hands under the counter again when Jethro snarled, "Left hand only." The lips puckered below the hairbrush moustache and the man bit his cigar in two. Still, the bartender struggled with temptation. Then he shrugged, waddled down the counter, picked up Jethro's silver dollar and slid it toward him.

"Price is good," Jethro said, pocketing the dollar. Then he drained the mug, backed to the door and while easing through, said, "You really do need to change the spelling on that sign."

Billy Benbrooke whooped with delight when he opened his cabin door. "Jason Frost, m'lad! Is it really you?" He looked past his visitor and said, "Where's Gunnar?"

"Working. Where else? You ever know him when he wasn't?"

Benbrooke laughed. "No, no. I'm buggered if I know why he let you free."

Jethro took his map from his pocket and flattened it on the Australian's table. "This is your claim," he said, pointing to where Walter Hopkins had drawn Benbrooke's "X". Billy bent over the map, nodding. Jethro pointed to another "X" and asked if that claim belonged to Gutierrez.

"No," Billy said, "Krajcyk."

"Then this one is Gutierrez's?"

"Aye. His is a claim they're wanting, but they'll have to kill for it."

"Tell me about the man."

"Anton Gutierrez—there's way more to the name than that. Claims he's some sort of ... I believe he calls it a 'grandee'. Came up from Mexico. He's a mining man with hardrock experience. A proud man. Done to the nines most times. Has no trust in man nor beast." Benbrooke gave a nervous laugh. "He frightens me, mate. And I think he puts the wind up Whittle, too."

"What's Krajcyk like?"

"He's as stubby as a wombat; wide as he is tall. The bloke is still here because he's seen hardrock on the Comstock and thinks there's something to this mountain, though he can't make head nor tail of it any more than me."

"Do you think Gutierrez can?"

"Questions, questions," Billy said. "Look, mate, I'd shout you a drink, but the whiskey ran out last week, and m'rum yesterday."

Jethro smiled. "That's all right, Billy. I had a beer at the Emporium and that'll get me by."

"Fancy lot, aren't they? Did you get on with Chalkie?"

"You must mean the bartender."

"Aye. Surly bugger isn't he?"

The bronzed visitor's gray eyes twinkled. "He's that. He's also drawing cards to a busted flush."

Billy stuffed his stove with kindling, touched a match, and put on a pot of coffee. When he returned to the table, Jethro said, "How is it I was lucky enough to catch you at your cabin? I thought you'd working your claim."

"I'm marking time, mate," Benbrooke said. "They've offered me three-fifty, but I'm holding out for four." The Australian avoided his visitor's eyes, but dejection and defeat were etched into the miner's squared-off face.

"Your claim might be worth more, Billy."

Benbrooke's eyes traveled the room, finally settling on Jethro. "And it might be worth nothing to a bloke who wants to go home."

Jethro studied steam beginning to rise from the coffeepot. Benbrooke said, "M'mind came clear the night they sprinkled porcupine quills over my toilet seat."

Jethro laughed. "That's a new one."

"Not at all pleasing to the touch, though. You ever

tried to pull porky quills outen your own arse? In the dark?" He chuckled. "I wasn't keen on hobbling half-mast to my neighbors and asking for help, y'know, 'specially when one is given to talking to himself and the other a Spaniard with pretensions of grandness."

Billy and Jethro spent several minutes, chuckling over the Aussie's porcupine discomfort and the ingenuity of the one responsible. Then Billy again mentioned the Spaniard and how the grandee would not take the issue in good humor.

"Which reminds me," Jethro said. "Do you think Gutierrez knows what might be in the outcrops?"

Benbrooke pushed back the empty dynamite box he used for a stool and jerked the boiling coffee pot from the stove. He held the pot and a couple of heavy mugs while pondering. "You know, he just might. He's a mysterious one, that." While pouring, he added, "A lot of good it'd do us, though. That's one bloke who'd rather get stuffed than help another."

The two men chatted inanely about weather, price of dynamite, the distance to cultural attainments. Finally Benbrooke could stand it no longer and blurted, "Okay, mate, I've went along in order to get along. Now *what* in bloody hell are you doing up at my place, in Placerville, in the middle of the day, away from Gunnar and his claim?"

Jethro set his empty mug down and eyed his table companion. "Gathering information, Billy. Trying to figure out if the ones who're left have a chance in hell of holding on to what they have."

"Well, you needn't count me in. I've made up m'mind that I'm going back Down Under and that's the end of it."

"And you wouldn't rather go back with a pocket full of double-eagles?"

Again Benbrooke laughed. "Right now, mate, all

Gunnar's Mine

I'm looking for is steerage money."

Jethro pursed his lips and eyed the Australian. Directly he said, "How about trotting down to the Emporium with me and I'll buy the beer."

Billy grinned. "Now wouldn't that be decent of you? I'd do the buying, but I'm a little shy until m'ship comes in."

Jethro followed Benbrooke into the San Miguell Emporium at a quarter after two on a Friday afternoon. Peering around Billy, he saw four men at the bar, none at the tables. Then he detached himself as the Australian's shadow and approached the bartender. "Your beer was so good I've decided on another draft. One for my friend, too."

The audacity of it caught Chalkie by surprise and the rag he carried fell from his hand. Then Andrew Whittle turned from the bar and said, "Well, well, if it isn't my friend, Einarssen's drudge."

The bartender's hands dipped below the bar's surface and Jethro's voice turned ominous. "Damn, I get tired of telling you this, Chalkie—now lay your hands on top of the bar until you see how this plays out."

The sleeves came up, garters and all, until the hands lay atop the bar. Whittle glanced at the bartender and his eyes narrowed. "You've already met, I see." He pushed from the bar to face Jethro, hand brushing the jacket flap from his gunbutt.

Benbrooke turned for the door, mumbling, "I'm buggered if I want in on this."

Jethro laughed and caught him by the arm. "Naw, Billy, we're going to have a beer. And these men will drink with us." There was a pause, then Jethro said,

"You will, won't you, Whittle?"

Andrew Whittle considered. He scrutinized the absence of fear in the man facing him, noted the tied-down gun and its oiled holster. Try as he might he couldn't avoid the cold, gray eyes and the challenging smirk on the bronzed face. His gaze returned to the gun and the splay-fingered hand casually hooked into the belt only inches from its butt. "Why not?" he said. "Eat your food, drink your beer ... sounds all right to me."

Jethro had to push Benbrooke to the bar, but as soon as the Australian clasped a mug of beer, he turned convivial.

His friend— 'Einarssen's drudge', as Whittle had called him—stood at his side, smiling mildly, gunhand and revolver both hanging free. This time the bartender took Jethro's silver dollar and replaced it with several coins of lesser value.

Whittle and his cohorts all hoisted their beers, as did Jethro. Then Whittle stuck out his free hand and said, "I don't know if I've heard the name. As you already know, I'm Andrew Whittle."

The dark man took the offered hand and when Whittle clamped down, jerked, and shouted, "Get the sonofabitch!" Jethro threw his beer in the other's face, kicked him in the crotch, vaulted the bar and grabbed the shotgun he knew was hidden there. Cocking both sawed-off barrels, he pointed the gun at the three men still milling beyond the gasping Andrew Whittle, hissed to the bartender that he'd better remain still, and reached back for what was left of his beer.

His voice caught the Australian halfway through the swinging doors. "C'mon back, Billy. It's not good manners to let a beer grow stale."

Benbrooke crept back to the bar. "Strewth!" was all the Aussie could say before he drained his draught in one open-throated swallow.

Gunnar's Mine

Whittle, still bent over and grasping his crotch, finally looked up, pure venom dripping from his dark eyes. Jethro laughed. "Approach," he ordered. The man straightened, wincing, then stepped nearer.

"Your beer's getting warm," Jethro said, nudging him in the chest with the twin shotgun muzzles.

He had nerve along with his venom, Jethro had to admit as the man picked up his beer and drained it, then used a forefinger to push the yawning barrels to the side. "What now?" Whittle asked.

"Now?" Jethro said. "Now I'm going to tell you that if I ever see you or one of your men on Gunnar Einarssen's claim again, I'm personally going to come up here and slit your nut-bag, run your leg through it. Then I'm going to drive you to hell up Telluride way at a fast lope."

Whittle stared through him, then turned and shuffled painfully from the Emporium. Whittle's friends still milled beyond the bar.

"Your beer is getting warm, too, boys," Jethro said.

Billy Benbrooke and Jethro Spring stopped at Tobe Krajcyk's cabin and found no one home. Antonio Gutierrez was in his cabin, but the man said he wasn't receiving. Jethro tried a word or two of Spanish he'd picked up in New Mexico, but was met only with silence.

So he bade Billy Benbrooke good night, swung by the Emporium for another beer, wholly to establish trust with Chalkie, then trotted back to Gunnar's cabin, arriving a few minutes after Gunnar had snuffed out the candle.

After the dog had sniffed his feet and he'd clambered

into bed, Gunnar's voice drifted from the darkness. "Yew have good day?"

Jethro smiled and said, "Ya!"

Chapter Six

Gunnar Einarssen and Jethro Spring worked from first light to evening shadows without exchanging a word. At lunchtime, Gunnar simply took the drill bit and hammer from Jethro and began pounding into the tunnel headwall while Jethro crawled out and walked to the cabin. The dog trotted behind.

She also sat watching Jethro eat, even taking a crust of bread from the man's hand—a tremendous leap forward in their relationship. However, the black and white mutt still wouldn't let Jethro touch her, and when he finished his dinner and returned to the mine, he discovered the dog was already there.

Back at the tunnel headwall, the young man reached for the drill and hammer and the older one let him take it without a word. When darkness at last drove Jethro Spring from the mine tunnel, first to the creek and at last to the cabin, he found Gunnar dishing up tasty potato paste over rich slices of ham.

"Good," the dark-faced man said a half-hour later as he pushed back from his pine block.

Gunnar grunted, ran fingers through his thinning white hair, washed his dishes, then turned into bed.

Thus went the evening and morning of Saturday, the 25th day of March, 1882.

Sunday, a day of rest, followed Saturday. Jethro was first up, firing the stove, frying sidemeat and flipping flapjacks. The cakes were served with the last chokecherry syrup from his Grand Junction foray, in November.

"Goot," Gunnar mumbled as he pushed back from the table and pointedly patted his belly.

Jethro grunted, jerked a pot of hot water from the stove, and washed his dishes. Then he pulled on his jacket, picked up his Winchester, and slipped from the cabin.

Gunnar stuffed his pipe, then tamped and fired it, all the while staring at the closed cabin door. Finally he took a deck of playing cards from one of the dynamite-crate cupboards and laid out a hand of solitaire.

Meanwhile, Jethro made a circuit of Gunnar's claims, meticulously studying the ground for any sign of intrusion ... not that he expected any so soon after his face-off with Whittle. The man would first have to digest the new dimension of Jethro's presence. Then he'd have to consult with whoever issued his orders. Even so, (and the gray-eyed man grinned at the thought) 'Einarssen's drudge' never doubted that Whittle would strike back some day. The hatred in the man's eyes sent that message loud and clear. Now, however, there was a question: would Whittle strike first at the drudge, or at the drudge's boss?

After satisfying himself that Gunnar's claims were safe, Jethro Spring laid the barrel of his Winchester over his shoulder and trotted off up-slope. He'd caught a whiff of spring on his to-and-fro jaunt to Placerville and wanted more. The man climbed steadily, pausing often

Gunnar's Mine

to breathe deeply of the pine-scented air, exclaiming "Ahh!" more than once. With the sun at its zenith, Jethro threw himself down in the grass of a sun-warmed hillside and slept until an ant tickled his nose.

He sat up, yawning and stretching, then rolled to his feet with the Winchester in hand, and began casting about for deer sign. The hunter in him came from good stock. Progeny of a mountain man father and a Blackfeet mother, Jethro Spring learned to track from masters of the craft, experts at reading the subtlest of signs ... bent blades of grass, broken brush stems, turned-over stones.

While moving stealthily through the scattered pine, juniper, and aspen, Jethro's thoughts turned inevitably to his parents who taught him so much of the nuances of woodcraft. Unable to control paths his mind followed, Jethro thought of his parents' deaths, and of the bloody massacre of an innocent band of Blackfeet too riddled with smallpox to flee.

A pine squirrel chittered from a tree limb above, breaking Jethro's despondent mood. He paused to stare up at the saucy creature who several times switched directions on the limb, all the while flipping his tail in a circular motion. The man grinned, pitched a pine cone upward and continued his stealthy advance.

He was back at the cabin by mid-afternoon, carrying a yearling mule deer buck. "Thought a little venison liver might give us a change of diet," he said to the little Swede who looked up quizzically from his card layout.

Gunnar nodded, rose from his pine block and said, "Ay will see if Walter, he has an onion."

Jethro waved a handful of tiny bulbs. "Found a few wild ones on the hillside. They'll taste a bunch stronger than any farm-grown ones, but they cost nothing and some is better than none."

Gunnar shook his head. "Ay will still see if Walter, he

has one."

Later, as both men shoveled in slices of fresh-fried liver and onions, Gunnar, eyes on his plate, said, "Walter, he tells me of things ay don' know."

"Really," Jethro said. "What kinds of things?"

"Walter says two days ago, one of my mans is in Placerville."

"Interesting."

"Walter says one of my mans gets into trouble at saloon. Trouble was with Andrew Whittle."

"Really?"

"Walter says one of my mans made an enemy of Andrew Whittle and the man who owns the saloon." It was only then that Gunnar's watery blue eyes left his plate and found Jethro's gray ones.

"Which one of your mans might that be?" Jethro asked, mouth corners twitching.

Gunnar continued, "Walter, he thinks maybe ay won't have trouble with Andrew Whittle after all."

"Hmm," Jethro said.

"But yew want to know what ay t'ink?"

"Mmm-hmm."

"Ay didn't hire yew as guard. Ay hired a mans to work in mine. For a guard ay have no money."

Jethro stood, then headed for the stove. "Why tell me this, Gunnar?" he asked with his back to the table. "I'm just what Whittle calls a drudge. Why not tell your mans who kicked off the ruckus—whoever the hell he might be?"

The little Swede followed his drudge to the dish washing bucket, then went to his bed.

With communications restored between Gunnar and his employee, work progressed steadily in the Nordic Summer. The tunnel inched into the mountain at a rate

Gunnar's Mine

of four feet a week. Though the days lengthened and daylight increased, the tunnel length at last grew so long that light dimmed until Jethro and Gunnar had to resort to candles throughout their working day.

"Some day," Gunnar observed, "so long will the tunnel grow, candles will not burn. Then we get the lamps of carbide."

Each day following their dynamite blasts, Gunnar carried the carefully shoveled gravel from the old streambed out for washing, then returned the washed gravel back to the tunnel floor. The detritus was bucketed laboriously from the mine and thrown into an ever-growing pile that snaked almost to Fall Creek.

It was three Sundays after Jethro brought in the venison that he decided another call on Placerville might be in order. It was after breakfast when he asked Gunnar if he'd like to amble up to Chalkie's place for a mug of beer.

The little man turned from the bucket of dishwater, his face etched with deepening lines. "Do not do this t'ing," he said. "For me ay don't want dis done."

Jethro clapped his little friend on the shoulder. "I'm not doing this for you, Gunnar; at least not for you alone. I'm doing it for me and Billy Benbrooke and Tobe Krajcyk and Anton Gutierrez." He paused thoughtfully, then continued, "And, strangely enough, I'm doing it for Andrew Whittle who needs to learn that might doesn't always make right."

Gunnar sighed and his expressive face took on even more lines. "Dat is what ay t'ink, too. About what yew say—might and right. But yew don't believe it. Yew want to show dem yew got most might."

Jethro's hand had still not left the little man's shoulder and it stayed in place for a full minute longer before squeezing and dropping. "No, pardner," he said at last. "I'm just showing them they're not the only ones with might—and I think that's the best thing we can do."

Jethro Spring heard the San Miguell Emporium before he saw it—a low murmur, punctuated with higher-pitched cries and finally a gunshot. Pausing at the batwing doors, he pulled his hatbrim down low over his nose and closed his eyes until they'd adjusted away from the bright daytime sun. Then he tilted his hat back, flicked the leather thong from the hammer of his low-slung Colt, pushed through the swinging doors and opened his eyes.

Chalkie's place was crowded, with all three tables filled and pushing, shoving men three deep at the bar. In the few seconds it took for Jethro's eyes to finish adjusting to the dim light, a hush fell over the throng and every eye turned his way. He remained rooted, giving everyone ample time to look him over. Meanwhile, his tight lips relaxed into a half-smile and his head swung slowly back and forth as he took the measure of every face. At last he strode forward, right thumb casually hooked over his belt buckle.

The crowd magically parted allowing the newcomer access to the bar rail. Chalkie was there as before, chewing on a dead cigar, hands spread atop the polished surface of the bar and flat, black eyes boring a hole over Jethro's right shoulder.

Just then a shout filled the low-ceilinged building. "Jason!" And a wave erupted along the bar as first one man, then another was shoved aside until at last, a wobbling Billy Benbrooke thrust his forehead onto Jethro's shoulder and said, "What blessed luck to have m'all-time bes' mate show up just when I'm bound back t'the land of 'roos an' reprobates."

Jethro lifted Billy's head from his shoulder and the Aussie would've fallen had Jethro not caught him against the bar.

To the waiting Chalkie, Jethro said, "A beer."

Gunnar's Mine

The barkeep's eyes flicked to Billy. "Him, too?"

Jethro shook his head. "Not until I see if he needs it."

The Australian jerked away from the bar and said to the bartender, "Give m'mate whatever's best in the house."

Jethro shook his head. "The beer will do."

Chalkie's eyes flicked from one to the other, but they stayed with Jethro as the man said, "You drinkin', Billy?"

"Do I look like a teetotaler, for gawd's sake?"

When Chalkie slid Jethro's beer and a water glass filled with an amber liquid to the Australian, he studiously ignored the newcomer's dime to ask, "You buying, Bill?"

Benbrooke fumbled in a trousers pocket and pulled out a wad of money, dropping several bills on the floor.

Jethro reached the money before Chalkie. Then he smiled sweetly and said, "Take the dime for my beer, and keep the change." Then he saw a man beyond Billy bend to the floor, so he pushed Benbrooke aside and stepped on a gold certificate—along with the man's fingers. To Chalkie, he added, "And tell me the price of Billy's bar swill."

"Five ..." Chalkie began, then took note of the steely look in his dark-faced customer's eyes and ended with "fifty cents."

Jethro slid a silver certificate across the bar and waited for Billy's change. While doing so, his gaze again swept the room. This time no face was turned his way.

Billy tried again to inject some good will into the scene by slapping Jethro's back and saying again, "What luck t'have you show up just when I'm heading back to the colonies."

The bartender returned with fifty cents change as Jethro lifted Billy's whiskey to take a sip. He licked his lips, shook his head, and said to the barkeep, "It's good enough to destroy my faith in my own judgement. He thought Chalkie's eye corners crinkled, but when he looked again, there was just only a fat, mustachioed, moon face chewing on a dead cigar.

While still staring at the dimly wriggling cigar, Jethro said, "Let's take our drinks outside, Billy. Maybe down to the river. I'll bet it'd be all right with Chalkie if we promise to bring the mugs back."

In answer, Chalkie waddled off down the bar, swiping at the top with a dirty rag as he went.

Jethro swept up the remaining bills that'd fallen from Billy's hand to the floor. Then he picked up both his friend's water glass and his own mug in his left hand, and, right hand hanging free, motioned Billy ahead of him as he backed to the door until the batwing doors blocked his view.

"How much did you get, Billy?" Jethro asked. The two men sat on boulders bordering the San Miguel. The site offered a clear view of all approaches.

Benbrooke chuckled. "They gave in when they saw Billy Benbrooke didn't ha' the backbone of a jellyfish." He took a big swig from his glass, threw a stick into the swiftly flowing stream and concluded, "I should've asked more—maybe five hundred."

Jethro's gaze followed the bobbing stick until it disappeared downstream. "When did you sell?"

"Ahh, just this morning. I planned to drop by your cabin on m'way out, but first I said to m'self, 'Billy, you deserve a tot.'"

"So they paid you in cash?"

"That they did. Never had so much in m'life."

"How much do you have left, Billy?"

Gunnar's Mine

Benbrooke snickered. "I'm buggered if I know." He turned his pockets out. Bills fluttered onto the rocks and Jethro scurried after them.

When he returned, Jethro said, "Is this all, Billy?"

Benbrooke eyed him. "Far as I know, mate. Why?"

Jethro counted. When he quit he said, "Billy, there's only fifty-four dollars here. Where's the rest of it?"

"Fifty-four dollars! Tell me you're joking!"

"How much is a ticket to Australia?"

The question went unanswered as Billy frantically searched each empty pocket. Finally he stared drunkenly at Jethro, muttering, "This cannot be true."

Jethro said, "When do you have to be out, Billy?"

Benbrooke dropped his face into his hands. "Today, Whittle said." Then he looked up, tears coursing down a forlorn face. "Andrew also said now I'd come into such wealth, that we could pop down to the Emporium so I could stand him a drink."

"And you stood the house a round."

"God, Jason, there … it might have been more than one."

Chapter Seven

"Ay don't want him here!" Gunnar Einarssen stood with an armload of split stovewood, effectively blocking the doorway to his little cabin. "If to Andrew Whittle he sold his birthright, ay want no t'ing to do with him."

Jethro and the little Swede stared down at the hapless Australian who sprawled dejectedly, face in hands, against a tree.

"Gunnar," Jethro said at last, "he has no place else to go. Whittle and company cleaned him out before the day was over. They had him drunk and buying rounds for the house."

Gunnar carried his armload of wood on into his cabin, then returned to block the door. "Ay won't have a … a …"

"Quitter?" Jethro prompted.

"A quitter, ya. Ay don't want a quitter on my claim."

"He had to get out of his cabin today. We picked up

his clothes and other stuff."

"And I brought back your drill bits," Billy added, lowering his hands.

Jethro's voice dropped almost to a whisper. "He's got enough money left to take a stage to the railroad and maybe enough to get to San Francisco, but right now he needs a place to sleep."

"No room is dere in dis cabin."

"We'll make room for the night, Gunnar."

"No. Ay will not ..."

Jethro gently lifted his little boss from the doorway and set him to one side. "Come on Billy," he called.

Benbrooke scrambled to his feet and hurried into the cabin.

The little black and white dog growled, standing uncertainly between her master and Jethro. Gunnar gestured to the dog while squinting angrily up at his hired man. Some measure of understanding seemed to pass between them as Gunnar's anger faded and his lined face turned even more melancholy than was his usual mien. "Yew would do dis t'ing, knowing ay do not wish it?"

Jethro nodded. "It's the right thing, Gunnar."

"Yew do many t'ings dat to yew is right but to me is wrong. Ay am the one paying yew. Yet, still yew do dese t'ings, even when you know ay might fire yew."

Jethro grinned. "Wouldn't make any difference, Gunnar. Fire me and you've still got a couple of house guests for the night."

A twinkle flashed in the watery blue eyes. "A man who gives up ay still do not like."

"Then little pardner, you'd ought to love me, 'cause I ain't much of a quitter, am I?" Then Jethro murmured, "He'll only be here for a night or two. Surely you can find it in your heart to tolerate him for that long."

But a week later, Billy Benbrooke was still at the

cabin on Fall Creek. And the Rio Grande Southern had bridged the Gunnison and began grading toward the Gunnison-Dolores divide.

One thing the little Swede stuck to his guns about—he would not permit Billy Benbrooke in his mine. But that suited the Australian fine; Billy simply took over cooking chores for his hosts, rising before daylight and bedding after dark. He worked around the cabin, too, sawing and splitting wood, washing clothes and bedding, scrubbing the cabin floor and, when not otherwise engaged and Jethro was nearby, following the bronzed man around like a faithful puppy.

Noting that the Nordic Summer's drill bits were in need of sharpening, as were the two he'd returned, Billy volunteered to take them to Telluride.

As the Australian strode from the cabin, Jethro appeared at his side. "Billy," he said, putting a hand on the other's shoulder, "are you taking the rest of your money with you?"

Benbrooke patted one of the pockets in his trousers. "S'all safe, mate. Right here in m'pocket."

Jethro held out his hand. "I'll hold it for you. It'll be safer that way."

Billy chuckled. "No, mate. I know what you're thinking, but I have m'self in hand now."

"The money, Billy."

Benbrooke squared his shoulders, throwing off Jethro's hand. "Nobody tells Billy Benbrooke what's …"

"The money." A smile spread slowly across the dark face, white teeth glistening in the early morning light.

Benbrooke wilted. He dug in his pocket and withdrew a fist filled with bills. Jethro counted, then held out his hand for the rest.

"You'd deny me a pint? Surely not!"

"The rest, Billy. I know Gunnar gave you enough to

pay the blacksmith and to get a room and grub. You'll make a pint out of that. You don't need more."

Benbrooke sat down, pulled off a boot, and silently handed Jethro a gold certificate.

That night, while Billy was gone, Jethro jogged from Fall Creek, heading down the San Miguel, through Placerville and on to the Redvale farm of Vidkun Bloomquist. Over one shoulder hung saddlebags heavy with gold double eagles. Over the other lay the barrel of a Winchester Model '73 in a .44 caliber. A well-oiled Colt, also .44 caliber, swung from his right thigh.

The following morning, just as Gunnar and his dog Odina were rising for the day, the weary traveler knocked on the Bloomquist farmhouse door.

An hour later, Jethro Spring and Vidkun Bloomquist had the farmer's forge up to fire to begin shoeing a sorrel mare and a gray gelding.

Jethro napped in mid-afternoon, as Billy Benbrooke was rising from his Telluride flophouse cot, and about the time the hung-over Australian was setting out from the blacksmith's for Gunnar's cabin, Jethro saddled his two ponies for the first time in five months.

"Dey are goosey," Bloomquist said.

Jethro grinned as he swung into the saddle. "Maybe I'll stick." He reached down a hand. "Thanks a bunch, Vidkun. They look good. Gunnar will be in touch."

Bloomquist's already sunburned face reddened more with the praise. "Gunnar, he is a good man. Maybe dey not kill him."

Shadows were deep as Jethro turned the sorrel mare south and west from the Bloomquist farm, heading at a ground-eating trot up a seldom-used freight road, bound for the low pass between the San Miguel and the upper Dolores. Man and horses passed through Gypsum Gap in the wee hours and went into camp along the Dolores River before daylight.

Off again during the waning hours of day, Jethro and his ponies forded the Dolores at Slick Rock, climbed to the Escalante Plateau, and plodded tiredly into the bustling old Spanish city of Cortez just as night fell.

In Cortez, Jethro Spring purchased enough flour, beans, bedding and needed replacement clothing to fill a pair of packsaddle panniers and a top pack.

It was after midnight when Jethro's little cavalcade slipped out of Cortez, ostensibly heading east toward Durango, but swinging north to lose itself in the wild foothills and desert country of southwestern Colorado.

It was, however, a solid ten days before a chagrined Jethro Spring returned to the little cabin at Fall Creek. "Got lost for a couple of days over on the upper Dolores," he said to Gunnar and Billy as both men turned out in their underwear to help unload Baldy. "Pretty country, though. Wouldn't mind going back some day."

Billy said, "Gunnar told me you ran off with m'money." He stopped with a pannier in his arms. "You didn't, did you, mate?"

Jethro laughed. "Well, I did take it with me, Billy. How else could we have paid for all these groceries?"

The Austrailian shrugged. "At least it went for some good, eh?"

Gunnar held up the lantern to study Baldy, affectionately rubbing the big gray's nose. "Walter, he knows dey come."

But Jethro shook his head. "Let's just jerk the saddles tonight, then take the ponies down first thing in the morning."

"Horses, dey need grain," the little Swede insisted. "Walter has grain. Ay have no grain."

"But I have grain," Jethro said, taking the feedbags hanging from Baldy's packsaddle and digging into his own saddlebags. "It'll get 'em by tonight." Jethro

Gunnar's Mine

glanced out into the darkness. "Besides, no longer'n it is 'til daylight, they don't need much."

None of the three men slept during the remainder of this night. Jethro returned Billy's fifty-four dollars, offered up a pint of brandy to the festivities, and sat benevolently by while Billy and Gunnar sorted through the supplies. It was after daylight, as the Australian cooked breakfast, that he turned from the stove and said, "I'll be a dead dingo if I can see where you got the money for this. Gunnar, is your mine a paying proppo?

The Swede's head snapped up. "Money ay had when I get off boat."

Billy laughed. "Money I had when I popped off the boat, too, mate, but both bills went down when I wrapped up wi' a fandango dancer before the dawn of a new day."

It was mid-afternoon before a refreshed Jethro Spring slid in beside Gunnar at the tunnel's headwall. The first thing the Swede said was, "If about the Nordic Summer, dat man finds the truth, us he will hurt."

"So what's the truth? Face it, Gunnar, the Nordic Summer isn't paying big. That's the truth."

"Dat is not what will be believed. To others ay will not be crazy. To others, the Nordic Summer will be rich and dey will want it."

Jethro sighed, taking the hammer and bit from his mining mentor. "What do you think we should do?"

"Home he wants to go. Let him go."

Jethro swung the maul. "He doesn't have enough money left to" (bang!) "get there. Best he could do, maybe," (bang!) "is get to the coast. Then what?"

Gunnar's head had been wagging ever since Jethro started swinging. "Ay do not want him here, Jason. Us he will hurt."

Jethro laid down the hammer and bit. "All right. But we've got to make sure he gets plumb away before talking to anybody else. The only way that's going to happen is if one of us goes with him to Grand Junction, then makes sure he's on the train west."

Gunnar hugged his knees as he considered. "You go. Dese t'ings ay don't know how."

Jethro Spring and Billy Benbrooke caught the mail hack at Placerville and rode it to Ridgeway. Then they caught a stage downriver to the tiny farming community of Montrose and finally, Grand Junction. Here, Jethro bought Billy a ticket on the D&RG to eventually hook up with the Central Pacific for the final leg to San Francisco.

Just before boarding, Billy said, "I don't know how I'll make it to Aussie land from San Francisco, but Jason, m'mate, I want you to know how much I think o' you for what y'did."

He held out a hand as the conductor yelled, "BOARD!" Jethro took it, shook it, then pulled his hand away to push Billy up the steps as the train began to move. Billy stood rooted in the car's vestibule, staring down at his hand until the train rounded the first bend. What lay in his hand was a heavy gold nugget!

Gunnar was preoccupied as he stalked among the scattered pines surrounding his little cabin. As if to punctuate his thoughts, tiny puffs of smoke burst randomly from his pipe. Jethro sat on a pine block watching, waving half-heartedly at a particularly pesky mosquito or two. When Gunnar took his perch on a block nearby, the younger man said, "Hot."

"Dose trees, dem ay want to cut."

Jethro nodded. "Makes sense. Close to the house. We'll get'em before fall."

"Now, ay t'ink we should cut dem down."

Gunnar's Mine

Jethro blinked. "Okay, you have a reason. What is it?"

"Is dry. Soon things burn too easy. If drive us away is what Whittle wants, is easy to set fire in trees. Ay t'ink we cut trees into wood, den burn little fire around cabin."

Jethro nodded. "That's called a backfire, Gunnar, and it's used to fight fires. Ay t'ink you one smart Swede."

The little man slapped his knees. "Tomorrow is when."

"Tomorrow? Tomorrow is Wednesday. What about the mine?"

Gunnar waved dismissively. "Yew want to sleep dere? Already has gold waited long time. For us, it will be better if we have cabin while we wait to find all dat gold."

Smoke from Gunnar's backfire wafted from the little clearing around the Swede's cabin on Friday. On Saturday, the two men were again hard at work on the tunnel's headwall. On another brutally hot day in early June, Tobe Krajcyk's cabin burned to the ground from a forest fire of unknown origin. And Antonio Garcia killed a man who was loosely handling matches while on the touchy Castilian's mining claim.

"Who was he?" Gunnar asked Walter as the owner of the eating place set steaming platters before the two Fall Creek men.

"One of the new men Whittle brought in for work on one of his exploratory adits." The storekeeper shrugged. "They're building up a big crew. They tell me Whittle's miners already outnumber cowhands in Chalkie's saloon. What it's going to be like when the railroad gets here is anybody's guess."

"Is the sheriff going after Garcia?" Jethro asked.

"Not the way I get it. The Mex just blowed away both of the firebug's hands with a shotgun, then held his face in his own fire until he smothered to death." Walter wiped the palms of his hands slowly across his flour sack apron and added, "I reckon it'd take one brave, stupid sonofabitch to go up on the Mex's claim. And our sheriff ain't neither one."

Tobias Krajcyk did what Gunnar Einarssen suggested might be his and Jethro's alternative were their cabin to be fired. He moved into his mine. Jethro found him there, reading in the uncertain light from the tunnel mouth.

"Yes?" Krajcyk said as he appeared at Jethro's halloo.

As Billy Benbrooke once described him, Krajcyk was almost as broad as he was tall. Though he couldn't have stood five feet in his bare feet, the old Comstock hand's neck and shoulders might easily have borne a draft horse's collar. Nor was there any tapering from what must be described as a barrel chest, down to the broad hips. And the legs! It was obvious that the man had to re-sew overalls, adding whatever denim material was cut from the length to fit between side seams. His face was as round as a drum and blank as newly stretched rawhide. Surprisingly for a man who worked underground, the face appeared sunburned, giving it the appearance of cherubic innocence. Large wire-rimmed glasses perching on the end of a button nose did, however, give it an owlish cast.

"I'm Jason Frost," the newcomer said. "I work for Gunnar Einarssen."

"My claim is not for sale."

Jethro spread his hands, palms up. "I work for Gunnar Einarssen, Mr. Krajcyk. I'm not interested in buying any claim, only in finding out if those who have ones that aren't owned by Andrew Whittle's outfit wants

Gunnar's Mine

to keep them.

"Come." Krajcyk stepped aside.

One pine block provided the only seating inside the tunnel. A pile of straw scattered off to one side appeared to be the sleeping accommodations—tolerable during mid-summer, Jethro thought, but what about winter?

There were a few blackened pots and pans. Scattered chunks of charcoaled wood amid a pile of ashes revealed where the blocky miner sited his cooking fire.

Krajcyk took the pine block, leaving Jethro to stand. It was soon apparent the host was not an accomplished conversationalist, so Jethro cut through the niceties. "Here's what I know or have heard," the visitor began. "I know you, Gutierrez, and Einarssen are all the independent claimholders left north of Telluride. I've been told that no matter how much pressure is applied you're stubborn and likely to stick."

Jethro waited vainly for the man to respond. Continuing, he said, "I've heard you have Comstock mining experience, that you believe there's something to these crazy rocks, but that you haven't figured it out."

Still, Tobe Krajcyk sat in silence on his pine block, peering up at his visitor through the outsized glasses.

"Well, it seems to me that Tobe Krajcyk, Anton Gutierrez, and Gunnar Einarssen better stick together if they don't want to get run out separately."

"How?" the other asked, his first word since inviting Jethro inside.

Jethro ran fingers through his thick mop of dark hair. "I suppose the first thing would be to compile a list of all the offers to buy, when they escalated to threats, then to their actions to drive you out, such as your cabin fire."

The light in the tunnel was tricky and the upturned face appeared even more cherubic than earlier. Jethro had the impression that the man's axle turned very slowly.

"What does the Spaniard say?" the blocky man asked.

"I've not talked to him. I wanted to see what you thought before I did."

"And the Swede?"

Jethro shrugged. "He's as independent as the rest of you. Thinks he can go it alone against all the money and rotten bastards in the world. Thinks they won't bother him if he doesn't bother them, even though they've already done plenty to bother him. But Gunnar will listen, and if you and Gutierrez are willing to support each other, the Swede will go along."

Tobe Krajcyk's massive head swung to the sidewall, then dipped as the man seemed to study the clasped hands he held between his knees.

"So are you willing to get together with Gutierrez and Einarssen and write down what's happened to the three of you since Whittle's outfit moved into the San Miguel?"

Krajcyk's moon-round face turned upwards. "You get Anton Gutierrez and Gunnar Einarssen, and Tobe Krajcyk, he will join you."

Chapter Eight

During the week following Jethro's positive contact with Tobe Kracyk, grading crews for the Rio Grande Southern Railroad reached the Gunnison-Dolores divide. While those crews labored, Jethro Spring tried repeatedly to speak to the third surviving claimholder in the Placerville-Fall Creek district. Each time, the haughty Spaniard either refused to acknowledge Jethro's presence, or ordered him off the premises. At last, Jethro simply squatted outside Gutierrez's cabin to outwait the man. He waited all night.

At dawn, Gutierrez stepped from his cabin holding a sawed-off double-barreled shotgun in twelve gauge. The man wore a white silk shirt with a button-on collar, black string tie, and dark woolen trousers tucked into elegant calf-skin boots. "You will leave," he ordered.

When Jethro made no move, the other eared back both hammers. As first one clicked, then the other, the Spaniard repeated, "You will leave. NOW!"

Jethro shook his head. "Not 'til I have the chance to talk to you."

"Ha! One such as you will never have that chance." However, he eared the shotgun's hammers down, stepped back inside his cabin and slammed the door.

Jethro pushed to his feet, stretched, then settled back on his heels to wait.

Hours passed. At last, puzzled, the waiting man clambered to his feet and knocked at the cabin door. No answer. He circled the cabin, pausing frequently to place an ear against the wall. Gradually it dawned upon him that Gutierrez had a second cabin exit. Jethro again circled the cabin, studying the walls even more carefully. Rifle slits there were, but no windows … and no second door. Convinced there were no outlets except the front door, he extended his search beyond the cabin, casting about for a hidden tunnel exit. He found nothing.

At last, Jethro shuffled back to the cabin's tiny clearing and stood pondering Gutierrez's nearby mine tunnel. Then he grinned at the Spaniard's shrewdness. Undoubtedly there was an adit from the mine to the cabin. Perhaps there was a second opening from the mine itself. Perhaps the Spaniard was somewhere in the aspens behind, chuckling at the younger man's confusion. Jethro jogged home to Gunnar's cabin.

For his part, the little Swede disliked Jethro's absences. Even so, the little mine owner grudgingly accepted his workman's efforts to enlist Kracyk and Gutierrez into a plan to counter Colorado Basin Holding Company's tightening grip—especially when Jethro made it clear he planned to continue with or without approval. Besides, Gunnar decided, his employee's increasing proficiency with a singlejack meant the mine tunnel snaked on into the mountainside at a reasonably steady rate, despite his man's occasional absences. Even more to the point, Gunnar was finding

Gunnar's Mine

additional things to like about his quiet companion. And finally, Odina, his one-man dog seemed increasingly to accept Jethro, even condescending to wag her tail at the younger man's approach.

"Maybe yew someday even touch her," he said at the little dog's latest advance to smell Jethro's leg.

"I already have. I scratched an ear last week."

"Yew see the Spaniard?"

"I saw him."

"What did he say?"

"He didn't say anything. He won't talk to me."

"For why?"

"Search me. Not good enough to wipe his boots, maybe. Got two heads, maybe. Maybe he's just touchy."

"Maybe too much yew expect."

"Maybe."

But two days later, Jethro Spring waited outside the Gutierrez cabin, this time hiding behind the tiny outhouse. The little building was located some fifty feet directly across from the cabin's door. His wait was gratifyingly brief. When the Spaniard exited the outhouse, it was to confront Jethro, crouching on his heels, across the trail.

Gutierrez strode around Jethro and returned to the cabin.

"Damn you!" the younger man shouted. "I'll see you in hell."

Three things transpired: There came a bark from a rifle slit, and dirt flew from the ground in front of Jethro, slapping his leg halfway to the knee. Then the cabin grew silent.

An hour later, Jethro took the sledge and drill from Gunnar's hands. To the Swede's question concerning Gutierrez, he shook his head without comment.

The following morning Jethro was sitting in the doorway of the Spaniard's cabin when he exited his toilet. Gutierrez strode directly to his mine tunnel.

Antonio Gutierrez began using his outhouse during the darkness of night and it took a few days for Jethro to catch on. But on the fifth night of nocturnal visits, the outhouse door had just closed behind the Spaniard when Jethro dropped a lariat loop over the entire building and pulled the door tight. "Now will you listen?" he asked.

His answer was the whisper of a knife blade through a crack in the logs and the lariat fell loose.

Gunnar quit asking the results of Jethro's visits to Gutierrez. But each time his workman returned, he raised an eyebrow. The unspoken question was always answered with a brief shake of his friend's head.

Finally, in desperation, Jethro spread a rope snare across the outhouse trail, triggered by a bent sapling. The following night a #15 beartrap was laid across Gunnar's mine trail.

Odina discovered the beartrap. It was not hidden and the dog drew back growling. Gunnar ordered Odina behind before throwing a stone on the pan. Both dog and man jumped when the jaws of the washtub-sized trap clanged shut.

The little Swede, lugging the forty pound beartrap, met Jethro as the younger man jogged homeward after another fruitless attempt to converse with the Spaniard.

"What the hell...!"

"Far enough dis has gone," Gunnar snapped. "Yew can come with me." The little man's tone brooked no argument. Neither did he allow Jethro to take the trap.

When they reached the cabin, Gunnar hammered on the door.

"He's in his mine," Jethro said.

The little man whirled and, still carrying the heavy trap, started for the mine with his dog trotting behind.

"He says he'll kill anyone who steps across the

Gunnar's Mine

threshold."

Gunnar never bothered to reply. But he had no chance to test Gutierrez's threat because the Spaniard stepped from his tunnel to meet them. Gutierrez was armed with his sawed-off shotgun. He drew himself regally to full height.

It crossed Jethro's mind that they made a ludicrous sight—the runted little Swede, without a shirt, wearing only patched and soiled overalls with knees blown from both legs; Gutierrez in a white shirt and black tie and this time, wearing light gray trousers with a stripe down the outside of each leg—Confederate Army issue, perhaps.

"What is it you wish?" the Spaniard asked, gazing disdainfully over his callers' heads, at distant mountains.

"What ay want is for the two of yew"—and here Gunnar pointedly turned to glare at Jethro—"to stop dis game dat is go on."

Not only was there a solid foot of difference in their height, but the Spaniard stood three feet higher on the trail to the mine mouth. And he used this advantage to portray arrogance. "If you, senor, have accomplished your purpose, be so kind as to remove yourself from my presence."

Gunnar's head was tilted back as he glared up at Antonio Gutierrez. He ignored the Spaniard's command, choosing instead to step up the trail to another level.

The shotgun's twin barrels swung to yawn between them, though Gutierrez continued to gaze into the distance.

Jethro said, "Easy does it, both of you."

"If ay see yew on my claim," the little Swede growled, "ay will take dis piece of iron and ay will club you with it until yew are yelly." When the haughty Spaniard's gaze remained distant, Gunnar added, "Dat is what ay will do."

Then Gunnar Einarssen spun on his heel, pushed past Jethro and strode down the trail, shoulders still jerking in anger.

Only then did Antonio Gutierrez's black eyes shift to the little man. "My trap, senor!" he called. "Do me the kindness of leaving it at my cabin."

"Yew can go to hell!"

The click of one of the shotgun's hammers being eared back carried to Jethro. The younger man stepped further to the side, his Colt appearing magically to hand. "You pull that trigger or move that barrel, and you die."

Gutierrez's gaze never wavered from the retreating little Swede, but he said clearly into the bright, sunshiny morning, "You, senor, I have never doubted."

Jose Antonio Gutierrez de Valdez y Mendoza first blinked to daylight at the Hacienda de Esperanza por Tierra de la Suavedad, near the city of San Pedros de las Colonias in the State of Coahuila, in north central Mexico. The year was 1831; the month, August. Young Antonio was the first-born son of the first-born son for many generations, tracing their Gutierrez lineage back to 1540 and a young officer in the entourage of Mexico's first Viceroy, Antonio de Mendoza; and through the officer's wife, the beautiful fair-haired youngest daughter of Mendoza, ultimately to the Court of Castille itself.

The Hacienda de Esperanza, at the time of the latest heir's birth, was owned by his grandfather, an autocratic sovereign with absolute power over an estancia the size of which he declined even to measure. The vast estancia included mines drilled in spurs of the Sierra Madre Occidental in the states of Zacatecas and

Gunnar's Mine

Durango. That the Hacienda de Esperanza had survived twenty years of turmoil, beginning with Father Hidalgo's "Cry of Sorrows" through Iturbide's declaration of Mexico's independence and the consequent overthrow of Iturbide as Emperor Augustin by General Lopez de Santa Anna, could be attributed to the political and diplomatic skills of grandfather Gutierrez.

Unfortunately, Antonio's grandfather's great heart gave way at the same late-October moment when news was received that rebellious Anglos, little more than guests dwelling in Coahuila-Texas, had revolted and overwhelmed a Mexican Army detachment at the caserio de Gonzales.

Finally free of his own father's innate caution, and since the Anglo rebellion in the north clearly constituted an external threat instead of internal upheaval, Antonio's father felt safe in aligning the Hacienda de Esperanza with Santa Anna as that seemingly invincible general moved a powerful army north to crush the upstart rebels. Pedro Bartolome Gutierrez de Valdez y Mendoza even answered his motherland's call to arms by raising a regiment of Coahuila neighbors to join the vast northward moving army.

Captain Bartolome Gutierrez proved a commanding figure as an officer, and a brave one under fire. It was he who was first over the walls of the Alamo, first to suggest moving cannon to within point-blank range of the defenders' last redoubt in the powder storage room, and first to shield the Alamo's six survivors—the three women, two children, and a black slave—from the wrath of his comrades.

Captain Bartolome Gutierrez also accompanied the detachment of Colonel Juan Morales, whose men were sent with cannon by Santa Anna to reinforce those of General Urrea as they invested the fortress at the place the rebels called Goliad. And it was Captain Bartolome

Gutierrez and his unit of stalwart Coahuila regulars who turned those same rebels from their sought-after forest sanctuary during the Battle of the Lost Woods, the one the rebels called Coleto Creek.

Sadly, it was Captain Bartolome Gutierrez who, eight days after the rebels surrendered, was disgracefully ordered by General Santa Anna himself to use his Coahuila regulars to shoot the unarmed rebel survivors, made to stand alongside trenches they'd dug for their own graves.

And finally, it was Captain Bartolome Gutierrez who was shot by that same firing squad for refusing to obey his commanding general's order.

The women of Hacienda de Esperanza por Tierra de la Suavedad tried heroically to keep the Gutierrez holdings together after Santa Anna's disastrous defeat at San Jacinto, as well as during the turmoil that overtook Mexico throughout the subsequent decade. With the family's fortunes in decline, the wolves descended. Headed primarily by the very Coahuila regulars whom Captain Bartolome Gutierrez had initially led to glory in the Texian War of Independence, they stripped the estancia, bleeding it of a mine here, a pasture there, water stolen from the next valley.

Jose Antonio Gutierrez de Valdez y Mendoza entered the Mexican Military College in 1842, as a cadet. He was eleven years old. His sole purpose was to become a general like Santa Anna; to control the government through coups and intrigues—even murder—to become dictator. When Antonio Gutierrez achieved such power, then Captain Bartolome Gutierrez and his family would be avenged.

Young Gutierrez's plan hit a snag in December,

Gunnar's Mine

1844 when a coalition of political moderates and Federalists forced the dictator Lopez de Santa Anna into exile, establishing a constitutional democracy. Unfortunately the Federalists' timing turned sour when, two months later, the United States of America annexed Texas and a wave of patriotism swept Mexico.

Santa Anna, who, as early as 1843, had warned that Mexico would consider U.S. annexation of Texas as 'equivalent to a declaration of war' was recalled and appointed commander of the Mexican Army. In December, 1846, General Lopez de Santa Anna was re-elected President of the Republic of Mexico.

In January 1847, Santa Anna moved north with an army of twenty thousand to block a smaller army of Norte Americanos approaching the central highlands through Monterrey. At the Hacienda de Esperanza, the battle was joined. The bloody two day fight, later known as the Battle of Buena Vista, proved inconclusive. Though Mexican casualties were much higher, the smaller American force was so reduced by bullet and disease that it was forced to lie fallow at the Hacienda de Esperanza in order to recover strength and purpose.

Meanwhile, Santa Anna was unable to exploit his enemy's weakness for the very good reason that he had to return south to counter a U.S. naval-borne invasion of Veracruz, threatening Mexico City itself.

The Central Mexican Campaign was a litany of disasters for the beleaguered army of Santa Anna: Veracruz, Cerro Gordo, Puebla, Jalapa, Contreras, Churubusco. Until Chapultepec.

During the invasion, the young cadets from the Mexican Military College seethed at their inability to join in the defense of their country's sacred soil. No cadet was more critical of Santa Anna's disastrous leadership than the sixteen-year-old senior, Jose Antonio Gutierrez de Valdez y Mendoza.

In early September, the invaders approached Mexico City, and it was at the fortified citadel of Chapultepec that cadet Jose Antonio Gutierrez de Valdez y Mendoza reached for immortality by marshalling his fellow cadets in defense. The final battle began with an artillery bombardment on September 12, followed the next day by a massed infantry assault. Even in defeat, the heroic cadets of Chapultepec, with well over half their number killed or wounded, represented Mexico's finest hour. The American General Winfield Scott was heard to say, "I'm grateful the enemy command never turned that bunch of children loose on us earlier in this war. Things may have been different."

Meanwhile, Santa Anna fled Mexico City with the remnants of his troops. The day of his flight was the day General Lopez de Santa Anna was deposed as head of the Mexican State, and the day his successors sued for peace.

Within a week, Jose Antonio Gutierrez de Valdez y Mendoza limped from an American Army infirmary to the Mexican War College where the youth was handed an early diploma in military engineering as reward for his heroism and leadership in defense of the Citadel of Chapultepec.

Thus the boy returned to the Hacienda de Esperanza a man, a certified engineer, a hero. To the remnants of his family, to his neighbors in southern Coahuila, and perhaps to himself, Jose Antonio Gutierrez de Valdez y Mendoza returned as the avenger who exacted retribution for his father's murder.

Home was hardly the same for the returning hero, however. With the fall of the familia Gutierrez from favor among the powerful elite, the stripping of the estancia by neighboring farmers and townsmen upon his father's disgrace and death, then occupation for over six months by a bivouacking hostile army, the Hacienda de

Gunnar's Mine

Esperanza was but a hollow shell of its former glory.

The young Gutierrez tried. Oh how he tried! With the mien of a hero that he'd earned in savage combat and the carriage of the military officer he'd become, he cowed his neighbors into again giving to the Gutierrez family an obeisance their heritage demanded. With unflagging vigor and great personal effort the Hacienda's essential buildings were repaired, fences mended, trespassers evicted. One year passed. Two. Three. Through Antonio's stewardship, the Hacienda de Esperanza, though far from exhibiting its former dimensions and assets, made its slow way back to a modicum of prestige and prosperity. Seeking more financial security than that gained by raising cattle and grain, young Gutierrez turned his engineering skills to mining. He turned out to be quite good at it.

As luck had it, the original bounds of the Hacienda de Esperanza penetrated into some of the richest mineral regions in Mexico; to the Torreon in Durango and the rich gold fields of San Luis Potosi. Though the Gutierrez family had been stripped of its former mine holdings, there existed a nucleus of loyal and competent mine managers and engineers awaiting only inspiration from a bonafied Gutierrez who was a jefe, a hero, an officer, an engineer. Jose Antonio Gutierrez de Valdez y Mendoza assembled these mining men from the compass points to which they'd drifted, enthused them, sent them off to explore, analyze, and assess. His instructions were to locate promising new properties and to acquire old properties with potential. Then he went with them, studying their work, learning their expertise and their methods. And the Compania Descubrir de Mineral prospered.

Then, in midsummer of 1853, Santa Anna returned as Mexico's 'Perpetual Dictator', sold southern Arizona to the United States, and began confiscating the holdings of wealthy liberals who'd previously persecuted him. The Gutierrez family, thorns in the dictator's side after his defeats against the Texians and Norte Americanos, was high on his list.

Though the dictator was overthrown in but two years by liberals led by Melchor Ocampo and Benito Juarez, the confiscation and destruction of the holdings of the family Gutierrez was virtually complete.

Jose Antonio Gutierrez de Valdez y Mendoza joined the forces of Ocampo and Juarez, who were pleased to obtain the services of the 'hero of Chapultepec'—a well-known hater of Santa Anna. It was at San Serta that Captain Gutierrez, with fire in his eyes and hatred in his heart, led a mob of untrained rabble to disaster against Santa Anna's disciplined troops. Thereafter, Gutierrez's soldiers became the best trained in all the rebel army, and the officer leading them was assigned more and more responsibility. He was promoted to Major; then Colonel.

When Lopez de Santa Anna was again overthrown, Jose Antonio Gutierrez de Valdez y Mendoza rode in the second rank, behind Ocampo and Juarez, as the victorious rebels entered Mexico City.

But all heart went out of him when he returned to the Hacienda de Esperanza and saw first-hand the destruction that had been wreaked upon it. Gone, too, was Compania Descubrir de Mineral, stripped and sold to Santa Anna hangers-on and foreign elements.

Also gone during his absence was Antonio's mother, dead of a broken heart at the tragedies enveloping her family.

Returning to Mexico City, this time as a solicitor, Gutierrez discovered Ocampo and Juarez had, in an attempt to right Mexico's shattered economy, decreed that the Church must sell most of its land and that Indian communal lands had to be distributed to individual peasants. The liberals' hopes for a rising middle class failed to materialize amid a new revolt, this time led by the Church. As a result, Ocampo and Juarez had all on their plates they could handle. Though Antonio Gutierrez had access to the seat of power, he soon discovered the leaders were too busy to demonstrate much interest in the affairs of one of their erstwhile commanders. "Besides, Colonel Gutierrez," President Benito Juarez said, "at this time of disorder, shouldn't you report to your command?"

The Colonel stormed from Juarez's august presence and took the first boat from Acapulco to Peru, thus missing the invasion of Mexico by the French during the United States Civil War. As recompense, Antonio Gutierrez discovered considerable demand for the services of a trained mining engineer amid the Peruvian Andes. It was there, during the benign Presidency of Ramon Castilla that Jose Antonio Gutierrez de Valdez y Mendoza polished his hardrock mining training. Then Castilla retired and a period of internal disorder, corruption, and increasing foreign debt overtook Peru.

The rootless Gutierrez migrated first to Bolivia, where he fought off bandits bent on taking over the mine he managed; then to Chile, where first one junta seized power then another; first one robber baron held sway, then another. Gradually Gutierrez became embittered, reclusive, as touchy as a wounded snake. Throughout all the turmoil, however, Antonio Gutierrez extended his knowledge of hardrock minerals and mining.

At last, in 1874, news reached the remote mountains of central Chile that Mexico's Presidente Benito Juarez, the man Antonio felt had most betrayed him, had died. Gutierrez decided to return to his homeland. He was slow in doing so, however, finally arriving in Mexico City in 1876, only weeks before General Porfiro Diaz seized power.

That was the last straw! Jose Antonio Gutierrez de Valdez y Mendoza headed north, to the *Estados Unidos*.

When the man he knew as Anton Gutierrez dropped the muzzle of his shotgun to point at his own feet, Jethro Spring asked, "Now are you ready to talk?"

As if coming out of a dream, the Spaniard's black eyes wandered from Gunnar Einarssen's retreating back to envelope the gray-eyed man standing below. Jethro holstered his Colt while the imperious Jose Antonio Gutierrez de Valdez y Mendoza sighed and said, "You, Senor, might someday wear an *hidalgo* down." Then he spun on his heel and disappeared into his mine.

Chapter Nine

The atmosphere permeating Gunnar Einarssen's holdings on Fall Creek was frigid for several days. For one thing, the beartrap, leaning against the wall between Gunnar's and Jethro's beds stood as a mute reminder of the moment the Swede lost his temper at the antics of his workman and the Spaniard, Gutierrez.

For his part, the little man said nothing, rising as usual each morning to eat breakfast, then, followed by his little dog, heading for the mine tunnel. His workman would clean the table, scour the pots and pans, then join Gunnar in the tunnel.

That Jethro cut down on his efforts to speak to Gutierrez, helped breach the coolness. Finally, in the early afternoon of the Fourth of July, Gunnar came to watch Jethro finish single-jacking shot holes in the tunnel's headwall and said, "Yew leave and the charges ay will set. Den we celebrate t'rowing out dat bad king with our own firework. What you t'ink?"

Jethro picked up his canteen and tools. "Sounds good to me. You want I should bring up the dynamite?"

"Ay have it. And the fuse, too." Then Gunnar patted the bib pocket on his overalls and added, "The caps ay have here."

Jethro's white teeth flashed in the dim candlelight.

"Den when ay finish and we watch, we take bath and to Walter's we go for supper. Fun we will have, ay t'ink."

When Jethro merely stood gazing at him, Gunnar added, "Is time we had fun, don' you t'ink?"

A half-hour later, when the little Swede exited the tunnel mouth, he found the younger man sitting on the tailings heap. Jethro pushed up and the two men, one a head taller, trailed by the dog, ambled to Fall Creek and the pool Jethro had formed with a dam of rubble rock. They'd just sat down to remove their boots when the explosion came, followed immediately by a cloud of dust blowing from the mine mouth.

"Old man," Jethro murmured, "you timed that one a little close."

Gunnar stood to unclasp one of the straps on his overalls. As he shucked them, he said, "Fuse, she cost money."

Jethro glared at him, then saw the twinkle in his friend's eye.

Minutes later the two lay sprawled in the pool, soaking in its coolness, letting muscles relax, willing newness and energy back into tired bodies. Then Odina growled and Gunnar stood to peer over the streambank. When he dived back to the water, Jethro, cursing, scrambled for the gunbelt he'd placed at the shoreline.

"My, my," the woman said as her head popped above a streamside bush, "I don't think I've witnessed such a display of vigor since that standardbred ran away with my pacing buggy."

Her face was pale and her hair the color of spring

snowbanks—even, Jethro noted as he squatted in shocked surprise, the eyebrows. He looked down. Water covered only his ankles.

She moved closer. Gunnar, whimpering, crowded his skinny frame against the cutbank while Odina, not understanding, licked his exposed shoulder and buttocks and the bottoms of his feet.

The woman moved on out to the edge of the cutbank and stood, hands on hips, apparently merely gazing into their pool. She was a large-boned woman. Her blouse-waist was a man's red silk shirt, unbuttoned at the neck and without a collar. The waist was tucked into a stylish, tailor-made walking skirt of a dark-striped material. A strangely detached Jethro noted that neither the hem of her skirt, nor her shoes, appeared wet. Had she crossed the San Miguel with skirt raised and shoes in hand?

"Delightful," the woman said. "Doubtless you come here often during this weather."

Then she looked squarely at Jethro and said, "I do wish you'd point that gun elsewhere."

Jethro stared stupidly down at the Colt. His knuckles were white. He was also unaware that the muzzle had unwittingly followed the woman as she stepped from her sheltering stand of young cottonwoods. He lowered the gun and muttered, "Sorry."

She smiled, shifting her pale blue eyes to Gunnar, then to Odina. "What a cute little dog. Does she have a name?"

Gunnar whimpered and cradled his head tighter against the crumbling cutbank. "Ma'am," Jethro began, "if you'll excuse us...."

"I will not," she replied. "I've not had so much fun since the girls from my finishing school trapped two farmboys dipping in a stockpond."

Jethro's gray eyes snapped, but with no other alternative, he pushed to his feet and reached for his trousers. When he'd pulled them and his boots on, he hopped up the bank and took the woman by the elbow, roughly steering her from the pool's bank so Gunnar could dress.

"Feel lucky," she said when he'd taken her to the trail. "We took the farmboys' clothing."

"You might've done that to us, too, except Odina caught you sneaking."

She giggled. "I might have."

Her teeth were glistening-white, more so, even, than hair and eyebrows. Jethro saw that, despite her gracious good looks, the woman was much older than he'd first supposed. "Who are you?" he growled.

She gasped in mock surprise. "Sir, I cannot share my name on the basis of a chance meeting with two total strangers."

"Wait here," he ordered. "I'll get my shirt."

But when he returned, she was gone.

It was a half-hour before Jethro could coax Gunnar to come from behind the shelter of the cutbank. When the little man finally emerged, it was with the furtive features of a midnight thief.

Upon reaching the cabin, Gunnar plopped a near-full whiskey bottle on the table, uncorked it and poured himself three fingers in a tin cup. "Who was dat woman?" he blurted after he'd downed the whiskey. "Maybe ay should t'ink it is another game yew and the Spaniard play."

Jethro grinned and poured himself a liberal dose from Gunnar's bottle. "Whoever she was, she caught us with our pants down."

"Ay will never wash in dat place again."

"Oh, I dunno, old man. I kinda enjoyed it."

Gunnar poured another for both of them. "At first, ay t'ought she was an angel."

"On second thought, I'm not sure she wasn't."

"She was, how yew say, boot, boot...."

"Beautiful."

"Yah."

Jethro poured more. "How the hell would you know? You had your nose pushed so deep into the bank it growed roots."

"Ay looked from my eye, the side of."

"You didn't neither."

"Ay did!"

An hour went by. Another. The bottle was emptied, knocked to the floor. Another magically appeared.

Walter was on the point of closing when the owner of the Nordic Summer and his hired man, each dripping water from the knees down and supporting the other, staggered in for supper.

"This ought to be worth stayin' open for," the waystop proprietor said, arching his eyebrows and pouring three cups of evil-looking coffee from a blackened pot.

"We ... we are sell ... sell ..." That's as far as Gunnar got before he hiccuped.

"Celebratin'," Jethro finished for him.

"That I can tell," Walter said. "Does that mean this afternoon's shot put you into color?"

Gunnar drew himself up to his full height, pointed a finger at the rough board ceiling and made a lengthy speech in pure Swedish.

Walter chuckled, while Jethro sagely nodded.

"Okay, boys, what'll it be? I need to get to bed sometime tonight."

When Gunnar gave another lengthy Viking discourse, Jethro said, "Steaks, Walter. The biggest and best steaks in all southwest Colorado."

Walter fired his stove, then disappeared to his root cellar for several minutes. In the interim, Jethro poured

Gunnar and himself more coffee.

Gunnar's Swedish diatribe rose amid a far-off stare, then began to run down into garbled muttering. At last, the little man laid his head on his arms and closed first one eye, then another. A half-hour went by. Eventually, Jethro asked, "Gunnar, you want I should go get the rest of that bottle? Or are we not celebratin' no more?"

Gunnar snored softly in response.

Then Walter plunked heavy pewter plates on the log counter. The plates overflowed with gigantic, still-steaming steaks. There was a bowl of baked potatoes, too, with butter, and beans. "How about some buttermilk, boys?" the proprietor asked. "Fresh this morning."

"How about it, Gunnar?" Jethro asked as the little man lifted his head. "Want buttermilk?"

Gunnar replied in Swedish, staring over Walter's head at some imaginary distant spot. "Talk American," Walter said. "I ain't no Norwegian."

"She ... she vas boot ..."

"Beautiful," Jethro supplied, prior to filling his mouth with a slice of dripping meat.

Walter laughed. "So you met her, huh?" He turned to the stove to clean up, saying, "She stopped in here lookin' for your claim, Gunnar. Said she'd heard a lot about you two. Said the way she'd heard it, you were both big enough and tough enough to slay elephants, each with one hand tied behind your backs."

The rich smell of the steaks aroused Gunnar so the little man attacked his meat with gusto. But Jethro stopped chewing. "She came in a buggy, right Walter? From which direction?"

"Didn't see one. No horse either. I think she walked up."

Jethro laid his knife and fork down. "That means Placerville?"

Walter shrugged. "The way I figured, too. We'll find

Gunnar's Mine

out soon enough, I guess. Woman with that much glitter'll be talked about some."

Gunnar sighed. "Ay t'ink she was angel."

Jethro said, "Maybe we will take some of that buttermilk, Walter. The bitterer, the better."

Neither employer nor employee enjoyed crawling into the Nordic Summer tunnel the morning following their meeting with the fair-haired angel. Jethro's head banged with each hammer blow to drill bit, while Gunnar was heard retching twice while hauling buckets of rubble from the tunnel.

The second, near-empty whiskey bottle stood in the middle of the table as both men picked at the soup and beans Gunnar laid out for dinner. It's cousin, the empty bottle, lay half under Gunnar's bed, where it'd been kicked the evening before.

When they'd eaten what they could, Gunnar grasped the table bottle, looked around for the missing cork, then shrugged and said, "Yew want some of dis, ay leave it."

The straight line of Jethro's mouth turned down as he rushed to the door to retch. After Gunnar ran the missing cork to ground and, while sitting on his bunk, pounded it into the bottle neck, the younger man said, "Look, old timer, you lay down on that bunk for a snooze and I promise you I'll do the same on my bunk."

Gunnar eyed his workman as if he was a leper, then he stretched out on his bunk and sighed.

Two hours passed. Three.

"Hello! Is anyone home?"

Jethro's eyes popped open, colliding with a wide-eyed stare from Gunnar. Odina growled. Then Jethro's mouth curled into a sneer.

"Hello! Is anyone home?" Knuckles rapped the door.

Odina barked. Gunnar drew a blanket over his head. The rawhide straps holding his straw mattress squealed as he did so.

"I hear you. You're in there; I know you're in there. I came to visit. If you're not decent, I can wait."

"Go away!" Jethro shouted.

"Is that any way to treat a lady? Of course I won't go away. I wish to become friends."

"Go away, dammit! Just go away." Then he added, "Please."

She giggled. "Mr. Hopkins said you gentlemen might not be feeling your best." Meeting silence, she persevered, "He said you might not even be working today. That's when I thought I might be able to minister to the afflicted."

A groan came from the blanket-covered mound on Gunnar's bed.

"Perhaps I should just come on in if you're unable to reach the door. I will, however, wait an appropriate interval in case you need time to dress properly."

Jethro leaped to his feet and jerked open the cabin door to glare at their visitor. First to be seen were her dimples as she stood on the stoop, smiling at him.

"My, you do look disheveled, Mr. Frost. May I call you that? Or would you prefer Jason? Tell me, does Mr. Einarssen appear as badly worn as you? I must say, it's difficult to believe you had such spirit and vigor less than twenty-four hours ago, especially in lieu of your present appearance."

Jethro ran his hand through his hair. "What do you want?"

She placed hands to hips and cocked her head as the dimpled smile broadened. "Why Mr. Frost! Such brusqueness! I only wish to better acquaint myself with those within the valley. To visit them, if you will. Apparently you do not mean to invite me inside, nor to offer coffee. Is that also Mr. Einarssen's attitude toward his neighbors?"

Jethro pushed on outside, backing her from the stoop, pulling the door closed behind. He had to admire her sense of place and balance as she stepped backward off the stoop to the ground. "I don't believe you," he said, biting the words. The man was a head above the woman now, glaring down. "What do you want with us?"

This time she was dressed in a creamy lawn dress with an off-the-shoulder waist trimmed in cardinal embroidery and narrow black ribbon. Daringly, the dress reached only to her ankles and provided maximum flounce for free movement. Again, its hem was free of moisture—as were her walking shoes and stockings.

Then Jethro heard movement in the cabin behind him, the stove door opening and closing. He continued to glare down at the woman. "Well?"

She glanced up at the chimney. "Ah, smoke. Perhaps Mr. Einarssen recuperates more quickly than you, Mr. Frost." She shifted her vision to bear upon him. "Is he making coffee for courtesy's sake?"

The dark-faced man was suddenly conscious that he had a hole in the toe of one stocking. He took a deep breath before again asking—this time in a more moderate tone, "What is it you want, ma'am?"

Her smile broadened. "That's better. I merely wish to become acquainted."

The coffee pot clanged on the stovetop. Jethro once more ran fingers through his hair. He thought her smile more leer than good humor, as he continued to do battle with his temper. "Just why is it you wish to become better acquainted?"

She said nothing, but continued to smile up at him.

He whirled, pushed through the door and slammed it in her face.

Gunnar, stoking the fire under the coffee pot, turned to peer at Jethro, eyebrows arched.

Jethro spread his hands and opened his mouth to tell the little man he'd learned nothing, when the door rattled to renewed knocking. The younger man dropped his face into the splayed fingers of one hand as Gunnar pushed past to swing open the door. Jethro sank onto a pine block and dropped his head onto arms folded across the table, as she chirped, "Oh there you are, Mr. Einarssen. I was hoping to get a chance to visit with you, too. May I come in?"

Though the woman continued to render Gunnar speechless, he moved aside and she swept into the room, pausing briefly to take in the cabin's interior, then settling onto a pine block across the table from Jethro. "So!" she said, flouncing on her stool.

Despite the insect hordes common to Colorado mountain country in July, Gunnar left the door ajar as he shuffled back to the stove and coffee pot. Jethro briefly met the woman's wide and seemingly guileless eyes, then sighed and began studying the stocking hole where his big toe thrust half-out.

"Tell me about yourselves," the woman said.

Again, Jethro sighed, uncrossed and recrossed his arms, all the while staring at his toe.

She turned to the little man who remained with his back to the visitor. "Mr. Einarssen, you are Swedish, yes?"

Gunnar lifted two tin cups and a milk can from the dynamite-box cupboard, saying as he did, "Ay from Sweden, ya."

Her smile brightened. "Well, I do declare. That's a start. From where in Sweden?"

The coffee was beginning to boil. Gunnar pretended to stir the fire. Without turning his head more than was necessary, he peeked at the woman. "Gotland, it is where ay lived."

"Goat land. Is that in the mountains, Mr. Einarssen? Or can I call you Gunnar? Did you herd goats?" Then she clapped her hands. "Do you yodel, Mr. Einarssen?"

The little man nodded, still without looking squarely at her. "Gunnar is my name. No mountains. Gotland is island in Baltic Sea. Ay do not know dis t'ing, yodel. What is?" He looked to Jethro for an explanation.

Jethro ignored them both.

Gunnar set the coffee pot aside for the grounds to settle. The woman resumed, "An island. Were you a fisherman? Do you have family there? Why did you come to America?"

Jethro exploded, "My God, woman!"

Gunnar filled the cups and the tin with steaming coffee, then brought them one by one to the table, reserving the milk tin for himself. At last he took the third pine block and said, "No. No family, dere is. My mama was maid to the Sven of Visby. Brought from Denmark, she was. My papa, she did not know who was. Dead for long time, mama."

The woman's face reddened and she touched Gunnar's arm. "I'm so sorry."

Gunnar's watery blue eyes lifted to meet her pale ones. A stillness fell over the tiny cabin, broken when she took a deep breath and said, "Do you know your eye's are fascinating, Gunnar?" Then her gaze wandered to Jethro. "Almost as fascinating as the gray ones belonging to Mr. Frost."

She lifted her coffee cup to sip.

"Why are you here, ma'am?" Jethro asked, squinting narrowly at the woman.

Her smile was radiant once more. "My, my. Is there no quit in you, Mr. Frost? Surely you know you two are subjects of mystery and suspense in Placerville and Telluride. You, Mr. Frost, are said to be more daring than Lancelot, and our friend, Gunnar, is thought insanely mad and supremely cunning. These are the kinds of things that just naturally turn a girl's head."

Suspicion and disbelief were so mirrored on Jethro's face that she added, "Surely you wouldn't begrudge a lady some curiosity, would you?"

Gunnar murmured, "Dere is no cake or cookies. Ay can make cornbread toast, and yam dere is."

She placed a hand over one of the little man's. Had he moved it nearer so she could reach it? "Thank you, Gunnar, but I need nothing, except the opportunity to learn of others."

A faint grin quickly swept Jethro's face, then disappeared. He pushed to his feet and went to the door, opening it even wider to stand and gaze outside for a full minute. Two. Then he returned to the table and the woman and Gunnar. She still covered Gunnar's hand with her own. The door remained wide open.

"... and you built this cabin yourself, Gunnar? Where did you learn to work so well with wood?"

"Ostersund is where. Ay worked in logging camp when ay leave Gotland."

"And then you came to America?"

"What is your name?" Jethro suddenly demanded.

She removed her hand from Gunnar's and fixed the younger man with her dimpled smile.

"You'll have to admit this is no longer a single chance meeting," he said, voice dripping with irony. "Nor can you claim we're two total strangers, since you already know our names. Now, what is yours?"

"Oh all right—Abigail."

"Abigail what?"

"Your persistence lacks taste, sir."

"Abigail what?"

"Dimity."

He seemed to ponder for a moment before asking, "And where are you from?"

Her dimples deepened. "Originally from Boston, but most recently from Placerville."

He stared her up and down. Ring on the third finger of her left hand, no powder and only a little rouge. Aged well, maybe fifty, certainly bold around men. Yet there's an undefinable something that says she's not what I think she is. And the light, almost white hair. Even eyelashes. Is she what one would call an albino, if an animal? He remembered how the plains Indians thought white buffaloes sacred and was, for a moment, diverted.

"Have you looked at me long enough?" Abigail Dimity asked. She turned to smile at Gunnar, then stood. "You gentlemen are fascinating, but I'm afraid I've used all my allotted time. Will you forgive me if I beg your leave?"

Gunnar and Jethro both stood. "Yew are welcome to once more come," Gunnar said. Then his eyes took on a mischievous glint. "Except when a bath ay take."

Her pealing laugh echoed around the room.

"Hold on," Jethro said, "and I'll get into a pair of boots and walk you to wherever it is you're going."

She moved swiftly to the door. "No need, sir. Thank you, however."

He overtook her at the river crossing, as she removed shoes and stockings. "Mr. Frost, I'm afraid you will require a great deal more training than most men. Apparently you didn't hear me when I said I needed no escort."

"Either I didn't hear, or I didn't listen."

"The second being the more likely of the two, I'm afraid."

Walking beside her, Jethro was struck again by the

woman's height, which brought her nearly eye-to-eye with him. She was slender, though, and her stride like a man's ... swift and lengthy.

When they reached Walter's, she turned to face him. "Thank you, Mr. Frost. I appreciate your kindness."

"I'll get your horse."

Her smile was fleeting. "I have no horse, thank you. I enjoy walking. But you needn't concern yourself."

He shook his head. "Placerville or Telluride?"

She giggled. "Placerville. Oh my! We'll have to retrace part of our journey won't we?"

They covered the first mile to Placerville in short order, then he asked if she would like to find a shaded place along the river and rest. She eyed him for a moment, then said, "Yes, I believe so."

After they were seated facing each other on large stones, he asked, "Why do you visit Gunnar and me?"

She laughed. "You worry that like a dog worries a bone, don't you, Mr. Frost?"

"And your name is Abigail Dimity?"

"It is."

"But Dimity is your middle name, isn't it?"

Her dimples deepened. "And you're unusually perceptive. Yes it is."

"Are you connected to Andrew Whittle?"

"I'm his mother."

He gazed off towards the river. "Uh-huh. I guessed it was something like that."

"Something like what, Mr. Frost?" When he didn't answer, her voice turned indignant. "Do you think I visited you at Andrew's instigation? If so, you're wrong. I came because I'm intrigued by what Billy said about you."

His head whipped around. "Billy? Billy who?"

"I believe his name is Billy Benbrooke. Apparently he's Australian."

Chapter Ten

A chill settled over Jethro Spring at Abigail Whittle's disclosure that the Australian, Billy Benbrooke, had returned to Placerville. *How long has Billy been back?*

"May I ask when you arrived at Placerville, ma'am?"

"Three weeks ago, I believe; perhaps a little more. I rode to end of track. Andrew sent a man to meet me there."

"This may be getting personal, ma'am, but what do you know of Andrew Whittle's activities here?"

"The question is not just personal, sir, it's impertinent!"

He nodded. "Nevertheless, I'd appreciate it if you answered. You see, you've already been impertinent towards us. Twice. So the way I figure that gives me the right."

She saw he was serious, perhaps even disturbingly so. "Mr. Whittle—Andrew's father—and I were married for twenty-five years. Andrew was a young child when he was brought to his father's second marriage. But he was long gone when Harvey died. I can tell you he was certainly surprised when I decided to join him in the West." Abigail sighed. "This isn't the most stimulating discussion one can imagine. Shouldn't we continue on, Mr. Frost?"

He came immediately to his feet, offering her a hand. As they walked, she talked—mostly of the East, of Boston. But he heard little. Once, he interrupted her to ask if Billy Benbrooke worked for her husband.

"Yes, I believe so."

"Then do you know what he does?"

She didn't.

On the outskirts of Placerville, he took his leave. "You'll be safe enough from here on, I'm sure."

She didn't smile as she took his hand. "I'd hoped I might see you and Andrew meet. There are tales of those occurrences and I find it intriguing that someone could beat Andrew at anything."

He scuffed a boot toe into the packed road and said, "Won't happen today, ma'am. Benbrooke's return means the ante's been upped. And as soon as it's known that we know, a bunch of hell might break loose." His gray eyes flashed. "And I reckon you'll let'em know that we know soon as you can."

Her forehead wrinkled, but she smiled through it—a sorrowful blend of concern and attempted cheer. "I like fish who swim upstream, Mr. Frost. You and Mr. Einarssen seem like interesting individuals. Neither my stepson—nor the company he works for—needs my help; nor me theirs." She paused to take a breath, then continued, "I'm an observer, Mr. Frost, not a player. For some reason, I get the impression you are both."

Gunnar's Mine

Jethro Spring did not return immediately to Gunnar and the cabin and mine. Instead, he sat by the San Miguel, tossing pebbles into the stream until the sun dipped toward the La Sals to the west. Then he jogged to the Fall Creek crossing, and in the last vestiges of light, did a perimeter check around Gunnar's mine.

He was up first the following morning. When he flipped the wheatcakes to plates and straddled his pine block, he said to the little man across from him, "Gunnar, we've got to talk."

His employer carefully crosshatched his stack of cakes, spread syrup evenly throughout, speared a forkful and said, "To listen, ay will do."

"Billy Benbrooke is back."

Gunnar dropped his fork to the floor, Odina licked up the remains. Then the little man sighed. "To let him come to us, we should not."

Jethro nodded. "You said it was wrong at the time. It was me that brought him here."

Gunnar picked up his fork, let Odina finish licking it, then wiped it on the leg of his overalls before meditatively returning to his breakfast. "He did not see inside the mine. He does not know what we do."

"He might, Gunnar," Jethro said softly.

The Swede stopped chewing. "Yew did not tell him!"

The younger man shook his head. "But I might have done worse. I gave him the nugget you used to pay me. I wanted to see the poor bastard get back to his home and ..." His explanation choked to nothing before he finished.

"Dis t'ing about Billy. How you know?"

"Abigail told me."

Gunnar's stern features softened and his eyes became distant. Finally he murmured, "An angel, she is."

"She's also Andrew Whittle's mother." Again

103

Gunnar's fork clattered to the floor.

Several minutes passed before the older man's head lifted from his chest and he reached down to pick up the Odina-cleaned fork. The dog licked his knuckles as he did. Gunnar did not again touch his food.

It was a measure of respect for Jethro that the little Swede didn't question why Abigail Whittle gave his hired man such information. Instead, he asked, "Was she sent for us to spy?"

"It's possible, Gunnar. But for some reason, I don't think so. At least she says not. Too, she's the one who told me about Billy—not knowing a thing about the past. Said it was him that got her interested in us."

"Den dat means he works for Andrew Whittle. And dat means Whittle knows we have somet'ing."

"That's the way I see it, too. I'll kill him, Gunnar, damn him! I'll kick the living shit out of him."

Gunnar seemed not to hear. At last he said, "What kind of mans would send his mother for us to spy?" The Swede set his plate on the floor for Odina to clean, before carrying it to the stove and dumping it into the simmering wash bucket. "I knew he was no good. I knew dis from first." He shuffled behind Jethro, then added, "From first, almost, anyway."

The darker man spun on his block to face his boss. "Gunnar, we're going to have to lever watching out for them bastards up a notch."

The little man shot him the briefest of glances, then strode to the door. "Dat yob is yours. Ay have a tunnel for to dig."

Jethro washed his plate and utensils, poured himself another cup of coffee and drank it slowly. Then he buckled on his Colt, picked up his Winchester and telescope and made several circuits around the cabin, the tunnel mouth, and the nearby hillside. Then he waded the San Miguel, climbed the hillside to the east, then jogged off

Gunnar's Mine

crosscountry to Placerville. On a promontory above the hamlet, the dark-faced man took up a sheltered position with a decent view.

Luck was with him as he spotted Benbrooke leaving Chalkie's for the outhouse late in the afternoon of his first day. From there, Billy staggered to a nearby board-and-batten cabin, wobbled inside and slammed the door.

Jethro kept watch on the cabin until nightfall, then slipped nearer and waited until the morning star climbed overhead. He used a cat's stealth as he slipped through the cabin's door, then paused to ensure no one else but Billy was inside, then pushed the point of his boot knife against the sleeping man's jugular, saying, "Make a sound and it'll be your last."

Only the whites of the Australian's eyes glistened in the darkness.

It took several minutes for the two men to clear Placerville and reach the banks of the San Miguel. Then it took additional minutes for the barefoot, underwear-clad Benbrooke to be prodded to the river's west side. And it took several more minutes before the frightened Benbrooke could find his voice.

Jethro patiently waited, cleaning his nails with the knife he used to get Billy's attention.

Finally Benbrooke choked out, "Ja-Jason Frost, me l-lad, fancy m-meeting you back in Placer...."

"You bloody rotten double-whipping two-timing piece of sour owl shit. You bastardizing sonsabitchin' sick piece of horse dung not worthy to be called a man. You ... aw shit! You're too low to waste time on."

Benbrooke's head hung at half-mast.

"Dammit, you sodlovin' skunk-stinking lowdown

drivel-driving backstabbing excuse for a pig. What do you have to say for yourself?" Then Jethro's voice dropped to an ominous whisper. "Speak, dammit, or I'll cut your tongue out and feed it to your ass, bloody end first."

Benbrooke whimpered. "I don't know how I got here, mate. One day I just woke up in Chalkie's. I didn't mean to."

The first light of dawn kissed where the two men crouched. Tears rolled down the Aussie's anguished face.

"Where's my nugget?"

Benbrooke threw up an arm as if expecting a blow. "I ... I lost it in a monte game in Virginia City."

"That nugget was to get you home to Australia. So you lied to me, lied to Gunnar, lied to everyone you'd already told goodby."

"I meant to go home. I wanted to. Jason, you must believe me! It just happened!"

"And then you came back here to sell information on us to Andrew Whittle."

"No, no. I've got m'weaknesses, mate, but filching on friends I'd never do."

"What did you tell him?"

"Jason, I swear I told him nothing. What could I tell him? I was never in Gunnar's mine."

"So he hired you out of the goodness of his heart?"

"Aye. The man has a conscience after all. He knew he'd used me and felt sorry about it."

"Did you tell him about the nugget?"

"No, no. I'd never do that!"

Jethro stood, flipped the knife end-over-end, caught it by the handle, then drove it to its hilt between Benbrooke's feet. "If you've just told me another lie, you sonofabitch, you've signed your death warrant."

Blood drained from the other man's blotched and

blocky face as he fell to one knee while wagging his head from side to side and gasping for breath. At last he said, "Maybe I let it drop, Jason, but I didn't mean to."

"And I suppose you told him about my going out for supplies."

"Y-yes." Billy was on both knees now, peering up imploringly at his former friend. "I only wanted to show him I knew something worthwhile. I didn't think about hurting Gunnar."

"Hand me that knife."

Billy reached to pull the knife from between his knees, finally using both hands to jerk it free. Then he handed it, handle first, to Jethro.

The dark-faced man took the knife, slipped it into his boot, picked up his Winchester, kicked Billy Benbrooke full in the face, and waded back across the San Miguel.

An hour later, Jethro took the hammer and drill bit from the smaller man's hands. "It's as bad as we thought, Gunnar."

"Ya? So?"

"I talked to Billy. He spilled his guts all over Whittle's lap. That means the bastards will be after you like buzzards wanting raw meat."

"Dey might try, but ay still won't sell."

Jethro's hammer blows were especially savage for the rest of the day.

That very evening Gunnar placed another angular nugget in his plate. It was even bigger than the first, and it carried a small strip of quartz along one edge. "I don't want it," Jethro angrily said. "You've already paid me more'n enough."

"Yew gave dat one away. So dis is yours."

He took his empty plate and the nugget, dropping

both into the bucket of dishwater.

The little Swede shrugged and went to bed. The following morning, and each morning for a week thereafter, the nugget was in the younger man's plate. Each morning, he returned it to the dishwater. Eventually, he thought it must be the cleanest nugget in all Colorado and dropped it in his pocket.

There came a day late in July when Gunnar crimped dynamite caps to lengths of fuse with his teeth, then slit sticks of the explosive, inserted the prepared fuses and pushed them into shot holes Jethro had drilled. The younger man watched with a morbid fascination, queasy about being present at such a sensitive stage in the hardrock process. At last, he gathered up his tools and headed for daylight.

"The woman, she is outside," Gunnar said as he left.

Jethro stopped. "Woman? Here? Outside the tunnel? Why?"

"Ay had nothing to say to her."

When Jethro exited the tunnel, she was perched on the slag heap. "Well, there you are, Mr. Frost. Are you not speaking to me, too?"

He clambered to his feet, grinned, and dusted off. Then he offered his hand and she took it, eyes questioning, as he pulled her to her feet and guided her down the trail. "Pretty quick there's going to be a big bang and a cloud of dust will blow out the tunnel mouth. You sit back there, ma'am, and you'll need a bath, too."

"I see. However, I know there's a nice bathing pool within walking distance."

"True," he replied as they strolled down the trail, "but it's private and belongs to men only."

Gunnar's Mine

"Hmm. That's unfortunate. What's a lady supposed to do?"

His eyes twinkled when he turned them on her. "I won't say what comes to mind, ma'am, for fear you'd do it."

She laughed. By this time, they were sitting on the bank, throwing twigs into the pool. Gunnar hurried by on the trail. "What did you tell Gunnar to turn him against me?"

"Only your name."

She sighed and distantly said, "The name is an accident of marriage. I shouldn't be held responsible for whatever Andrew has done to evoke yours and Gunnar's animosity."

"How about for what he will do?"

She turned to face him. "What a strange thing to say. Please explain."

He tossed another twig into the pool. "Who does your son work for?"

"A very large mining company."

"Which one?"

"I'm afraid I have no idea. Is it important?"

This time it was he who sighed. "Are you aware there's an attempt underway by a large mining concern to gobble up all the claims in this district?"

"Surely you don't think ..."

"Are you aware claims have been jumped? That claimholders have been ..." (he pulled out the notebook from his shirtpocket and consulted it) "... coerced into selling? Even killed?"

"And Andrew is responsible? That's absurd."

Neither he nor she broke eye contact until he snapped off another twig and tossed it into the pool. "For some reason or another, I don't think you believe what you've just said, ma'am."

"Well! I certainly would not wish it to be otherwise."

He handed her the remaining end of his twig, which she pitched into the pool. "Enough of that," he said. "So tell me, why are you here?"

Her laugh seemed forced. "Mr. Frost, do you play only one note?"

He smiled. "Tell me why and I'll play another."

"All right. I'm in need of stimulating conversation. Despite what you might believe, Placerville is not exactly a lodestone for intelligent repartee."

This time he chuckled. "That's a stretch; to expect Gunnar and me to talk up a high-toned storm."

She shook her head at his irony. "You'd be surprised how I'm kept tucked away up there. Naturally I can't visit the high faluting San Miguell Emporium, as do all the other inhabitants of this district. Andrew seems much too busy to spend time talking to his stepmother, and apparently he has the men who work for him so cowed, they dare not talk to me. That leaves only the dissidents."

He took out his notepad and wrote 'D-I-S-A-D-E-N-T' in it, asking what it meant as he did.

"You mean dissident? It means someone who dissents—who differs from the ideas of a majority."

He tapped his notepad with his pencil, as if to drive the word home. Then he asked, "Have you visited other dissidents besides me and Gunnar?"

She shrugged. "Mr. Kracyk, unfortunately, is given to silence even more profound than that of Gunnar's. And Mr. Gutierrez won't receive me." She turned her head and smiled at him. "So that leaves just you and Gunnar. And now he won't talk to me because my name is that of a pariah to him."

P-A-R-I-A. She leaned closer to look. "Pariah ends with an 'H'. It means someone who's avoided by others."

Gunnar's Mine

"Well, I'm not avoiding ..."

Suddenly there came a roar from the mountain. Dust and debris blew from the tunnel mouth. "Goodness!" she exclaimed.

He watched the dust settle. "You talked to Billy Benbrooke before; why not now?"

"He's no longer there. It's rumored you did something to him. Did you?"

He broke off another twig and pitched it. "How long has he been gone?"

"Since just after I told you he was in the district. As his presence was so disturbing to you, it must be a comfort to know he's gone."

"Too late," he replied. "He sold us out and I found out too late to stop him."

He thought it to her credit that she didn't ask leading questions about the substance of Benbrooke's 'sell out'.

They sat silently staring into the pool for a while, then she softly asked, "May I talk to Gunnar?"

"You can try."

"He wouldn't talk to me outside the mine tunnel an hour ago."

"He goes by his own set of rules."

She stared in the direction of the cabin.

He said, "I know he was taken with you, so all you'll have to overcome is your name being suspect."

"Will you help me?"

He pulled her to her feet and led the way to the cabin. Smoke wafted from the chimney. He left her outside while he made sure Gunnar was decent. The little man stood by the stove, stirring a pot. "Lady wants to see you, Gunnar."

"Ay am too busy."

"She won't take 'no' for an answer."

Gunnar whirled from the stove and, carrying his

spoon, swung open the door. Abigail Dimity Whittle stood just beyond the stoop. Neither immediately spoke.

Then she said, "I hoped that I could talk to you, Mr. Einarssen. If so, I would tell you that I'm not responsible for the behavior of any person other than myself. If another person has sinned against you, it's wrong to hold that act against me. I'd also like to tell you that I find you and Mr. Frost to be kind and intelligent individuals, and a comfort to visit."

When Gunnar said nothing in return, she asked, "Mr. Einarssen, may I come in?"

"My name is Gunnar," he said, leaving the door open and returning to his stove.

The man they knew as Jason Frost picked up his Winchester carbine, leaving Abigail and Gunnar to themselves while he made his perimeter patrol. When he returned, she was preparing to leave.

"I'll walk you home," he said.

"Oh dear!" she replied. "I'm terribly sorry, but my card is filled. Gunnar offered and I accepted. He's changing shirts now."

Chapter Eleven

When Gunnar Einarssen returned from escorting Abigail Whittle home he said, "A footbridge across the river, we need. Tomorrow we build, ya?"

Jethro grinned. "Aw, I sorta liked the thought of all our lady visitors having to hike their skirts."

The shadow of a smile swept over Gunnar's long face. "The water, someday will be too deep. Without bridge, no more ladies will come."

It took them two days. The spot was a half-mile upstream, almost across from Walter's. There was a high rock shelf on the west side of the stream. On the east, they labored all one day building a log crib and filling it with stones. The following day they felled two trees, trimmed them to the right length, then by main strength and awkwardness, managed to get them into position spanning the stream. Walter and two of his passing patrons helped with the big lift onto the rock crib.

Gunnar spent most of a third day adzing the two logs flat on top and building a handrail.

Meanwhile, grading crews for Rio Grande Southern finally punched through the narrow Gateway Canyon in late August, and began blasting and scraping a railroad grade down the long descent to the Dolores River. With luck, they expected grading to reach the San Miguel and track to be laid to the Dolores, before work had to be suspended for winter.

In early September, Tobe Krajcyk began a tiny ten-by-twelve trapper-style cabin, using fire-killed aspens for logs. Kracyk planned the cabin to be four feet high on the sidewalls, six feet to floor-level from its ridgepole. In one corner, stones from his mine tunnel were laid for a hearth, while one roof corner was hinged and could be made to swing out to allow smoke to vent. All in all, the Krajcyk's cabin was only adequate for bare survival.

Tobe Krajcyk finished the cabin by the end of October and, on the second day of November, was brutally beaten by a team of masked men carrying pick handles. The new cabin was burned to the ground.

Gunnar and Jethro heard of the Krajcyk beating on November third. They'd emerged from the Nordic Summer tunnel and were on their way to the cabin after having washed at the creek.

"There was no apparent reason," Abigail Whittle said, angrily tossing her head. "Mr. Krajcyk was a harmless recluse who could in no way have made enemies."

The three stood outside Gunnar's cabin as the last light dimmed. A fine dusting of snow had fallen during the day. Jethro dug a hole through the skiff and into the dirt with the toe of his boot. Gunnar stooped to bury a hand in Odina's scruff while he stared up at the indignant woman.

"Where's Tobe now?" Jethro asked.

"I have him at my home. It's the only place available."

"Is that also Andrew Whittle's home?"

"He is my *son,* Jason. Of course it's Andrew's home. But I have an entire wing of three rooms, including a sleeping room. I had the men who brought Mr. Krajcyk into town for attention, carry him into my sleeping quarters." Then she added, "If you're wondering about its propriety, I've had a cot placed in my sitting room for the duration."

"Ma'am, I wasn't wondering about that at all. What I was wondering about was Tobe. How bad is he?"

"Dear me, I wish I could say. He's still unconscious. The attack must have occurred sometime yesterday, but God only knows. He's been beaten badly about the head. Several teeth were knocked out. It must have been terrible for him."

Gunnar straightened and said, "A fire ay will get. Den yew can come in."

"Oh, Gunnar, I must get back." Nevertheless, she made no move to go. Jason could tell the woman's distress was real.

"Did he give anything back? Do you know?"

"I don't know what you …"

"Was his knuckles skinned? What did the ground look like where it took place?"

She stared through him. "I … I don't know. I didn't look." Then she shook her head. "I'm no good at this kind of thing, am I?"

"But you were up there?"

"Yes. I went as soon as I could; as soon as I heard. But it had begun to snow by then and the ground was all tracked up by the men who found him."

"Who found him?"

"Andrew did. That's why I know he had nothing to do with this."

Night had fallen enough so they could see sparks rising from the newly ignited fire. Jethro pondered the stovepipe for a full minute. "They must have left him alive so he could serve as a warning to the Spaniard and the Swede."

"Who are 'they'?"

Before Jethro could answer, Gunnar swung open the cabin door. He'd struck a lantern and its glow cast a more cheering light on the somberness of the group.

"Well," Abigail said, "I'll come in for just a moment, then I must return."

Gunnar had the two cups and the milk tin on the table. There was also a half-filled bottle of Pike's Magnolia. He raised an eyebrow at the lady and when she said, "Oh my, yes," he poured a finger for her, one for the workman he knew as Jason, and one for himself. They raised their cups simultaneously. Jethro murmured, "To Tobe."

"To Tobe," the others echoed.

"Who are they?" Abigail persisted.

Jethro looked at Gunnar. The Swede dropped his gaze to Odina.

The lady stamped her foot. "I want to know! Who are they?"

Jethro carefully set his cup on the table, then stretched to his full height and said, "I should think it pretty clear, ma'am. 'They' are whoever would profit the most by having Tobe Krajcyk out of the picture."

"And who would that be?"

"Aw, for God's sake!"

Gunnar, still looking down at Odina, said, "Jason or me, it was not."

"Of course not."

"Walter Hopkins, why would he do it?"

"Don't be ridiculous!"

Jethro took up Gunnar's reasoning: "Anton Gutierrez is clean on this one because you said there were obviously several men in on the attack."

"Yes. But I don't see …"

"Who has a bunch of men, Abigail? Robbery wasn't a motive because Tobe Krajcyk had nothing. Do you think it was just a bunch of boys out having a little fun?"

She bit her lip, then said, "I must go home."

"It's dark now."

"I know it's dark. But I also know Tobe Kracyk is lying there, perhaps in need. Andrew's housekeeper is with him, but I'll feel better if I *know* he's being properly cared for."

Jethro shrugged. "I'll take the lantern." He looked at Gunnar and asked, "Can you get by with a candle tonight?"

"Ay will do it, you betcha."

The younger man placed a hand on his friend's shoulder. "I might not be back tonight, Gunnar. In fact, I won't be."

When the little man nodded, Jethro said, "I want you to sleep with the door locked and a rifle at your side. I think they've upped the ante and I don't want to lose you while I'm trying to run down what's happening."

"Ay will do it." Then he placed his own hand over the one still gripping his shoulder. "Ay want yew to come back all right."

Jethro grinned. "Yah, ay will do it, you betcha."

The younger man snatched a coat, his rifle, a few biscuits, and the lantern. Its light was welcome at the footbridge, but no longer needed after they hit the roadway at Walter Hopkins' place. Jethro snuffed the lantern and hung it from an aspen limb.

"You think Andrew had something to do with this,

don't you?" Abigail asked as they trudged down the road.

"Process of elimination, ma'am. Who else, if not the big outfit?"

"That does not make Andrew complicit."

Jethro dug in his shirt pocket for a pencil and paper, then gave up the idea because of the dim light. "'Complicit' must mean 'in on it', or something like that."

"Yes. Just because you think the company Andrew works for may have been responsible for Tobe Krajcyk's beating, that doesn't mean my son is involved."

"That could be true, ma'am." But his tone of voice left no doubt as to what he believed.

She persisted. "After all, Andrew found Mr. Krajcyk. That doesn't seem consistent with your suspicions."

Jethro said no more and neither did she until they reached Placerville. Then Abigail halted abruptly before they approached the first outlying hovel. "Tell me, do you feel you and Gunnar are in danger?"

The night had become very dark, so much so that their noses were but a short distance apart. His white teeth flashed. "Sure do," he said, then added, "And you must feel so, too, otherwise you'd not have come all the way to Fall Creek to warn us, knowing you couldn't get back before dark."

Despite the inky darkness, she walked on with the calm confidence of a person on familiar ground. Meanwhile he walked beside her, equally at home as a result of his experience as a hunter-stalker. Light came from her window. Before she reached its glow, she held out her hand. "Thank you, sir, for seeing me home."

He took her hand and leaned close. "Check on Tobe," he whispered. "If he's awake, come to the door and wave me in."

She turned without a word to enter her home, was

gone for a few moments, then returned holding a lamp and wagging a hand back and forth to indicate there was no change in the injured man's condition.

Jethro would've been at Tobe Krajcyk's burned cabin site at first light, except that he found the Spaniard's outhouse so comfortable he overslept. Surprised by the owner's footsteps, he sat up and quickly judged it to be already daylight. Jethro's surprise was nothing compared to the shock Antonio Gutierrez received when he jerked open his outhouse door and found himself staring down the snout of a .44 caliber Colt revolver. "Okay, Gutierrez," the younger man said, "your hiding days are over."

The Spaniard, after his initial shock, smiled fleetingly. "Ah, my friend, you have been absent so long, I am unprepared."

Jethro admired the other's quick recovery. The younger man came to his feet. "Gun?" he asked.

"But of course, senor. Do you take me for a fool?"

"Where is it?"

"Again, do you take me for a fool?"

"I know you have a knife—at least one." Jethro wagged his Colt. "Move aside. Let me out."

Gutierrez stepped back and Jethro edged past, as tense as if he held a rattlesnake by the head.

Gutierrez bowed and entered the outhouse. A few moments later, he emerged to find Jethro sitting on his cabin stoop. The Colt was back in its holster. "You know about Tobe?" the younger man asked.

"*Si.*"

"What do you know that I don't?"

"That it was Whittle; who else?"

"Can you prove it?"

"No, but I don't need to prove it to know it to be true."

Jethro sighed. "Well, Senor Gutierrez, what are we going to do? I don't see how we can be more vulnerable. There are only two of us left now and we live almost three miles apart. Gunnar's better off than you are, because he's got me. All you have is you."

Gutierrez approached to within three feet of the seated intruder. His arms were crossed and a haughty scowl adorned his face. When the Spaniard said nothing, Jethro continued, "I know you're tough and I know you're mean. But are you tough enough and mean enough? If you think so, then you're a fool."

"What do you propose?" Gutierrez asked.

"What we should do is get together on one claim or the other. Maybe work one for awhile, then the other. Pool our assets and our labor just to make sure that we're all together." Then Jethro grinned as the other man's scowl deepened and darkened. "But Gunnar would never agree to such a plan and I can see you won't, either. So we got to get back to what we can do."

"And that is?"

"For starters, like I told Tobe Krajcyk, we make a list of when and how each approach was made to buy your claims; the dates, the methods involved. Note when the offers petered out and threats began. We try to recollect when all the others in this district got run out, when and what kinds of pressure they were under, what was done to finally run'em off ..."

"Or kill them," Gutierrez murmured.

"I think if the whole history was pulled together, it might be impressive enough to get a Governor's attention."

"You are foolish, senor."

"Can you suggest anything better?"

Gunnar's Mine

"Unfortunately, no."

"Will you try my idea, then?"

Gutierrez motioned Jethro aside and entered his cabin, leaving his door open. The man was back in a few moments to hand Jethro a paper.

"Well, I'll be ..." the younger man muttered. The paper was a meticulous list of each approach Whittle's company had made to buy Gutierrez's claim. Also included were threats and attempts at destruction, including several of which Jethro was unaware.

He looked up and shook his head at the haughty hidalgo standing rigidly in the cabin doorway. "Looks like you're ahead of me on this," the younger man said. Then his gaze wandered around the little clearing. "Any more ideas, Anton?"

None of the haughtiness was gone, but a certain speculation had been added. "This I must think about, senor. If we are to work together, we must have a plan."

Jethro grinned. "God, I hope you're not as tough to approach the second time as you was the first."

The Spaniard's scowl was replaced by a fleeting smile—then he slammed the cabin door in the younger man's face.

It took Jethro two hours to circle Tobe Krajcyk's claim and identify where the three outposts were. The first was only too happy to leave his post as soon as he felt the muzzle of Jethro's Winchester on his neck.

So was outpost number two.

Outpost number three wanted to play it brave, so Jethro dispatched him with a swift kick to the nether region and a couple of well-aimed rabbit punches to his neck. The man's neckerchief and belt served to keep him mollified until Jethro finished searching the ground around the destroyed cabin site.

Yesterday's snow was long gone by the time Jethro began his search. The ground had been trampled by many a miner's boot and horse's hoof, but there was enough evidence for a skillful tracker to see that a struggle had indeed taken place. Near the cabin, several aspen seedlings had been broken off, and low limbs had been snapped from pines, as if the struggle had raged for considerable time over a considerable area.

As he moved meticulously around the scene, Jethro's mind turned back to Lincoln County and the way he'd studied the ground where his friend John Tunstall was murdered. For a moment, his mouth pinched. *Of the four men who'd murdered you, John, three are dead: Buck Morton, Frank Baker, and Tom Hill. Morton and Baker were killed by Billy the Kid, and I got Tom Hill myself when I caught him robbing a sheep camp and about to kill the Indian herder.* He pushed to his feet and began systematically moving in an expanding circle. *Only Jesse Evans is left, John, and I couldn't get him, even though I tried.* Then he chuckled. *But he never got me either, and God knows, he tried.*

Jethro crouched over two bootheel prints that had been gouged into the soil, near one corner of the burned-out cabin. It was obvious that the heels had been planted and dug in, then twisted first one way, then another, each time sinking deeper, as if much weight had been piled on the person wearing those boots. Jethro grinned at the thought of the blocky Tobe Krajcyk refusing to go down, even though he was surrounded by men beating him with clubs and piling on to bring him to his knees.

Yes, Tobe resisted the bastards here. His gaze rose to take in the broken trees. And there!

So the dark-faced man returned to the sentry he'd

Gunnar's Mine

trussed. The man was awake and terror-stricken. Jethro pulled his Colt, eared back the hammer, hooked the barrel in the cringing man's left nostril and said, "I want answers."

Chapter Twelve

The only thing on the sentry that wasn't tightly bound was his tongue and it warbled volubly as Jethro Spring held the muzzle of his cocked revolver up the bound man's nostril. The sentry said eight men were detailed to attack Tobe Krajcyk, but swore he knew only six by name—which he spewed forth. He said the eight were armed with pick handles and shot-loaded saps. Even so, he said Krajcyk had put up a formidable fight.

"Did Andrew Whittle give the order?" Jethro murmured.

The man moaned, "Who else could it be?" Then he took another look at the hard face of the avenger crouching over him and said, "I don't know that for sure, but nobody moves in Placerville without Whittle's say so."

Jethro glanced at the sun and knew his time was running out. He let the hammer down on his Colt, holstered it, then trotted off down the hill toward

Gunnar's Mine

Placerville.

He met the first skirmishers when he was halfway to town. Those he spotted were all bearded miners armed with shotguns and rifles. They were already spreading out, intending to surround Tobe Krajcyk's claim. They were a ragtag bunch, most apparently unfamiliar with firearms, cursing, shouting to their comrades, and shooting at the chitter of pine squirrels or the scratch of a cottontail. Some of the skirmishers, aware of the reputation of their quarry, proved more reluctant than others to go forward at all, thus the skirmish line became ragged, and with giant gaps. It was easy for a cautious half-Indian, half-mountain man to lie hidden in the underbrush while the clumsy miners shuffled past.

Chalkie opened the doors of the San Miguell Emporium at high noon on the fourth day of November to a crowd of three cowboys who were anxiously awaiting just such an important event. Jethro Spring let five minutes elapse before he, too, pushed through the batwing doors of Chalkie's establishment. He went no further inside than was necessary to let the doors swing closed behind him, then slid three feet to the left, his Colt a magical extension of his right hand.

Surprise was complete. Chalkie busied himself in one of the room's corners, lifting down chairs from atop card tables and positioning them. The cowboys were grouped together on the near end of the bar, a bottle of whiskey and partially filled shot glasses before them.

"This won't take long, boys, and it won't hurt you to listen real careful."

Chalkie dropped the chair he was lifting and began edging back to the bar. "No, Chalkie, that means you, too." The barman stopped as if he'd ran into a wall.

"Now that I have your attention," Jethro said, "I want you all to know that I'm looking for Marshall Kleppner, George Peters, Tom LaFranch, Kels Johanson, Gerhard Schmidt, Britt Wobley, and two others that I don't know by name—yet. If I find these low-life bastards and they're lucky, I'll just beat the living shit out of them. If they put up one sign of a fight, I'll kill them."

Nothing and no one moved, not even a dust-devil in the street.

"The reason I'm going to do this is because these are the scum-sucking bastards who beat Tobe Krajcyk. The fact that eight of 'em did this to one man pisses me off—as it should you, too, if you've got more than porridge for brains."

All four men faced him; all eight hands were in plain sight; all four men worked hard to keep all eight hands from shaking.

"Now the reason I'm telling you this is because I want word to get out. I want those eight bastards to know I'm coming after them. I want them to know the only chance they've got is to run far away from here—and do it damned fast."

Then Jethro sidled to the right and backed through the batwings. As he turned, he bumped into Andrew Whittle, who chanced to be on his way in for a morning refresher. Whittle leaped back in surprise. The gun Jethro held kept the mine manager from attempting anything foolish.

"Mr. Whittle!" Jethro exclaimed. "We were just talking about you." He waved grandly at the swinging batwings. "Please go on in and enjoy yourself—if you can."

A red-faced Andrew Whittle slipped through the batwings, closing the interior doors on his way. Jethro used his time to dash to the end of the block and turn right, then left, and right again. Then he knocked at Abigail Whittle's door.

"Oh my God," the woman said as she opened the door. "Are you insane?"

He held a finger to his lips, then pushed into her kitchen before whispering, "Tobe, how is he."

"He was awake a short while ago," she whispered. "But he's sleeping again now. I'm hopeful for him, however."

Jethro pulled the sheet of paper Gutierrez had given him and handed it to Abigail Whittle.

"What is this?" she asked.

"It's from Antonio Gutierrez. It's in his hand."

"But it's not signed. How do I know it is his?"

"You don't—if you won't trust me."

By then she was deep into the account. "I don't believe a word of this," she said without finishing, handing it back.

"I can understand. But you do see the format, don't you? I've already talked to Tobe about compiling his own, but I'm not sure if he did it. I know he can read and write, so nothing can keep him from it if he wants to make out one of his own—except death. What I'm asking, Abigail, is that if he does come to his senses enough to remember, can you help him draft his own timetable? Or maybe I should ask, *will* you help him do one?"

She peered thoughtfully at Jethro, then sighed and said, "Let me see that paper again."

After she'd thoroughly digested the Gutierrez report, she again handed it back, saying, "Some of Andrew's men came here two hours ago. They said you had gone crazy and were attacking the guards Andrew had posted on Mr. Krajcyk's property."

He smiled. She continued, "Andrew ordered men out to apprehend you. As a consequence, you must see that you are not safe here. I'm not even sure if you'd be safe at Mr. Einarssen's cabin."

Jethro's smile stayed in place as he said, "Actually, Abigail, your Andrew and I are in the process of negotiating that point right now."

She caught the irony, but declined to pry. Instead, she asked, "Have you had anything to eat? I know you had no supper yesterday, and I doubt that you've eaten anything today." She could tell she'd struck a positive note by the interest in widening gray eyes. "I have some ham. It's quite salty, but I can make some punch to go with it."

"What about your own safety?"

"*My* safety? Are you questioning the safety of Andrew Whittle's mother? If you're not insane, then, Mr. Frost, you certainly are odd."

His teeth flashed. "Have you considered the fact that you might be harboring a criminal?"

She placed hands to hips and asked, "Are you a criminal, Mr. Frost?"

He shook his head, but he could not help thinking of a military fort and a major who'd murdered Jethro's parents. He remembered the blast of his father's buffalo gun and how the major had died with a hole blown through his chest. Then there was his escape, the chase, and all the 'WANTED-JETHRO SPRING, DEAD OR ALIVE!' posters distributed throughout the West. *If you only knew, ma'am,* he thought to himself.

But he said, "If your Andrew finds me here, or even learns that I've been here, you might suffer."

"Andrew has never been an easy child to handle," she said, "but I have, after all, had several years of experience." The woman busied herself with setting out the ham and stirring up the punch. She even sweetened the punch with a dash of vodka before pouring it up for Jethro.

Gunnar's Mine

After he'd finished eating, Abigail Whittle said, "I believe it would be foolish for you to leave before dark. Since that's only two or three hours away, I suggest you lie down and sleep until then."

He nodded. "Where?"

"My cot is in the sitting room."

He shook his head. "Too easy for your Andrew or his maid to walk in on me there. How about if I crawl in under Tobe's bed?"

"I'll get a blanket and pillow."

Jethro awoke to faint voices. A flowing, crocheted bedspread pulled over Tobe Krajcyk's blankets fell almost to the floor. The hidden man lifted the spread with the muzzle of his Winchester and saw it was not yet dark.

"I stopped by to see how he is." *Whittle's voice!*

"Do you mean Mr. Krajcyk?"

"For God's sake, Mother, who else could I mean? Is he awake?"

"If you keep on shouting, he soon will be. Please lower your voice."

They moved farther back into the kitchen and Jethro could no longer decipher what was being said. But he drew his Colt. *At least now,* he thought, *we'll find out whether Abigail will sell us out, me and Gunnar, and probably the Spaniard, too.*

After several minutes of lowered conversation, the kitchen discussion began to heat up again.

"What are you accusing me of, woman?"

"Andrew, I'm accusing you of nothing. I'm simply asking you how Mr. Krajcyk's beating could have taken place without the involvement of some of your men?"

"My Lord, do you think I know the inner workings

of every bandit and thug in this valley?"

"Andrew, I'm only asking who of your men could've been involved?"

"None. At least none on my orders."

"Gracious!" she exclaimed. "I should hope not!"

There was a lag in the conversation until Andrew Whittle declared, "I should never have allowed you to bring him here in the first place."

"Oh, Andrew, where else could the poor man go?"

"They have a doctor in Telluride."

"You know it would've killed him to have been transported that far in a wagonbox."

"Well, he can't stay here."

Abigail Whittle's voice had a ring of finality about it. "He will stay here until he can be moved."

"This is my house."

"And I'm *your* mother."

They were both angry now. In addition, they'd moved more closely to the sleeping room where Jethro lay hidden.

"You must return to the East sometime," an angry Andrew Whittle said. "Perhaps sooner is better than later."

"One thing you can be sure of Andrew," she said, "I'm not leaving this house until Mr. Krajcyk is able to do likewise."

Jethro heard the front door slam. In a few moments, Abigail Whittle was in the bedroom soothing Tobe Krajcyk's forehead with a damp cloth. "It's almost dark," she cooed. "The maid usually comes in at six-thirty with my supper. Then, you poor man, she'll stay to clean up."

Is she talking to me or Tobe?

"So perhaps the best time for you to leave would be within the next ten minutes, or else wait a few more hours until after the whole town goes to sleep."

Gunnar's Mine

A sliver of a moon crossed the night sky while Jethro Spring stealthily circled Gunnar Einarssen's cabin, making certain there were no Whittle men lying in ambush. Finally, in the wee hours, he knocked on the cabin door.

Odina barked, then apparently sniffed Jethro's presence through the door and began scratching. Gunnar threw the bolt and swung back the door. "Ay know yew it was. Odina said so."

When the little man struck a candle, a tired Jethro set the lantern on the table. "Sorry I was so long getting this back, but there were a few developments."

Gunnar held the candle close to Jethro's face, saw the lines and the weariness and said, "To bed, yew should go. Tomorrow is soon enough for talk."

"I accept—on the condition that you get me up at daylight. There are no Company boys around here yet, but we can count on'em coming. We don't want to be caught in the cabin when they do."

Gunnar shuffled back to throw the door bolt, then blew out the candle. Jethro was sprawled fast asleep on his bunk by the time the little Swede returned to his own bunk.

The Company didn't strike back as quickly as Jethro supposed it would. One reason for the lack of quick response might have been a strange series of events that in some observers' minds seemed unnatural.

The first occurred two days after Jethro Spring had issued his threat in the San Miguell Emporium, a day when a sudden blizzard roared down from the frozen North. The blizzard caught Tom LaFranch and Eugene Heisner on a routine trip to Telluride to fetch a wagon load of sharpened drill bits. Though their team returned to Placerville pulling the loaded wagon, the men were found frozen beneath the lee of a cutbank. Two empty whiskey bottles lay nearby.

Heads were wagged and 'tsk, tsks' were said until someone recalled that Tom LaFranch had been named by that maniac from Fall Creek as one of the men who'd beaten Tobe Krajcyk. Then someone in the know claimed Gene Heisner was one of the two unnamed men involved.

'Coincidence', it was said. However, the very next day, a drunken George Peters staggered out into the middle of the main street of Placerville at the same time the Telluride stage came thundering into town. There was no way the driver could've avoided what occurred.

Whatever the reason for the accidents (or 'on purposes', so several tongues whispered), Kels Johanson and Marshall Kleppner decided to quit the country. Unfortunately, neither had sufficient resources to take them beyond the junction of the San Miguel and Dolores Rivers, where the winter camp of the Rio Grande Southern grading crews was located. While stopping over at the camp, Johanson and Kleppner decided to make an unauthorized withdrawal from the last payroll shipment of the season to the railroad's grading crews. The response of the crewmen to the unsuccessful robbery attempt was predictable and Kleppner's and Johanson's bodies hung from the same cottonwood limb for most of the winter as a warning to other would-be thieves that a railroad camp was not the place to practice their specialty. At least the bodies hung until the ravens, magpies, and crows had so worked over the remains that the skeletons separated of their own weight.

With Kleppner's and Johanson's demise, only Gerhard Schmidt, Britt Wobley, and a man later identified as Harry Brown were left from the thugs who'd

Gunnar's Mine

beaten Tobe Krajcyk.

Gerhard Schmidt wasn't cowed. The hulking German was neither imaginative, nor believed in curses. Thus, Schmidt decided to take matters into his own hands. His mistake was in first shooting Odina, Gunnar Einarssen's dog.

It was mid-December and Jethro's and Gunnar's vigil had relaxed. Odina, however, was constantly on alert and on the day of her death, when she was let out for her morning constitutional, she immediately began barking. The volatile German lost his temper and drew a bead on the barking bitch. Odina's yelp was mercifully brief. Equally quick was the screaming little man who burst from the cabin, brandishing a shovel. Schmidt got one snap shot off at the berserk Swede before his hiding place was bracketed by a barrage of Winchester .44s coming from the cabin's open door.

Taking cover, the German's second mistake was assuming his opponents would do the same. Before he realized his error, the edge of Gunnar Einarssen's shovel caught him across the temple, neatly shearing one ear in half. Schmidt roared, dropping his rifle and leaping to his feet, blood flooding into an eye. The blinded eye happened to be the same one Gunnar's shovel targeted the second time around. That time, Schmidt's nose was broken and his blood-filled eye sliced from its socket.

Roaring, Schmidt made a grab for the shovel, missed, and was slammed by Gunnar's third swing, this time on the back of his neck. Collapsing to his knees, the German bellowed, "Enough, for Gott's...!" But that's as far as he got before the shovel's fourth swing severed his spinal column at the neck. There was a fifth and sixth swing, before Jethro gently took Gunnar in his arms and lifted the bloody shovel from him. "Let's look to Odina, little man. She deserves a decent burial, don't you think?"

Word of Gerhard Schmidt's fate, and how the man was beaten to death with a shovel, traveled the length and breadth of the San Miguel's wintertime valley. There were few who heard it who didn't believe Jethro Spring's curse played an outsized role in the deaths of all six men implicated in the Krajcyk beating. As for Britt Wobley and Henry Brown, they exited the San Miguel without letting their shirttails touch their backs.

Tobe Krajcyk recovered consciousness shortly after Jethro slumbered beneath his bed, and slowly began to mend. "He appears to have full use of his faculties," Abigail Whittle told Gunnar and Jethro shortly after word got out of Gerhard Schmidt's demise. "I believe he'll be moving soon and I intend to give him a celebratory Christmas dinner."

Gunnar, still grieving over Odina's death, sat dejectedly on his block of wood, elbows propped to the tabletop, head in hands. Jethro, meanwhile, whittled on a piece of pine wood.

"You two gentlemen will come, will you not?"

Jethro snapped his clasp knife closed and said, "This gentleman will not."

"And why not?"

"You mean put our heads in the lion's mouth?"

"Meaning Andrew's?"

"Meaning Andrew's."

She smiled. "Well, I anticipated that reaction. That's why I'm the bearer of special news of such significance that it may change your minds."

Jethro brushed shavings from his trousers. "And what's that?"

She paused sufficiently long for suspense to build before drawing herself up and announcing, "Andrew has delegated a crew of men to rebuild Tobe Krajcyk's cabin."

Jethro's eyes were veiled as he sought Gunnar's reaction. Gunnar, for his part, avoided looking at either the woman or his workman. "When?" Jethro asked.

"I'm told it will be ready by Christmas."

"But will Tobe be ready by Christmas?"

"My, but you're the skeptic, Mr. Frost. I trust Mr. Einarssen is more open to truth." She turned her wide-set eyes on Gunnar and he melted. "Will you come to my party for Tobe, Gunnar?"

"Ay will come."

"When is it?" Jethro asked.

"On Christmas day; ten days hence."

Jethro's smile never reached his eyes. "And I suppose you'll issue an invitation to the Spaniard?"

"It is my plan, Mr. Frost, to invite everyone in the district. Of course an invitation will go to Mr. Gutierrez."

He nodded.

She studied him. "Are you the brutal killer it's being rumored, sir? If so, you must know you have no further enemies left in Placerville. Therefore there's no good reason for you—or Mr. Gutierrez for that matter—not to come."

He let her run down, then stood and moved to the wall for a broom. "That, Miss Abigail, was cheap; not at all worthy of you."

She reddened. "You're right, of course, and I apologize. No matter what others might believe, I'm intelligent enough to know you had nothing to do with anyone's death except for that dog-shooting cur,

Gerhard Schmidt."

"Ay killed him," Gunnar quietly said. "Und if my shovel Jason had not taken from me, ay would have carved him into pieces no bigger than a potato."

Abigail stared at first one, then the other of the men. "I see."

Jethro opened the door and swept his shavings onto the stoop, then into the yard. When he came back in, he said, "No ma'am, you do not see. You don't see that Gunnar Einarssen, Tobe Krajcyk, and Anton Gutierrez are in the middle of a life-and-death struggle to hold onto what little of life and property they have left. I know you're being told one thing by Andrew Whittle and another thing by me and Gunnar and probably Tobe Krajcyk."

He paused because she began shaking her head. "I don't dispute everything you say, Jason. Don't you know that? How can I argue that it was some of Andrew's men who perpetrated Tobe's beating? But you are wrong to hold Andrew responsible. Wrong, wrong, wrong!"

Jethro leaned the broom in its place beside the door and returned to his seat. As he eased back on the wood block, he continued as if he'd not been interrupted. "In this life-and-death struggle Gunnar and Tobe and the Spaniard are in, they can win battle after battle, time after time, and still not be the victors." He leaned forward so she had to look at his stern, unsmiling face. "You see, ma'am, if they lose once, they're dead."

"I don't see what …"

"The outfit Andrew Whittle works for lost every time they tried to run the last three surviving claimholders out of this valley. They lost with Tobe Krajcyk and they lost with the Spaniard. And they've also lost with Gunnar. But you'd have to be…" he paused, "…to use your choice of words 'insane' to believe it's all over."

Gunnar's Mine

Her face turned scarlet as she struggled to hold her temper. "You must believe me, Mr. Frost, when I say Andrew Whittle has not been, is not now, nor will he be in the future, in any way complicit in trying to do you people harm."

Jethro sighed. "Nevertheless, ma'am, I do not wish to dampen your Christmas party. Therefore, I'll not be there."

Chapter Thirteen

Gunnar Einarssen did not, after all, attend a Christmas celebration in honor of Tobe Krajcyk's recovery. Neither did Jose Antonio Gutierrez de Valdez y Mendoza, nor Andrew Whittle and all the workmen of Placerville and its environs. The reason no one attended a celebration in Tobe Kracyk's honor was that Tobe Krajcyk was dead.

Abigail Whittle was dry-eyed and somber when, three days before Christmas, she brought the news to Fall Creek. She set a wriggling, little, black and white terrier pup on the floor, shrugged from a calf-length sheepskin coat, then told them of Tobe's death:

"I don't know what happened, Jason." She switched focus to Gunnar and said, "Andrew and I took the buggy to Telluride yesterday. I wanted to pick up this darling little puppy for Christmas ..." Her voice trailed off as she watched the pup waddle around the table, then squat to pee beside Gunnar's boot. "She is your

Gunnar's Mine

Christmas present, Gunnar. When I returned, Tobe was dead." She searched her friends' faces. "How could it happen? He was doing so well."

"He was made sick?" Gunnar ventured.

"Oh Gunnar, that's impossible. I left Tobe in Maria's care. She had explicit instructions to …" At last, tears filled her eyes and she sat abruptly on a block of wood near the stove.

"What about opening him up to see if there's any poison?" Jethro wondered.

"I asked Andrew about that when he came in this afternoon, but he dismissed that option. He says the doctor in Telluride, such as he is, is incompetent to do an autopsy and that Tobe's body would have to be transported elsewhere for a thorough examination."

"That's tough to do this time of year."

"'Impossible' is how Andrew put it. He sent to Telluride for the sheriff to hold some sort of inquiry."

The pup ran across the puncheon floor to the woman, but when Abigail reached for her, dodged and romped so ungainly back toward Gunnar that her feet tangled and she tumbled head over heels. Gunnar lifted her to his lap.

Jethro stared at the pup without really seeing it. "And Andrew Whittle was with you in Telluride?"

"Yes. He said he had some business to conduct. What's more, Jason, he never finished the business and stayed over while I came on alone." She bit her lip and added, "Indeed, if there has been any foul play, Andrew could not have had anything to do with it."

Jethro asked, "How trustworthy is this Maria?"

"Please, Jason, she's a good woman. My Lord, she's got to be seventy years old if she's a day. Have you not seen her?"

Jethro shook his head and Abigail continued, "She's plump, jolly, and caring. There's no way she could've been involved."

"But she's Whittle's housekeeper."

Both men watched the woman wrestle with her emotions. On the one hand was the crushing blow of Tobe Krajcyk's death when he appeared so well on his way to recovery; on the other, was the fact that this man, Jason Frost, persisted in insinuating Andrew Whittle was responsible for a litany of disasters that befell independent claimholders in the district.

At last, Abigail Whittle placed both hands on her knees and pushed to her feet. She smiled down at the little man and the puppy curled asleep on his lap. "I know she'll not replace Odina, Gunnar, but perhaps you can find it in your heart to love another."

Jethro Spring reached for his mackinaw. He was surprised to see a lone tear slide through the Swede's stubble as Gunnar swallowed and said, "Ay t'ank yew, Miss."

They were out on the main road before either Abigail or Jethro spoke. Finally he cleared his throat and said, "I suppose you'll be returning east?"

"I would imagine that to be the prudent thing to do."

He stopped abruptly, and so did she. "You've not exactly followed a sensible course ever since coming here, ma'am. That's why I think you'll stay."

She studied the mountains on her right for a moment, but when she turned to face him, her mouth was pinched into a fine line. She reached somewhere within the folds of her skirt to retrieve several folded sheets of writing paper. "I believe this is what you asked for. It's Tobe Krajcyk's account of the pressure brought upon him to sell his mining claim to, I assume, the Colorado Basin Holding Company."

When he reached for the papers, she maintained her grip on them and their eyes locked. "I shouldn't even give this to you. Andrew's name is mentioned promi-

Gunnar's Mine

nently throughout the list."

He continued to hold his end, conscious that he should breathe evenly, without emotion. "I wouldn't give them to you, Mr. Frost, except for what happened yesterday." She suddenly released her grip, spun on her heel and set off resolutely down the road.

When he was again alongside her, she sighed and said, "There is too much resemblance between Tobe's account and Mr. Gutierrez's and, I presume, Gunnar's to be mere coincidence."

He said nothing, so she continued, "I pray that Andrew's hands are clean, but I also must accept the possibility that they're not. Should that be the case, then I might better serve my husband's son by staying to support him."

He nodded. "I can see how you'd feel that way, ma'am, but don't get caught in the crossfire."

This time it was she who stopped. When they again faced each other, Jethro could feel a breeze beginning in gusts, puffing downriver. He knew the temperature was falling. A spit of snow swept past, heading for Telluride; then another. Their breaths came in little puffs now, rising between them. She asked so softly he had to strain to hear, "Will there be a crossfire, Mr. Frost?"

He nodded thoughtfully. "I'm afraid so, Abigail. I've always figured that whoever is behind this won't stop until they get it all. Earlier I thought Gunnar's mine might lay outside their target area, so I had hopes he might be left in peace. But when Billy came back and spilled the beans that Gunnar was actually taking a little color from his mine, that was the kiss of death."

Again she sighed. "How long do we have, young man?"

His gray eyes shifted from hers to the mountain slopes behind, not unconscious that she'd said 'we.' When he again met her steady gaze, he shrugged. "The

Rio Grande Southern will have grading crews to Placerville by mid-summer. Tracks will be laid to the San Miguel by then. They'll take the railroad on up to Telluride—which will be pure hell. But they'll want to do it before next winter. Whatever happens here will happen before then."

"A year perhaps?"

"No, not that long. I imagine the people behind the Colorado Basin Holding Company will want to have their bundle lassoed and tied off before that; say late-summer at the outside."

"And how will you fight them?"

He smiled grimly. "By trying to keep Gunnar alive."

"What about you?"

"Me, too. I can't keep Gunnar alive if I'm dead."

"And Mr. Gutierrez?"

He deliberately began walking on. More snow gusted past, borne on the wind. "I'd like to help the Spaniard. But that problem looks shakier to me. He's out there in the middle of their holdings all by himself. He's careful and he's tough, but I don't think he's got much of a chance." He paused, then added, "We don't either, but our chances are better than his."

"What will happen to Tobe's claim?"

"Well, he didn't prove up on it; at least not long enough. I suppose someone will file on it."

"What if that someone was me?"

He stopped abruptly, and when she turned to face him, he whistled. "Now wouldn't that be a shot across their bow?"

To think was to act for Abigail Dimity Whittle, so as soon as she reached Placerville, she harnessed the little carriage horse and backed him into the traces. Within minutes she was pounding past Walter's log-and-wattle way station and on for Telluride. She was too late to conduct business that evening, of course, so she took a room at the Ore Bucket Inn. The following morning, however, she was at the door when the county offices opened for business. Her report, later that afternoon, to Gunnar and the man she knew as Jason Frost was grim.

"I was too late. Tobe's claim had already been filed on."

"Were you able to find out who filed?" Jason asked.

She flushed. "Andrew Whittle."

Jethro backed to the stove, thinking. "So he filed the day after Tobe died—on Friday. But you were back in Telluride Friday evening. How was it you had the buggy?"

"Don't you remember? I told you Andrew stayed in Telluride Thursday while I came home alone."

"Then how could he have known about Tobe?"

Tears welled and began trickling down her face. "I don't *know!* I've been asking myself that question."

"Did you meet any riders on the road while you were returning last Thursday?"

"Oh, I'm sure of it. With all the mining traffic up there, it would be unusual not to do so."

Jethro walked over to the block of wood Abigail Whittle occupied and gently asked, "Did you recognize anyone?"

She was already shaking her head before he finished. "I wondered the same thing, too. But I had my hands full with handling the reins and with the puppy. I simply wasn't paying attention."

"So Andrew could've got word by messenger?"

"That's what must have happened."

"But still, wasn't it lucky for him to be at the right place at the right time?"

She began crying. The pup scampered across the

floor to pounce on the toe of her boot, then fled before she could respond. It was enough, however, for her to smile through the tears. She reached into a sleeve and pulled out an embroidered handkerchief. At last, she said, "If what you suspect is true, then Andrew is up to his ears in this thing. What's worse, if it's true, he has no qualms about disclosing his true nature to me, and is therefore, utterly without conscience."

Gunnar spoke for the first time, asking Jethro, "Is she safe?"

Jethro raised an eyebrow to the woman.

"My goodness," Abigail said, "I should *think* so. I pose no threat to anyone's plans. Besides, I *am* the man's mother."

Jethro wondered. What might have happened had this woman actually succeeded in filing on the dead Tobe Krajcyk's mining claim? Would it then have made any difference whether or not she was Andrew Whittle's mother?

Jethro's thoughts took a sudden turn. "Has the sheriff been to Placerville to do his investigation?"

"I don't know. I stopped here before returning." Then her eyes took a calculating turn. "Why?"

"If he hadn't filed his report, I wonder if Tobe could be considered officially dead?"

"Do you mean Andrew filed for Tobe's claim before he could legally do so?"

"Apparently the sheriff had not been to Placerville for an inquiry on Friday," Jethro said, "so if he's been there at all, it would have to be today, while you were gone. But if so, there's no way Tobe could've been declared *officially* dead until late today."

Gunnar's head had been swiveling from one to the other throughout the conversation, from one to the other. He said, "Dere is law what says man's family has rights, even before proofing." Then he dropped his head

Gunnar's Mine

and said, seemingly to the floor, "But proof up, dey still must do."

Jethro nodded. "That's probably pretty standard in mining camps, no matter where the camp is located. It's probably there just to keep this kind of thing from happening—someone being killed so the killer can take over his claim."

When Abigail resumed crying, Gunnar muttered, "Puppy, she needs to go out." The little man slipped into his coat, then eased into the night. As he went, he heard his man, Jason, say, "Tomorrow's Sunday, so the office will be closed. Monday is Christmas and it'll be closed then, too. If the sheriff hasn't already filed his report, then he'll have to do it Tuesday."

The door swung shut and Gunnar could hear no more. When he returned, Jethro was helping Abigail on with her sheepskin coat. The tiny black and white pup squirmed in Gunnar's arms as the woman scratched the little dog's ears. Then she bent to peck Gunnar on the cheek and said, "I want both of you to be careful."

Gunnar seemed startled that she was leaving alone. He turned to Jethro. "With her, you are not going?"

She said, "We already discussed it Gunnar. I have the buggy at Walter's. I will be fine."

Jethro caught Gunnar's eye and shrugged. But when the woman closed the door, he slipped into his own mackinaw, snatched up the Winchester, and followed her into the night.

Christmas would have been less cheerful had not Abigail Whittle knocked on the tiny cabin door at noon. She brought an armload of packages—two woolen shirts and heavy boot socks for her young friend, two pairs of blue canvas overalls and a new double-shouldered, wool plaid coat for Gunnar, a braided leather collar and a big ham bone for puppy.

The men were grateful they'd taken time to bathe and shave in honor of the Christ child. But they were shamed that they had thought to give the woman nothing in return—at least Jethro was. Gunnar shyly handed her a newspaper-wrapped bundle taken from beneath his cot. When she untied the string and folded back the papers, she cried in delight and held up a brightly flowered apron for Jethro to see.

Abigail also brought huge slices of ham and freshly baked cornbread. Jethro wondered aloud how many trips she'd made from Walter's to carry the packages. "Pshaw," the woman said. "I carried the packages in a tote sack and the food hamper in the other hand. I'm not exactly helpless, you know."

There was no wine, but an unopened quart of "Magnolia" appeared magically from the cornucopia that apparently existed beneath Gunnar's cot. While Jethro peeled potatoes, Gunnar put on another pot of coffee and opened what he called a 'yar' of 'yelly' for their cornbread.

Toasts were made and just before they took their places at the table, there came a soft knock on the door. Jethro opened it.

"*Buenos tardes, Senor Frost,*" said Jose Antonio Gutierrez de Valdez y Mendoza, bowing deeply. "It is my humble wish to offer Christmas greetings to the three of you." He then produced a package wrapped in paper stamped with green fir boughs and red holly berries. "My compliments, senor."

Jethro swung the door wide. "Welcome sir! Won't you come in and join us?" As Gutierrez stepped inside, Jethro went to the woodpile for another block of wood to use as a chair. While doing so, he wondered how the Spaniard knew there were three people in the cabin.

Gunnar's Mine

Had he been eavesdropping? Then he remembered Abigail saying she'd left her buggy at Walter's and to a seasoned warrior like Antonio Gutierrez, reading tracks from Walter's place to Gunnar's cabin would've been simple enough.

Both Abigail's and Gunnar's broad smiles apparently was enough to put Gutierrez at ease. While the man slipped from his coat and laid it atop Jethro's bunk, Gunnar wiped out an empty fruit jar with a rag and poured a dollop of whiskey so the newcomer could join the toast.

After Merry Christmases had been said and toasts drunk, Abigail voiced their predicament, "Jason and Gunnar, we must invite this gentleman to our Christmas dinner, but what shall we do for a plate and utensils?"

Jethro smiled. "If I know anything about Anton, ma'am, it's that he has his own knife. Beyond that, he can use the cornbread pan for a plate, and I'll give him my spoon."

However, the newcomer solved the problem by asking Gunnar to open his Christmas package. Inside was a four-place service of fine china, complete with utensils of silver, and wine goblets of crystal. A frown wrinkled Gunnar's forehead. Just then, Abigail gasped, "Why, they're beautiful, Mr. Gutierrez!"

"They are stamped with my family's crest," Antonio said of the dishes, "the last survivors from our *hacienda's* service for thirty. I bring them to you, little senor, since you are no doubt short of sufficient service to entertain another visitor for an extended period." As he finished, the newcomer's black eyes swept over the group, ending with Jethro. Still staring at the younger man, he added, "There is a bottle of fine burgandy in my coat. If you, senor, would be kind enough to hand it to me, I shall remove the cork and offer it for dinner."

While Gunnar cleared their old pewter dishes and

mismatched utensils, Abigail set Gutierrez's service, handling each plate and cup and wineglass and piece of silverware so lovingly that Jethro himself, watching the refined eastern woman, only then grasped the rarity of the treasure offered by the Spaniard. He waited until they'd finished their Christmas dinner before reopening the brief comment Antonio made about entertaining a visitor for an extended period, during their pre-dinner exchange:

"Senor Gutierrez, what prompted you to abandon your cabin?"

Both Gunnar and Abigail looked at the newcomer in surprise. Neither had understood him to say he was leaving his claim.

Gutierrez smile was fleeting. "I no longer have eyes and ears to watch what Senor Whittle does and plans. Without such eyes and ears I would be foolish to keep my head in the lion's mouth."

Jethro thought about it, then asked, "When did she leave?"

"Are you talking about Maria?" Abigail Whittle cried. "My God, are you talking about Maria?"

Neither Gutierrez nor Jethro batted an eye at the woman's outburst. The Spaniard replied, "Two days ago, while the Senora was in Telluride."

"Maria! My God, I thought she was spending Christmas with her family!"

Jethro said, "I presume she's in a safe place."

"She is from the family of one of my family's most trusted retainers, Senor. By now, we can both be assured she's beyond the reach of the Colorado Basin Holding Company."

Abigail Whittle leaped up and stood by the stove with her back to them, knuckles pressed to the sides of her head. None of the three men in the room paid her any attention, but the puppy ran over to pounce on the

Gunnar's Mine

toe of her boot. She smiled wistfully, picked up the animal, and returned to the table just as Jethro asked, "Was it poison."

"This she could not say. She believed so, but who can know? Senor Krajcyk died sometime during the night; peacefully she thought. So there is no way of knowing. It is possible that he was suffocated."

"Not without a struggle."

"Yes, without a struggle—if he was chloroformed during his sleep."

"Could this be done?"

Gutierrez nodded. "Maria slept in a separate part of the house. She does, I believe, sleep well—as all who have untroubled consciences should. The smell of chloroform would probably be gone by morning. In addition, my retainer is a simple peasant woman, perhaps without any previous experience of such a drug."

"Then even an autopsy by a qualified doctor wouldn't reveal that he was suffocated—if there was no struggle."

Abigail placed both palms flat on the table and said, "This is Christmas Day, for God's sake, gentlemen. I will listen to no more of this discussion!"

The Spaniard leaned back on his block of wood, jaw outthrust.

Jethro covered one of the woman's hands with his own and murmured, "Then, ma'am, if I was you I'd take a walk. What is being discussed here is a matter of life-and-death for everyone in this room but you. Unfortunately we three do not have the luxury of ignoring that we're tied to the tracks and a train is heading our way."

She jerked her hand from Jethro's grip and strode to a wall peg for her coat. Gunnar said, "Ay will go with yew."

After the two had departed, Jethro asked, "Who is

the Colorado Basin Holding Company?"

The Spaniard scoffed. "Have I not told you that I do not know, senor?"

Jethro stared at him shrewdly. "But, senor, you must see there's a difference between *knowing* and *suspecting*. Who do you suspect it might be."

There was a tight smile on the aristocratic face. "It could be one of five or six companies with the size and money to operate in such a manner. But there's only one—perhaps two—who might be so ruthless."

"And that is?"

"One is Amalgamated Minerals and Mining. They are headquartered in the east, but active in much of the west. Their past has been a history of ruthless adventure."

"And others?"

"Weymouth, also from the east. Hearst is heavily into Nevada and the Black Hills. This man's headquarters is in San Francisco. He is what you might think aggressive, but I would hesitate to call him ruthless." Gutierrez chuckled. "Hearst and Burroughs are enemies."

"Burroughs?"

"The one who owns Amalgamated Minerals and Mining."

By the time Gunnar and Abigail had returned, Jethro and Antonio Gutierrez were studying notes from the recollections of Tobe Krajcyk.

While the woman pulled off her sheepskin coat, she said, "Gunnar and I were just talking about those. He tells me that despite Jason's prodding, he has yet to compile his own list. Therefore, we've decided we'll spend the afternoon writing it."

Chapter Fourteen

The addition of Antonio Gutierrez to the tiny community of what Jethro Spring began calling "Gunnar's fort," proved much smoother than any of the involved parties might have predicted. The cabin was indeed cramped, with the Spaniard on a pallet near the door. But the solution came quickly the following morning when Gutierrez suggested that he sleep in the mine. Jethro expected the idea would receive short shrift from the little Swede who, instead, turned thoughtful while the other two discussed the plan's merits.

"The three of us should not be confined here," Gutierrez said, eyes wandering professionally over the cabin walls. "There are no rifle loops, no corner blocks for defense. If our enemy decides to strike, it will be easy for him." With Gunnar seemingly lost in thought, the Spaniard directed his attention to Jethro. "Two strong points would be superior to one, senor."

"No question of that," Jethro said, eyeing the little

Swede, expecting him to stomp angrily from the cabin. "But I wouldn't want you to sleep up there without heat."

"Nonsense!" Antonio drew himself up to his full height. With voice rising, he said, "I am an hidalgo from superior stock. I have slept in mines from the Chilean Occidental to the Cordillera Catalan. I had nothing but blankets during a winter storm on the Atacoma Desert. I have wintered at fifteen thousand feet in the Bolivian Andes. Do you, senor, dare tell me, Jose Antonio Gutierrez de Valdez y Mendoza, that I am too weak to ..."

Jethro held out a hand. "Anton, calm down. I didn't say ..."

"I could still take my meals here. With sufficient robes and bedding, it would simply be a place to sleep."

The younger man stroked his chin, remembering all too vividly how adamant Gunnar had been about having Billy Benbrooke on the premises. Finally he said, "There's no question that we'd all be safer if we had two strongpoints instead of one."

"Jason," the Swede interrupted, still staring at the floor, "has slept away from cabin if he t'ought he should do that t'ing."

Jethro sighed, seeing where the conversation was going. The cabin *was* too small for three. In addition, Gutierrez was right—it had glaring defensive weaknesses. Also, there were excellent reasons for having a rifle strongpoint outside the cabin. But he didn't for one moment believe Gunnar would allow the newcomer in his mine. That left it up to either the little Swede or his hired man. Jethro gazed fondly at his friend and threw up his hands. "Okay, I give up. I'll sleep in the mine."

Privately, Jethro considered the two older men a volatile mix; the proud Spaniard and the simple Swede had nothing at all in common except their enemy. Though Gutierrez was, in effect, an uninvited guest, all

Gunnar's Mine

parties recognized his presence more than doubled their security. However, the man's forceful personality, Jethro thought, was certain to collide with Gunnar's stubbornness. Eventually, their efforts to work together might be ruined.

Still, Jethro thought Gunnar could benefit from exposure to the widely traveled mining engineer's knowledge of ore and vein structure. But how much the Swede could learn without exposing the Spaniard to the Nordic Summer's secrets was anybody's guess.

Gutierrez seemed to sense the others' thoughts, so his voice was mild when he said, "I would not wish to dispossess you of your bed, senor, but on the other hand, it is possible that our friend here does not want an outsider in his mine."

Gunnar continued to study a spot on his floor, until Puppy scampered to him and tried to climb his leg. Finally he said, "Go faster would the tunnel if all time someone was outside to watch for Whittle mans."

Again Jethro sighed. If truth be known, he preferred perimeter patrol rather than single-jacking in the tunnel. But if patrolling was assigned to the Spaniard, that meant he'd be in the tunnel both day and night.

Gunnar picked up Puppy and cuddled her in his arms while peering up at Gutierrez. "Up to the mine we will go and begin a tunnel for Anton to sleep. Then all t'ree of us will work with the drills in turn and the patrols, the two of yew can do."

It took four days for Gunnar and Gutierrez to carve out a sleeping cubicle for the newcomer. During that time, Jethro alternated on patrol, building a cot and coatrack for the new room, and drilling holes in the headwall of the mine tunnel. When the cubicle was ready, despite Jethro's half-hearted protests, Jose Antonio Gutierrez de Valencia y Mendoza moved in.

It was Sunday, the last day of 1882, and it was snowing hard. Privately, Jethro welcomed the snow, knowing the white landscape would make it impossible to approach Gunnar's mine without leaving tell-tale tracks.

Abigail Whittle arrived in the middle of Antonio's move. "My goodness," she said, "I've not seen such activity since a fire drill at my boarding school." The lady was dressed in a heavy woolen walking dress and her calf-length sheepskin coat. In addition, she wore a scarf around her neck and another over her head. Her hands were tucked into a sheepskin muff. She discarded the muff and scarves and insisted on helping.

Gutierrez stepped aside, an ironic smile brushing his lips. Jethro shook his head and tried to block the woman from butting in until Gunnar handed her a small bundle containing a pillow and blanket. Jethro and Antonio carried the pole cot, then the two returned—the younger man for a block of wood to serve as a stool, Gutierrez for a straw mattress. Meanwhile, Gunnar lit a candle and took the woman on her first tour of the Nordic Summer.

Later, the four gathered in the cabin for end-of-year toasts and some cheery conviviality. Abigail effectively curtailed the festivities when she told them the sheriff's investigation into Tobe Krajcyk's death was dated the same day as the man's death.

"But that's impossible!" Jethro exclaimed. "There was no such report when you tried to file two days later."

"That is what I was led to believe, young man. But there is always the possibility that I was falsely led."

"So Andrew Whittle's filing could be valid."

"It may be worse than that," she replied. "The investigation report also disclosed that Tobe Krajcyk had no known relatives."

"Sonofabitch!" Jethro burst out.

A chuckle came from the Spaniard's end of the table. "Your emotion is unbecoming, senor. Even in a land

Gunnar's Mine

where law is manipulated, it must be obvious this sheriff's search is beneath scorn."

"Have you gentlemen composed your letter to the Governor?" Abigail asked.

Jethro shook his head.

"Then I suggest that is the proper task for the four of us to accomplish today." She pointed to Gutierrez. "Anton, I want you to make a second copy of your report. Meanwhile, Jethro can copy Gunnar's and I'll make a second copy of Tobe's. After that we will compose the letter."

Jethro thought of New Mexico, how honest farmers and ranchers had long suffered under the heel of the Santa Fe Ring. He recalled how they'd appealed in vain to the Territorial Governor, only to find that he was involved up to his eyebrows in the ring. Lastly, he remembered how only a blizzard of letters to federal offices had led eventually to the demise of the Santa Fe ring. "We'll need another copy of each list," he said, "and a second copy of the letter to the Governor to go to the President of the United States."

"Can an appeal to the President help when our problem comes under the jurisdiction of a sovereign state?" Abigail asked.

Jethro shook his head. He simply didn't know. New Mexico had been a Federal Territory, subject to administration from the Federal Government. Abigail might have a point. On the other hand, how much could they trust a six-year-old State Government to buck major mining companies when it, for all practical purposes, was founded mostly by mining interests. "What's this new Governor's name—Grant?" he asked. "Has he already taken office? Hell, we don't even know who to write to!" At last he murmured, "Can it hurt?"

Abigail's letter went through several drafts, passing under the careful scrutiny of each of the men. Though

Gunnar seemed in awe of the woman's composition, and Jethro made only a couple of pertinent suggestions, it fell to Antonio Gutierrez to bring science, mining law, and mining camp tradition into full flower within the letter. Gunnar and Jethro were amazed at the Spaniard's knowledge and logic. Abigail incorporated the man's suggestions and eventually a finished letter was created and copied.

"Now, how are we to deliver this?" Abigail asked. Each man looked at the other. "Come, gentlemen. We have but very little time. This letter must be delivered immediately."

"To trust the mail," Gunnar said, "ay would not do."

"No, senors," Gutierrez agreed, "the mail would be subject to tampering. We must find another way."

Jethro sighed, knowing he must be singled out. Just then, Abigail Whittle said, "I believe I should deliver it, gentlemen. Perhaps I could even get an audience to dramatize the serious nature of unfolding events in this region."

As far as the men in the cabin were concerned, Abigail Whittle's trustworthiness was beyond question. What caused them to demur, however, was the arduous nature of a journey across the main spine of the Rocky Mountains during the depths of winter.

"Can you gentlemen afford to wait until spring?" she asked. "It seems to me of paramount importance for this letter and its attachments to reach the Governor as soon as possible."

"I'll take it," Jethro said with finality, but to his surprise, the others shook their head. It was the woman who put their reservations into words: "I believe your presence here to be more valuable. You may be the only thing holding your enemy in abeyance."

"In what?" Jethro asked, fumbling for his notebook.

Gunnar's Mine

"Abeyance. It means ... oh hang what it means! I'm the only one who *can* go. Gunnar's command of English isn't sufficient to gain him access, nor articulate enough to argue the case if he did. Besides, he's not a citizen." She looked questioningly at Gutierrez and the Spaniard shook his head.

"I'm a citizen," Jethro said. "My command of English may not be as good as yours, but I'll try to make a case."

"Mr. Frost," she said, "we've already decided against you. It must be me."

"So the Spaniard, the Swede, and the Indian are out, and we must rely on our enemy's mother?"

She sighed at his irony. "My selection as emissary might not prove impractical after all. Andrew and I are becoming increasingly estranged as I become more and more your partisan. He's wanted me away from here since Christmas—actually, since I brought Tobe Krajcyk to his home after the man was beaten. He will, I'm sure, help me reach the rail line successfully, probably considering it good riddance."

"But see you again, ay will never do!" Gunnar exclaimed.

Jethro began drumming on the table with his fingers. "Have you considered that it might be *you*, ma'am, who is holding Andrew Whittle from 'obeying'?"

"In abeyance," she said through a restrained smile. "I have considered that, Jason, and will return as soon as possible. Andrew will be furious, but I still plan to do so in any event. The simple truth is neither your presence nor mine has prevented him and his employers and minions from pursuing their ends; only in covering his role in it."

"What will you do if he doesn't allow you to live with him after you return?"

"Then I must lodge in Telluride. Or," her dimples

deepened as she flashed her most engaging smile, "I might ask if I could stay with you gentlemen."

"In the Nordic Summer," Gunnar blurted, "ay and my mans will sleep."

With the upper San Miguel locked in winter, perimeter patrols turned routine and the men of the Nordic Summer were able to relax their watchfulness. With the addition of Antonio Gutierrez to their crew, headwall drilling continued without letup, and blasting took place every day.

As anticipated, the Spaniard soon worked out the reason for Gunnar's selection of a tunnel route. "And you hope to strike the source of placer gold?"

"Ay do."

The discussion took place at an evening meal, with both Gunnar and Jethro becoming intrigued by Antonio's mining knowledge.

"That means, little senor, that you are playing for unknown stakes."

"Ay am."

The Spaniard nodded, then gripped his crossed knees and leaned back on his block of wood. "And you've given no real thought to the ore in the mountain above you."

"Placer gold is all ay know."

"Yet real wealth awaits the one who can extract the minerals from these mountains."

Jethro propped elbows to the table and leaned nearer. "Anton, neither of us, Gunnar or me, knows a damn thing about hardrock mining. What minerals are you talking about?"

"Gold, of course, and silver. Perhaps manganese and copper and lead. But the trouble is, senors, those minerals are all mixed together and, as yet, no one has been able to reduce it."

"Is that the reason for somebody trying to grab it all; that they must be big in order to handle it?"

"Hah!" Gutierrez barked. "They want it because it is rich in metals, not because they are big. They want it because it will make them bigger so they can steal more and more."

"But Tobe didn't know how to reduce it. In fact, he didn't even know what he had. But he thought it might be a rich deposit."

"Rich enough it was," Gunnar said, "dat he was killed for it."

Over in the corner, Puppy wrestled with a battered bone, growling fiercely, pouncing on it, backing off, barking her high-pitched puppy yelp.

Finally Jethro muttered, "And others will die, too."

"It is possible the people behind the Colorado Basin Holding Company know of a way to reduce the complicated ore in this district. I myself have heard of a Belgium reduction firm who made technical advances that might be of service in this instance. But as of yet, no one has solved the problems." He paused for effect, then added, "It is my belief the company intends to begin here as soon as the railroad reaches Placerville. If so, they will build arrastras to crush the ore, then ship it to separation mills, perhaps in Nevada. This process will begin experimentally, but eventually someone will learn how to separate the minerals, thereby reaping fortunes."

"Okay," Jethro said. "I understand why they would want to acquire as many holdings as possible in the region, but kill for it? What could it hurt if one or two or three small claimholders out of dozens remained?"

Again the Spaniard barked. "You do not know these people, Senor Frost. They become so eaten up with greed, they will allow not even so much as one claimholder to profit from their efforts and expense."

Jethro nodded, more to himself than to the others. Suddenly he leaned forward and said, "Why haven't you tried to bring in another outside interest as a counter to this company?"

Gutierrez waved dismissively. "I have, senor. But it is too complicated for them, also. They say it would require too big an investment for my small claim."

"Then, from that point of view, the Colorado Basin Holding Company is doing the right thing."

Gutierrez nodded. "Except for their greed that drives them to excess."

"So what will you and Gunnar do? What is your plan, Anton?"

"There can be but one—maintain my claim until the ones behind the Colorado Basin Holding Company develop methods for ore reduction that will work for these mountains. Then I will be able to retire to a villa on the Sea of Cortez."

Gunnar slowly pushed to his feet, Puppy cradled in his arms. "The Nordic Summer is my life. Ay will not leave her."

"What about Gunnar?" Jethro asked. "What of his pursuit of a gold vein? His situation seems different from yours and all the other claims in the district. What of that?"

Gutierrez nodded before Jethro had finished. "This I have thought on, senor. Senor Gunnar does have prospects beyond those known to the Colorado Basin Holding Company. But how good are his prospects? This I do not know. The vein he seeks—even if he reaches it—may only be a small pocket; perhaps it may be a narrow band that tapers to nothing. Or it may be a *vena grande* with untold riches. But this I believe, senors, the great wealth of this mine, and of every other mine in this region, lies within the mountain above."

Gunnar's Mine

Gunnar set Puppy on his block of wood, then shuffled to his bunk. On his return he carried two quartz pieces wrapped in a red handkerchief. When he shook the pieces laced with gold loose on the table, Antonio Gutierrez picked one up, studied it, then laid it down to pick up the other. "When were these recovered, senor?"

"When ay washed the gravel, ay got them."

"But when? How long ago?"

Gunnar grinned at Jethro, then said to the Spaniard, "Today it was."

Again, Gutierrez returned to study the quartz. At last he laid them down on the handkerchief and said, "Then, senor, you are certainly close to a vein of some sort. But these streaks of gold are small and are possibly spiders from the main vein. It is certain you do not pursue a pocket but a vein. Exciting though it may be to you, this is still not enough to allow you to retire to a castle in Stockholm."

Gunnar picked up the pieces and folded the handkerchief around them. His movements seemed so dejected the Spaniard was moved to repeat, "Again, senor, you are close to something. It would be my guess that before the lava last flowed over this land, a ledge crumbled from someplace above into the stream course you follow. If you continue up this course and suddenly find no more placer gold, then you may assume the gold came from such hills as might then flanked the stream."

"What if the original stream forked?" Jethro asked.

"What of it? If Senor Gunnar wishes to pursue the placer gold, that is easy enough to answer. He follows the one with the gold in it."

"But if what you say is true, he might as well hunker down and wait for Amalgamated Minerals and Mining—or whoever—to lead the way to even greater riches."

"That is what I plan to do, senor."

"Ay will stay, too," Gunnar said. "Und ay will follow

the gold ay know."

Jethro shook his head. "What I don't get, though, Anton, is why stick it out here? Why not in Denver or Mexico City? Why don't both of you go to a beach in California, return to do enough work on your claims to keep them active, and wait for the big company to make you rich?"

Gunnar insisted again that he would not leave. Gutierrez ignored Gunnar's outburst, explaining, "Because, senor, they would not allow us to come back. You had a recent example of how the law works for Senor Whittle. With the company in control of our mines and representatives of the law accepting graft, what is left? As long as we are still here, still in one mine or the other, we maintain both claims."

"Yet your mine has the best defensive set up."

"Si, senor. But the little man will not come to me, so I must come to him. Besides, he pursues what I believe may turn into a strike, while I must await developments by the big company."

Gutierrez lowered the porcelain dishes carrying his family's crest into the wash bucket, washed them clean, rinsed them, then took his coat from a wall peg and prepared to retire for the evening. Jethro caused him to pause by asking, "What could we do here to increase security, Anton?"

Gutierrez pondered, then said, "I would buy two savage dogs and chain them, one to a tree near the cabin and the other to a tree near the mine. I would feed them and bring them water. But I would never let them roam free. And I would listen very carefully when they told me I should do so."

Three days later, a great, black beast, half wolf and half Siberian husky, was chained to a tree near the mine tunnel. Four days later, a bulldog-redbone cross was chained near the cabin.

Gunnar's Mine

And for weeks thereafter, it was a full time job for Gunnar to keep Puppy from either of the brutes' fangs.

Chapter Fifteen

The Colorado Basin Holding Company made its first move of 1883 against the region's last independent miners during an unseasonal, early-February warming period. Jethro was on outside patrol, climbing on the hillside above Gunnar's mine. Most of the snow had burned off in the face of a week of warm Pacific winds. Any remaining snowbanks hid behind exposed boulders or were packed into clefts in the rocks. Drenching rain had fell during the night, then tapered to light showers by morning, leaving a sodden and muddy mountain nightmare. Temperatures fell as the storm blew itself out. Showers turned to light snow.

The baying of the guard dog at the cabin was soon accompanied by the savage barking of the wolf-dog near the mine.

Jethro eased down the hill, using available cover in the manner Naiche Tana had taught him during his stay on the Mescalero Reservation. Finally he reached a point

Gunnar's Mine

where he had a view of the flat below. There were two men at the cabin, apparently talking, gesticulating, walking about the premises. Two horses were snubbed to trees at the edge of the little clearing. After some short discussion, the men started up the trail to the mine.

Both dogs seemed focused on the strangers alone and after first studying the flat, Jethro glided down the hill to stealthily trail the strangers. The men came to an abrupt halt when Gunnar emerged from the mine brandishing a shovel. "What is you want?" the little man challenged, glancing at Jethro, blue eyes twinkling.

"We're down from Telluride," the swarthy one replied. "Lookin' for work."

"We was told you might be hiring," the thinner, smooth-shaven one said.

"Told wrong you was," Gunnar said. "No work ay have."

While the men went through the motions with Gunnar, they were actually studying the layout of the mine's approaches. Jethro had watched them do the same at the cabin.

"Say, that's a cute pup," the swarthy one said, pointing at Puppy, who'd waddled from the tunnel after Gunnar. "It don't look to me like it fits with the one chained over there.

The one chained 'over there' continued to snarl and bark, lunging over and over against the end of his chain.

"Ay have no work," Gunnar repeated.

"We're good," the thin man said. "We're one of the best double-jack teams in all Colorado. We hear you're taking raw gold from …" The man's constantly swiveling eyes caused him to swing his head enough to spot Jethro standing behind. The swarthy one wheeled at the abrupt break in his friend's monologue, hand moving toward a revolver tucked into his waistband.

Jethro smiled, earing the Winchester's hammer back;

its muzzle pointed to the man's knee.

Swarthy's hand fell away, but he was not intimidated. "They even got Injuns here, Lon," he said.

Lon lifted his hands, followed seconds later by Swarthy, who added, "We'uns are just looking for a job, friend. That's all."

"Ay said dere is no yob here. Why would ay hire mens who don't hear?"

Lon said, "If you'll tell your Injun to move out of the way, we won't bother you no more, little man."

After the men had gone, Antonio stepped from the tunnel carrying his sawed-off double-barrel, saying, "Work they want. Hah! They were spies."

Jethro's mouth twisted in a wry smile that never reached his gray eyes. "I'll be gone a while, boys. Look after things while I'm away." Then he turned and trotted off, splashing across Fall Creek and later, fording the San Miguel, heading north through the foothills toward Placerville.

He was sipping a tepid beer in Chalkie's Emporium when Swarthy and Lon jogged their horses into town, tied them to the hitchrail out front, and strode in.

"Still looking for work, boys?" Jethro asked. "Placerville's a good place."

"Hey Lon!" interrupted a baggy-trousered miner who shouted from the bar's far end. "You're back. C'mon down and I'll buy you and Drogue a red-eye."

Chalkie leaned against his cash drawer, arms crossed, bar rag in hand, and an amused smile beneath his drooping moustache. Earlier, he'd filled Jethro's request for a beer, taken the coin offered, and promptly returned change. Then he positioned himself without threat to await whatever events Jethro's arrival always seemed to presage.

The man Jethro had just learned was Drogue was less fazed than his partner. Though he hesitated, he

Gunnar's Mine

shook himself, put his arm around his single-jacking partner, and strode on down to where they were offered a red-eye.

Jethro threw off his beer, then walked from the building. Within an hour, he was back at the Nordic Summer. "We figured it right," he told Gunnar and Gutierrez. "They came from Placerville; sent here to scout us."

"They did not have the fear of most of Whittle's running dogs," the Spaniard said. "Especially the bearded one."

"True. He was not the type to cringe. Have you seen either of them before?"

Both older men shook their heads.

"So Whittle is bringing in outside help, getting ready to turn the screws. You know what this means, don't you?"

Antonio nodded, but Gunnar's head swiveled between his companions. "What is?"

"It means they're getting ready to hit us; that we'll have to be ready, do more patrols, lay in more supplies, maybe tighten our defenses."

"How you mean, 'hit us'? Dey will shoot?"

Jethro gripped the little man's shoulders. "And it means we'll shoot back."

They came in the night, as Jethro and the Spaniard thought they would. Arrogantly, they first occupied Walter's way station, blindfolding the owner, tying him to a chair in his kitchen. The men were masked, and they were dressed alike in dark Union Army blankets with holes cut in the center for their heads to fit through. They did not fool the bulldog-redbone, who began baying sometime around midnight. The moon was in its last phase, a condition made to order for Gutierrez, as well as Gunnar's 'mans', who blacked their faces with charcoal when they slipped from their sleeping places.

The barking of the bulldog-cross turned to snarls just before he was killed with an axe while lunging at the limit of his chain. The axe wielder died seconds later, following the whisper of a Spanish throwing knife that lodged between his shoulder blades.

"Get'em boys!" came a lusty shout from the creek, followed by a rifle volley and the rush of many feet toward the cabin, where attackers were felled by a network of trip ropes. One of them screamed when Antonio's beartrap clanged shut on his boot, and yet another tumbled into a pit with sharpened stakes imbedded in the bottom.

Most of the attackers prudently awaited the results of their comrades' first rush and were terrified by the bedlam breaking out around the cabin. Then a terrifying scream came from off to their left, where the clearing turned into scrub pines.

Guns barked haphazardly, felling attackers with bullets from their own ranks. The leader tried to reassert command, but his shouted orders were ominously cut short in mid-sentence, lost finally in a gurgled scream. Still firing wildly, blanketed shapes fell away from the cabin. Flight became general, then descended into a stampede.

When daylight came, Jose Antonio Gutierrez de Valdez y Mendoza materialized from the early morning mist to pull his throwing knife from the body of a bearded, blanketed figure Jethro had once heard called 'Drogue'.

Jethro sat on his haunches cleaning his knife. At his feet lay two fresh scalps.

"Are yours yet alive?" Antonio asked, wiping his knife on his trousers as he walked past.

Gunnar's Mine

Jethro stood, slipped his knife back into his boot and said, "Wanted'em to. They'll spread more fear than a dead man."

The Spaniard gestured at a whimpering attacker who was curled in a fetal position—or as nearly as possible with a beartrap clenching his bloody leg. "And him?"

"Aw, let him go, too."

"It will take the both of us to depress the trap, senor."

Jethro grinned. "Shall we let him out first, or see to the one I hear still moaning in the pit?"

Gunnar came from the cabin, paused to stare down into the pit, then joined his friends where they worked at releasing the trap. "How's he?" Jethro asked, pointing toward the pit with his chin.

"Ay don't know." Then Gunnar spied their dead dog and asked, "Why him do they kill?"

The sobbing, blanket-clad attacker rolled away as soon as the trap was released, then scrambled for the trail back to the San Miguel, stopping abruptly when Jethro's belt knife thudded into a tree trunk just ahead of his nose.

"Wait for us to get your friend out of the pit," Jethro said. "Who knows? He might need help more than you."

The man in the pit needed very little help. He had a shallow puncture in his side and another in his thigh. But, given the sounds of terror coming from all around him, he'd opted to stay hidden in the pit.

"Name?" Jethro said, staring down into the hole.

"Walker, s-sir:"

"Walker what?"

"Luke. Luke Walker."

Movement caught Jethro's eye and he said, "Gunnar, why don't you take your shovel over there and beat the hell out of that sonofabitch who's trying to crawl away?" He turned back to Luke Walker. "Why are you here?"

"Be-because we were told to."

"What were you going to do?"

"Burn you out, I guess. I don't know." He put his hands over his face. "I only do what I'm told!"

The Winchester blazed. Sand and rocks leaped onto the man's spraddled trousers. "Look at me when I talk to you," Jethro ordered. "It's impolite not to look a man in the eye when he talks to you."

Tears streamed down the attacker's face, and though the eyes were closed, the face turned upwards.

Nearby, Gunnar's shovel clanged and the escapee howled. Then he started crawling back toward Antonio and Jethro. Jethro said to Luke Walker, "You do what you're told. Right?"

"Y-yessir."

"What if I told you to take Gunnar's shovel and fill up that hole while you were still in it. Would you do that?"

The chin sank to the man's chest, but bounced up again when another bullet "kle-klatched" into the Winchester's chamber. "Nosir."

"But you said you always do what you're told."

The prisoner remained silent.

"Who told you to attack us?"

"Gorney."

"Gorney who?"

"Brandon Gorney."

"What does he do?"

"He works for the company."

"Does he work *for* Whittle, or *over* him?"

"For him."

Jethro shook his head as Antonio raised an eyebrow. "Get out of there," he told the man in the pit.

"I can't. I'm hurt."

Gunnar's Mine

"You can, and you will or you'll hurt a lot worse." Luke Walker scrambled from the pit.

When Luke Walker stood unsteadily on the pit's edge, Jethro threw him a patch of hair. You take this back to Brandon Gorney and tell him the next time I catch him or one of his men on this property, I'll take both of his ears to go with his hair."

Walker looked stupidly down at the bloody scalp, then dropped it in horror.

"Pick it up. If you don't, the next thing you'll do is eat it." Walker did so in alarm.

"Now, Jethro said, "take your partner and get the hell out of my sight."

It was afternoon before the sheriff, accompanied by Walter Hopkins, paid an investigative call. He examined the bodies of the two attackers left behind, and that of the dead dog, looked at the bullet gouges in the cabin walls, and asked a few questions. He said he'd get to the bottom of what he called, "this incident," asked for help in removing the bodies, was refused, and left in a huff.

Walter said, "I reckon he ain't much for a sheriff. Says he can't believe Andrew Whittle had a thing to do with it. Hell, I *know* that ain't right and I ain't no lawman."

"Some names we have," Gunnar said, hitching his overalls and taking them up an inch at the shoulders.

Walter shook his head. "I guess I'm out of it, Gunnar. I can see which way the wind's blowing and I'm standing in the way. I sure as hell favor you boys, but this is a dyin' game that's being dealt here. I ain't got that much invested in my station, even though the land's deeded. Maybe I could make it through what's coming here, but I'll be damned if I can see where it's worth the risk."

With Walter's departure, there was no friendly face left between Redvale and Telluride. That changed, however, when one Sunday in late March, Abigail Whittle came striding to the cabin, pleated skirt swishing. Puppy yapped once, then boisterously began wriggling ecstatically, then jumping on the woman. Gunnar and Jethro were outside the cabin in their shirtsleeves, sawing and splitting wood. Abigail hugged an embarrassed Gunnar and kissed him on the cheek, then hugged Jethro.

Still holding Jethro, she looked around and asked, "Where's Antonio? I know he's here somewhere."

The Spaniard stepped from behind a tree, teeth shining beneath a pencil moustache. "The senora left her buggy at Walter's old station. Her *caballo* is a blood bay and is presently unhooked and in the stable. She arrived at precisely ten minutes after ten and, after seeing to her horse—which is a small gelding—came directly here."

She laughed gaily, and by the time Antonio trailed off, had also given him a hug.

The day began with one of those crisp, fresh March mornings when the temperature was too brisk for comfort but the day too pleasing to stay indoors. The center of attention, Abigail propped up a block of wood and sat upon it, cuddling Puppy in her arms. "The Governor," she said.

Gunnar perched on a block directly in front of the woman while Jethro and Antonio chose to stand either side of the little Swede.

"Governor Grant is, I believe, an amiable island surrounded by hungry sharks. He granted my request for an audience, listened carefully to everything I had to say, received your letters graciously, and said he would

Gunnar's Mine

review them with dispatch. Then he personally walked me from his office to the Capitol steps, took me by the hand and promised an investigation would be launched immediately. What he didn't say was that I would be visited by the Capitol lobbyist for the Colorado Basin Holding Company within sixteen hours, and that I would receive an unpleasant telegram from Andrew within forty-eight."

Gutierrez caught Jethro's eye, and the ends of his moustache lifted toward his cheekbones.

"So," Abigail continued, "I prepared to mail the second set of copies to President Arthur in Washington; but before I did, I wondered what might happen if they were lost? So I went to a respected Denver attorney and asked him to have someone on his staff make copies, and for him to witness their accuracy. Those were the ones I mailed to the President.

"Soon thereafter, I asked for advice concerning Governor Grant's investigation. His aides were polite, but not very helpful. Consequently, I petitioned for a second audience with the Governor." She paused, then added, "Those requests, unfortunately, led nowhere, despite a month of repeated effort.

"At last I returned to the office of Thomas Oglesby, the attorney who'd helped earlier with additional letter drafts. Mr. Oglesby made further attempts to secure an appointment with the Governor, but to no avail. So finally, I determined the only practical course of action would be to return here and join forces with you gentlemen."

When it was obvious that she'd run down, Jethro said, "And you were met with open arms by your late husband's son?"

She laughed merrily. "He locked me from his house. He even placed a guard to keep me away."

Gunnar glanced quickly up at Jethro, then said, "We

will move to the mine, my mans and ay."

Abigail's laugh again rang out and she pinched Gunnar's cheek. "You are wonderful—all of you are wonderful. But I already have accommodations. You see, on my return I met Walter Hopkins quite by chance in Grand Junction. He sold me his station. We're neighbors!"

Chapter Sixteen

To say that Abigail Whittle's revelation that the men of Gunnar's fort would have her as a neighbor shocked her listeners might be an understatement. Gunnar Einarssen, for one, cried, "Ya!" and began clapping. Jose Antonio Gutierrez de Valdez y Mendoza smiled, glanced at the overhead sky, began mumbling a 'Hail Mary' before kneeling to kiss the woman's hand, then trotting away on patrol.

Only Jethro Spring proved undemonstrative, merely studying the woman through hooded eyes.

"What is wrong, Mr. Frost?" she asked, surprised at his lack of response. "Are you not pleased?"

Actually, he had mixed emotions. He knew why Gunnar, blinkered by a growing infatuation for Abigail, was jubilant. And he suspected that Gutierrez presumed the woman's living nearby would offer a further shield from their enemies. But would Andrew Whittle be deterred from an offensive against the three holdout miners out of consideration for the presence of his own stepmother? No doubt the forces driving Whittle, the son, were too overwhelming to be blunted by the unexpected arrival of his mother. Besides, she'd already caused the son embarrassment by her Denver efforts on behalf of the beleaguered miners along the San Miguel. No, there was little doubt about it, if Andrew Whittle shrank from what his employers thought his duty, they'd simply bring in someone else to finish the job. Abigail Whittle's presence at Walter's station might cause no more than a blink in the eyes of Gunnar's enemies, and she could even prove a liability; another individual in need of protection.

Jethro smiled fleetingly. "Are you thinking of opening Walter's to serve the lost and weary, ma'am?"

"I certainly am. And I assume I can count on serving occasional meals to hungry neighbors, too."

"Ay and my mans will come, you betcha," Gunnar responded enthusiastically. "Both mans, even."

Jethro chuckled at his little friend, then asked, "What will you need to put the station to rights? Do you need help?"

"Perhaps. I don't know. There will be a wagonload of supplies arriving from end-of-track in less than a week. I'll need to go to Telluride and order a few interim things, as well as engage some laborers—if any are available. Should I need anything from you gentlemen, I promise to ask. But I warn you, I want to do this myself."

Jethro nodded, then asked, "Where is end-of-track, Abigail?"

"I wish I could tell you. Perhaps halfway between Gateway and Redvale...." She paused, thinking. "No, not that far. It's a frightful canyon and they've already bridged the—Oh, I know! They're halfway between Gateway and the junction of the Dolores and San

Gunnar's Mine

Miguel." When the younger man took too long digesting the information, Abigail asked, "Does that help?"

He nodded. "How about the grading crews?"

"I could see them from the wagon road. I believe they're on the bench west of the San Miguel. There's frightful mud."

Jethro could see it all—the fresnos, the powder monkeys and teamsters, the mules, the sweat, curses, shouts, and imprecations. His mind returned to the months he spent building a railroad up the Arkansas Royal Gorge, heading for Leadville. His gaze wandered up the hills to the east, over those hills and mountains—row upon row of them—and finally over the main chain of the Colorado Rockies to the river and sweating, toiling Chinese, who worked for less pay and accomplished more than the gangs of resentful, white workmen.

He smiled fondly. *Those slant-eyed, little bastards worked in their baggy blue pantaloons and cotton shirts, wore the big straw hats, and drank tea like it was the nectar of the Gods. But Lord, could they work!* He was so lost in thought that he shook his head. *They expected me to protect them and I failed.*

He'd heard the popping of guns while bending over the neck of his pounding horse. The sounds came from afar. Then he began seeing blue-clad figures darting through river-bottom willows, and the burning tents. Gunshots were louder now, and occasional bodies lay scattered about. Bullets began plucking at his clothing and whining past his ears. Then the big gray was staggered and when he finally fell. He saw himself vaulting from his saddle, intent on only one thing—digging his Colt from where it was buried in a suitcase in his burning tent, the words of his Texas Ranger friend still ringing in his ears: "Just don't bury your gun too far, hear?"

Instinctively, he patted the Colt that had seldom left his side in the years since. *He'd learned his....*

"Jason, what's wrong?" Abigail interrupted. "You look as though you've seen a ghost."

"Huh? I'm sorry."

"I said, you look as though you've seen a ghost."

He had. The ghost was of his friend, Ling San, whose lifeless body he'd cradled at the end of a senseless railroad race riot. Ling San Ho—the man who'd taught him about the simple values of peace and courage and tranquility, who'd taught him Chinese fighting skills and who'd twice saved him from bounty hunters....

"I'll go find Anton," he said, picking up his Winchester and trotting away, into the nearby forest.

"You are wrong!" Antonio Gutierrez said, angrily shaking his head. "She is an angel of mercy; one who will not stand by while the minions of *muerte* destroy us."

The men sat high on the mountainside above Gunnar's mine. In the distance below, the San Miguel shimmered in the noontime sun and wagons plied the road between Telluride and the rest of the world. The roadhouse roof and stable of Walter's old station was barely visible among scattered trees.

Instinctively, Jethro had climbed to this point, knowing somehow that the Spaniard would be there. He'd been surprised earlier at Antonio's show of emotion—the first he'd seen from the stern, forbidding mining engineer. Now the two men sat against a rock outcrop exchanging views.

The younger man learned the Spaniard's hopes had been revived by Abigail's reappearance. He listened quietly for a very long time as Antonio Gutierrez told the story of his life. He learned of the vast family holdings, plundered after the execution of Pedro Gutierrez, the valiant attempts of a young military hero to restore his family's position in society, and the adventures that brought Jose Antonio Gutierrez de Valdez y Mendoza a wealth of mining knowledge.

Lastly, Jethro learned how the aging mining engineer had finally turned to the *Estados Unidos* in a last attempt to practice his profession without interference from government or enemy; a place where one may, through his own intelligence and effort, achieve a destiny of his own making. Then came Andrew Whittle and the Colorado Basin Holding Company.

It shocked Jethro to learn, in retrospect, that an embittered Jose Antonio Gutierrez de Valdez y Mendoza had, in reality, only been going through the motions because this was, for him, the end of the line. After a lifetime of fighting for first one losing cause, then another, the Spaniard had finally decided to make this his last stand; the mining claim on the San Miguel was his sword line in the dust—like his father's decision to die at Goliad rather than implement an order that would disgrace him and his family.

Jethro understood now that Antonio Gutierrez had planned to die on the San Miguel, and that he for a time, saw Gunnar Einarssen's young mine worker as an impediment to that plan. Frost's stubbornness and courage and resourcefulness began pecking away at Gutierrez, until the man finally asked himself why he should not join the last of the district's holdout miners and cause his enemies as much grief as possible. "Why not," he asked himself, "join the Swede and the Indian in a last stand?"

But as events unfolded, it was a pleasant surprise to Antonio Gutierrez to discover that Jethro Spring was not merely courageous and stubborn, but also intelligent and an excellent listener. At the present time this intelligent listener occupied himself with what Jose

Antonio Gutierrez de Valencia y Mendoza was saying about the coming of Abigail Dimity Whittle. It was her efforts on their behalf—the woman's persistence in obtaining Tobe Kracyk's litany of attempts on his life and mining claim, her insistence on getting a similar report from Gunnar, and lastly, her audience with the Colorado Governor that had elevated Gutierrez's hopes.

"So you see, senor, I have now begun to think we have a chance. The Senora Whittle provides another factor to that chance." The Spaniard chuckled. "I am like you, senor, after all. I do not believe Andrew Whittle will be deterred for one moment by his mother's presence. And, like you, I believe if he were, his puppeteers would find another to do their bidding.

"What she does offer, senor, is credibility. If Senor Antonio Gutierrez or Senor Gunnar Einarssen, or even Senor Jason Frost makes claims against the Colorado Basin Holding Company, they can be dismissed as petty complaints by jealous competitors. But Senora Abigail Whittle has no such mining interests, no recognizable reason to make malodorous charges. If she makes the same claims as those we make, her charges—and ours—will carry much more weight. Do you not agree?"

"Yes, but ..."

"Our problem, senor, is how to withstand their next attack, and the next. That is how we should conduct ourselves—by trying to anticipate their next move and how we can prevent them from succeeding."

Gutierrez fell silent while Jethro stared into the distance at Utah's La Sal Mountains. At last the younger man asked, "What do you think they'll do next?"

By the time Antonio and Jethro returned to the cabin, Abigail Whittle had pumped Gunnar for a full accounting of the battle of Gunnar's fort. She had, of course, already heard the story from Walter, but Gunnar's tale was more colorful as he garnished the exploits of his two 'mans' beyond credibility. Still, she clapped and begged for more, and when Jethro and Antonio put in a late afternoon appearance, the woman told them how proud she was of their strategy and valor.

The occupation of Walter Hopkins' old station by Abigail Whittle came as much of a shock to Andrew Whittle and the Colorado Basin Holding Company as it earlier did to the three miners on Fall Creek.

First the woman was visited by Sheriff Richards, who politely explained that the property had been officially abandoned by the claimant of record and was under examination by his department for its tax status.

Abigail replied that the taxes were current and she had a transfer of deed witnessed by the duly appointed judge for southeastern Colorado, the Honorable Seth Sutherland, holding court in Grand Junction.

Sheriff Richards, hat in hand, begged Mrs. Whittle's pardon, saying he must further investigate the dispute. Then Barnabas Richards rode on to Placerville to report to Andrew Whittle.

Whittle demanded to know if the sheriff had actually seen the deed. The sheriff shook his head. "Then I would suggest you go back and ask to do so. If such a deed exists, take it to Telluride—use any damned excuse you can think of. I'll want to have our counsel examine it."

"What if she says no?" the sheriff asked.

"Then take it from her," Whittle said, voice rising. "Good Jupiter, you're the legally constituted law in this county. You can do what you want." Then he added, "What we can't allow her to do is record that deed."

But upon Sheriff Richard's return, Abigail Whittle would not produce her deed to Walter Hopkins' land holding, claiming it was locked up at the Nordic Summer. If the sheriff wished to accompany her to the mine on Fall Creek, however, she would ask Gunnar if he would produce it. Sheriff Barnabas, it turned out, was reluctant to confront the men of the Fall Creek enclave. Instead, he said he had to return to Telluride on urgent business and would plan to come back the following day. In the interim, the sheriff instructed Abigail to obtain the deed for his examination.

That's why Sheriff Barnabas Richards was surprised the following morning to see Abigail Whittle driving into town, accompanied by one of the coldest-eyed, meanest-looking bastards he'd ever set eyes on—the one who'd cowed Andrew Whittle and an entire bar filled with tough cowboys and miners, placed a curse on eight of Whittle's men, and singlehandedly (if one could believe what one heard) drove off a hundred-man attack on the men of the Nordic Summer. Thus, the sheriff prudently busied himself saddling and bridling his black gelding, neither seeing nor (he hoped) being seen.

Later, after the deed had been legally filed, the sheriff had ample opportunity to examine the records, reporting back to Andrew Whittle that all appeared in order.

The confrontation between Andrew and his stepmother was heated; at times even explosive.

"A whore! You're calling your own mother a whore?"

"You're not my mother. You came here without invitation, then started undermining me from the first day."

"You poor, misguided fool," she replied. "I tried to

Gunnar's Mine

save you from yourself, but I gave up the effort when it became obvious you've denied every bit of moral sense God and your father gave you."

"Don't bring my father into this!"

The station yard rang with her laughter. "You needn't worry, Andrew. He could never be brought into anything as sordid and underhanded as these things you're engaged in."

Andrew Whittle jerked the bridle reins loose from the station hitchrail. "I can't promise to protect you forever."

"Have you protected me—*ever?*" she shot back.

The man sighed in exasperation, thrust a boot toe in the stirrup, and swung atop his big bay. He paused to stare down at her, then said, "Mother, dammit, come to your senses. I will pay whatever you paid Hopkins for this place. I'll pay even more. But I want you out of the way before ..."

"Before what, Andrew? Before you send an entire regiment against the three, innocent holdouts at Gunnar's mine? An Army? Are you so insane as to think you can get away with whatever it is you intend to do?"

CHAPTER SEVENTEEN

Grading crews for the Rio Grande Southern Railroad reached the Redvale bench by mid-June and end-of-track pushed past the juncture of the Dolores and San Miguel Rivers only to bump up against yet another major bridge span, this time across the San Miguel's lower canyon.

With his knowledge of railroad construction, Jethro Spring knew that after tracklayers successfully crossed to the south bench above the San Miguel, that progress would be rapid. But he knew also that grading crews were heading toward their toughest work—cutting a grade back down into the San Miguel's upper canyon. He estimated the track should reach Placerville sometime in late August or early September, then punch on through to Telluride before winter set in.

That meant it would be two, perhaps three months before the company seizing control of the Placerville district would want to begin developing its holdings in

Gunnar's Mine

earnest. First, according to Antonio Gutierrez, they'd need rail sidings, then storage warehouses for machinery. If Antonio was correct, they would also put up large buildings for crushing the ore to concentrate. After that would come loading facilities for shipping concentrated ore to outside smelters.

All in all, their preparatory work prior to large scale mining should be completed before the depths of winter. Sometime between now and then, the faceless monopolizer would want all the district's loose ends tied up. That meant the Swede and the Spaniard must either sell or die.

Lying like a sunning lizard on an outcrop above Antonio's claim, Jethro could see Placerville. The town lazily flexed itself on the first hot day of the coming summer. Down below, workmen toiled. They seemed especially active on Billy Benbrooke's old claim, as well as the two adjoining it. Tobe Krajcyk's contested claim appeared untouched, but the 'sunning lizard' found it interesting that the Spaniard's claim had recently been worked—probably merely exploratory. He was, in addition, surprised to see Antonio's cabin still standing. But why not? It was sturdy and well-located, probably ideal as a mine office when work actually began.

During a previous night's foray, Jethro discovered ground actually being broken, possibly for the storage sheds Anton said would be needed. The new sheds would be located along the survey line established for the railway bed. So Whittle and his masters weren't letting any grass grow under their feet.

But when would their next strike come? And where?

The answer came the very next day when Mr. Jay Eldon Blackenby, accompanied by a hesitant sheriff, arrived at Gunnar's mine.

"Hallo-o-o!" came the cry.

Gunnar, scooping gravel into buckets, stopped shoveling to cock an ear. When the hail came again, he called to Jethro, farther back in the tunnel, to stop single-jacking.

"Halloo-o the mine!"

Gunnar trotted to the tunnel mouth. Jethro snatched up his Winchester and followed as fast as a stooped-over shuffle would permit. When he arrived near the mouth, he heard a stranger say, "And we'll pay both you and Mr. Gutierrez twice the purchase price of any of the other mining properties in the Placerville District."

The Swede shook his head. "Ay will not sell for any moneys. The Nordic Summer, she belongs to Gunnar Einarssen, and to Gunnar Einarssen she will stay."

The stranger chuckled and said, "I understand, Mr. Einarssen. I truly do. But the ore in this district is so difficult that only a large corporation can succeed in profitably extracting it. It is our ..." The stranger's voice trailed off as a dusty Jethro Spring emerged into sunlight.

"Hello, sheriff. What brings you down here to Fall Creek?"

Shuffling uncomfortably, the sheriff replied, "Well I ... I brought Mr. Blackenby down on a matter of business with Mr. Einarssen."

"What kind of business?" Jethro asked the sheriff, pointedly excluding the newcomer.

Jay Eldon Blackenby ignored the snub, striding forward with an outstretched hand. "You must be Jason Frost. I've heard of you young man ..."

Jethro ignored the man and his hand. "What is this man's business, sheriff?" he asked again, his voice dropping an octave.

The sheriff, taking courage from Blackenby's presence, made an effort to assert authority. "I'm not sure it's any business of yours, Frost. Mr. Blackenby's busi-

Gunnar's Mine

ness is between Mr. Einarssen and himself."

"Please!" Jose Antonio Gutierrez de Valdez y Mendoza said from close behind the sheriff. "I beg of you to listen to what the young senor says. I myself have seen him both in action and thought, and I have great respect for his abilities, as well as great confidence in him."

Blackenby, whirling at the Spaniard's entry, said, "Ah, Mr. Gutierrez, I'm pleased that you could join us."

The sheriff only stared at the ground.

"Now, let's try this one last time, sheriff," Jethro said. "What business does Mr. Blackenby have with Mr. Einarssen, that requires the help of a county officer?"

Blackenby focused again on Jethro. "I would advise you, young man, to demonstrate a little respect for due process. The person you are talking to is the duly elected representative of the law in San Miguel County."

Jethro sighed. "It does look like you are bound to become annoying, Mr. ... uh ..."

"Blackenby," the newcomer said. "Jay Eldon Blackenby, attorney at law." Blackenby again extended his hand. "I have the pleasure to represent ..."

Jethro once more ignored the hand, but this time he focused a pair of most disquieting gray eyes on the newcomer. "It does look like we're going to have to resolve the problem of what to do with you while Senor Gutierrez and I conduct our discussion with San Miguel County's representative of law and order."

"I just came down from Telluride to show Mr. Blackenby the way," the sheriff said, still focusing on the ground at his feet.

"And did Mr. Blackenby say what his business was with Mr. Einarssen?"

"He said he wanted to make an offer on the mines belonging to Gutierrez and Einarssen."

"And are you a part of this discussion, sheriff?"

"No." The sheriff's eyes jumped to Jethro at last. "Absolutely not. I got no place here."

"That's right, sheriff. You have no status here. But do you suppose your presence might be thought as lending support to Mr. What's-his-name's proposal?"

"Blackenby," Blackenby said. "I believe I might share ..."

"It might," the sheriff muttered, again staring at his feet. "I suppose it might, but that's not why I come."

"Ah, that! Then sheriff, why don't you share with us precisely why you did come."

"Well, I was trying to help you boys. Tryin' to avert trouble."

Both Jethro Spring and Antonio Gutierrez laughed. "Senor sheriff," the Spaniard said, "are you not talking to the wrong people? Surely the people of Fall Creek aren't the villains who prey on the people of Fall Creek."

"Tell you what you do, sheriff," Jethro said. "You trot on back to Abigail Whittle's place and have her set you up a big steak. Mr. What's-his-name will join you after Mr. Einarssen and Mr. Gutierrez hear his proposal and they make him a counter-proposal. How's that?"

"Well, I don't think I wish to ..." Blackenby began.

Jethro turned to him and smiled amiably. "How about if we said 'Please', Mr. What's-his-name?"

Blackenby's mouth pinched into a tight line and his eyes flashed, but Jethro gave him credit for guts when he said, "As you wish, gentlemen."

The sheriff left in a rush, verging on a run. The guard dog between mine and cabin—the one which had not ceased barking since the strangers appeared—increased his velocity, spiriting the sheriff's exit even more. The four men at the mine mouth watched until the lawman disappeared, then Jethro said, "Mr. Blackenby, if you'd be kind enough to wait in the mine mouth, I'd like to discuss the situation with my friends."

Gunnar's Mine

"I'm sorry, Mr. Frost," Blackenby said, restraining an impulse to offer his hand a third time. "I had no idea you were a principal in either of these mines."

"Oh I'm not sir. Not at all. What I lack in not being a principal, however, I make up in principle. And I do indeed have a stake in the outcome."

Jay Eldon Blackenby, mollified by Jethro's sudden change in attitude, stepped into the mouth of Gunnar's mine while Antonio, Gunnar, and Jethro ambled down the path toward the cabin. When they paused, Jethro said, "Let's face the cabin—he might read lips."

Gutierrez chuckled. "Drama is always welcome, senor."

"All right," Jethro said, "here's what I think: What we need is time. Time works in our favor. Our enemies would rather win without blood, so they've sent this Blackenby guy to make both of you a final offer. Don't turn him down cold. To turn him down means they'll move to the next phase, which will probably be a shotgun blast in the dark. What we've got to do is make him believe you're wavering."

Gutierrez's moustache ends curled up. "For me, senor, that would not be hard."

Jethro saw he was joking. "Please try to drag this out, boys. As long as Blackenby thinks you're honorably negotiating, he'll keep telling his bosses to keep their shirts on."

"How do ay do dis t'ing?" Gunnar asked.

"Okay, here's what I think. Let's turn around and walk back up there like we're in the middle of a big argument." Without further ado, the younger man started waving his arms and shouting at the others. Then he lowered his volume to say, "I'll be the bad guy. We'll argue all the way up there, then I'll get pissed and shout some more at you. After awhile, I'll turn around and storm back to the cabin. You can then go on and negotiate with the guy, but don't agree with him. Tell him anything. Tell him you have to think about it. Make him a sky-high counter-offer. Or tell him you want to talk about the sale terms and ask him to present a formal proposal. Anything that will leave him believing he's making progress."

When he ran down, Gunnar said, "Ay will try."

The Spaniard chuckled. "You are, I fear, a devious person, senor. Though I will join you, I do so only because I'll enjoy watching our enemies twist while they spring their trap." This time it was Gutierrez who put his nose next to Jethro's and punched the air with a forefinger.

Jethro jerked away, then wheeled back. All three men of Gunnar's fort started walking toward the mine mouth with the younger one obviously pleading and the other two just as obviously ignoring him. Finally Gunnar, seemingly at the end of his patience, shouted, "The mine, yew do not own! Ay do."

And with that, Jethro Spring wheeled away, striding for the cabin.

Gunnar stopped and stared after his 'mans', but Gutierrez grabbed his arm and dragged him to meet Blackenby. "Do not be alarmed, senor." Antonio told the barrister. "Workmen the world over are much the same. They soon believe they own everything."

"Oh that's all right," Blackenby said, smiling amiably. "It's all part of making the world go around."

"What yew mean, 'make the world round'?" Gunnar asked.

"Ha, ha. *Go* around, Mr. Einarssen. Everybody knows by now the world is round. But not everybody knows it ..."

"What yew say— 'world is round'?"

"Yes. Well, uh, shall we discuss your mines?"

"Ay want to know how yew t'ink world is round."

Gunnar's Mine

Blackenby raised an eyebrow to Antonio, then said, "Just foolishness, Mr. Einarssen. I should be more serious, don't you think?"

"About what?" Gunnar said. "Ay don' know dis t'ing, 'be serious'. What is?"

Blackenby turned from the little Swede to ask the Spaniard, who'd wandered back out into the daylight, what he thought his mine was worth.

"I am sorry, senor. I did not hear your question. As it turns out, I am distraught over our man's anger."

"*My mans.*" Gunnar said.

"Come now, little senor. Why do you think he's 'your mans' alone?"

"Because ..." Gunnar walked right up to Gutierrez, and stretched to put his nose at the other man's chin. "... ay hired him. While yew hide from our enemy is what yew did!"

"You old fool! Jose Antonio Gutierrez de Valdez y Mendoza has never been afraid to confront man or beast in his entire life!"

"Gentlemen, gentlemen," Jay Eldon Blackenby cooed, putting a hand between them. "Let's discuss your mines."

"Ya! Ay want to do that. But dis ... dis mes ... messy"

"Hah! Are you calling me a *mestizo?*"

"Ya! Ay call yew a mestizo. What yew do about it?"

"Gentlemen! Gentlemen!" Blackenby actually shoved between the two miners. "Please! Name calling will accomplish nothing."

"You are right, senor," a still angry Antonio Gutierrez agreed. "Let us talk about your company's offer for my mining claim."

"Ay will not stay and listen to any mans who says for Colorado Basin Holding Comp'ny." The Swede headed out of the tunnel mouth.

"Please don't leave, Mr. Einarssen," Blackenby cried. "I can assure you my representation goes beyond the Colorado Basin Holding Company." The attorney took stock, saw his announcement bore fruit, and continued, "I represent one of this country's premier mining companies—Amalgamated Minerals and Mining. Our investors' interests run very deep in this district. And I can assure you they are quite interested in both your properties; so much so, that I have been authorized to offer an extremely fair price for your holdings."

Gunnar sidled back into the mine. "How much is what ay ask?"

Blackenby glanced quickly at the third man in the tunnel, then said, "Twice as much as you've been offered before."

"How much is dat?" Gunnar demanded.

Blackenby, glancing back and forth between the drawn face of the Swede and the swarthy one of the Spaniard, was clearly reluctant to quote figures to one, in the presence of the other. Finally he threw up his hands and said, "Oh very well. They'll kill me for this, but I'll put their top offer on the table—one thousand each. How's that?"

Anton Gutierrez stroked his chin thoughtfully, saying nothing. But Gunnar snorted, "The Nordic Summer, she is wort' more."

"Oh come now, Mr. Einarssen. I have it on good authority that you've not been offered more than a third as much."

"Ya, but Billy Benbrooke, he got t'ree t'ousand for his."

"That's ridiculous!" Blackenby saw he'd made a mistake when Gunnar drew himself up.

"Yew should not call me liar," the little man icily said.

Gutierrez chuckled. "Little senor, you have not told

Gunnar's Mine

the truth since you've been on Fall Creek."

"No, no! Don't begin fighting again." Sweat was beading on the Amalgamated attorney's face. "Perhaps it would be best if I spoke to each of you alone. Perhaps you two cannot coexist civily. Is that it?"

Gunnar nodded. "It is my mans who makes us get along."

"That is true, senor. Senor Frost is the only one who can get both of us to cooperate while you present your employer's offer."

Blackenby said, "But isn't Mr. Frost opposed to you selling your mines?"

"True, senor. He mediates well between peacocks, but he makes no decisions."

"Very well. Can we get him back?"

So Jethro Spring was sought out and brought back to join the negotiations. As promised, the man was very helpful in aiding Mr. Blackenby to present his company's offers. He was equally helpful in enabling the attorney to understand that Mr. Gutierrez had a problem in making the transfer; a problem that was totally unrelated to money.

"It's his wife, Mr. Blackenby. The Senora Gutierrez de Valdez. Antonio promised her this would be his last mining venture. And since her family financed his expedition, he must obtain their approval before he sells the mine."

"A mere formality," Gutierrez added, shaking his head. "A courier could reach them in a matter of weeks. They dwell in Durango; that is, the Durango which is a city in Mexico."

When Blackenby threatened to withdraw the thousand-dollar offer if it was not accepted immediately, the Spaniard shrugged and said, "Very well, senor. Withdraw it if you must. It would not be the first time her family prevented me from making something of myself."

Gunnar, on the other hand, wanted more money.

Blackenby threw up his hands in disgust. "Mr Einarssen seems to be under the delusion that the Australian, Billy Benbrooke, received three thousand dollars for his claim. Will you please explain to him how ridiculous that idea is?"

"Gunnar, I thought he got four."

"No, t'ree."

"Well, hell, four seems fair to me. Remember, you've got a placer claim, as well as a hardrock claim."

"Und discovery rights, too."

"And discovery rights; that's true." Jethro turned back to the exasperated lawyer and said, "Did you not know the extent of the little man's claims, barrister?"

Blackenby turned to Gutierrez. "How soon could you get a letter off to your wife and her family?"

"I will write it now if you will allow me, senor. Then you can take the letter to Placerville and ensure that it is posted on the mail coach."

"If that suits you, Mr. Gutierrez, go ahead. I do not know if my company will wait so long for you to get word back from Durango, but I'm willing to try—if you're willing to accept the offer."

"I will be at the cabin, senor." Gutierrez paused after exiting the tunnel, to peer back inside. "May you have some success, senor, with that stubborn Scandinavian. His mother was a mule and his father a jackass."

Gunnar ran to the tunnel mouth and shouted, "Ay don't want yew in my cabin!" And as he turned back, he muttered, "Stinking 'mestizo'."

"Good heavens, Mr. Frost, are they always like this?"

"Like a cat and dog. They make that half-wolf outside look like a down comforter."

Blackenby rubbed his hands. "So now, perhaps we can get back to business. Just how much do you want for your claims, Mr. Einarssen?"

Gunnar's Mine

"Four thousand," interjected the man known to Blackenby and Gunnar as Jason Frost.

"Five t'ousand," the Swede countered.

Blackenby laughed. "Let's get serious, gentlemen. My people will never pay that kind of money for an unproven mine."

"Then how much will they pay?" Jethro asked.

"One thousand dollars. That's what I've offered and that's what I know they'll cover."

"But they might pay more. Right?"

"I'm certain they will not."

Jethro turned to Gunnar and asked, "Little man, will you sell the Nordic Summer for one thousand dollars?"

"Ay will not!"

"There you go, Mr. Blackenby. Your top offer is one thousand and Gunnar will not accept such a low price. I guess your discussion over the Nordic Summer has hit a rock. But your trip here might not have been in vain because it looks like the Spaniard might take you up on it."

"Ay will go back to work," said Gunnar and, trailed by Puppy, he bent over and disappeared into his mine.

"Well, Mr. Frost," Blackenby said after Gunnar had disappeared, "I guess that's that."

"I guess so, Mr. Blackenby. I'll walk you down to the cabin and turn you over to Gutierrez."

On their way down the trail, however, the Amalgamated attorney stopped abruptly and said confidentially, "Look, Frost, I'll try to get Mr. Einarssen more. But if Gutierrez finds out, it might spoil our agreement with him."

"I wouldn't fret over that, Mr. Blackenby," Jethro said. "One thing we do really good around here is keep secrets."

Chapter Eighteen

Because of the need for heightened security, work in the Nordic Summer slowed to a crawl. Interruptions also became more frequent. Gunnar insisted on eating three evening meals per week at the business Abigail Whittle formally named "Walter's Station." Word of the quality of the woman's food spread so far and wide that there wasn't always sufficient room for the three men of Gunnar's fort. When Rio Grande Southern's grading crews reached the Placerville-Fall Creek flat, it became impossible to secure a place at her table.

The Spaniard was, from the outset, hesitant to join Gunnar and his 'mans', thinking the risk too great for the three of them to be caught away from the mine at one time. Later, with the addition of the railroaders, came the risk to Jethro that one of them might have worked on the D&RG's Arkansas River tracks when he was employed as a foreman there under the alias 'Jed

Gunnar's Mine

Summers'. Subsequently, Jethro's visits also turned infrequent.

Abigail had done a splendid job remodeling Walter Hopkins' shabby buildings. The interior of the eatery was still log and the outside still wattle, but a month had not yet gone by when the woman disclosed she planned an addition. Less than three additional weeks passed before a connecting box building of sawn lumber and real glass in two windows, went up.

With the additional space and the added clientele that space afforded, Abigail had to employ outside help—an elderly couple who were both born as citizens of Spain. They became Mexicans with that country's overthrow of Spanish rule, then, with the Mexican War of 1846, citizens of the United States of America—all without leaving the confines of their little San Miguel Valley. The Zapapas, husband and wife team, took over the kitchen, the stable, and much of the cleaning.

Though Antonio and Jethro visited only sporadically, Gunnar's and Puppy's time at Walter's Station became more frequent. Finally Jethro broached the subject on a day when he and Gunnar bathed in Fall Creek, sipping port Abigail had sent home with the little Swede the evening before.

"Dammit, Gunnar," Jethro muttered, "one thing you can't do is develop a pattern in going to Abigail's."

"Ay can, too."

"All right! But you shouldn't."

"Why?"

"Make it too easy for someone to lay in wait and ambush you."

Puppy paddled out to where Gunnar sat neck deep in the pool, then turned and swam back to shore.

"Why would dey want to do dat?"

Jethro watched Puppy clamber onto the bank, then shake, water flying to the compass points. "Do what?"

he asked.

"Dis t'ing, 'ambush'."

"For your mine. Have you forgotten that Whittle wants the Nordic Summer?"

"He can't have it. Ay have it."

"He might get it if you are dead, dammit."

Gunnar threw off the rest of his port, leaped to his feet and shook like his dog, then stood knee deep in the pool until his upper torso dried in the mid-summer heat. A few minutes later, while dressing, the little man said, "The Nordic Summer, Whittle will not get. Ay will talk of dis t'ing with Abigail. She will say what to do."

Jethro shrugged, dressed, and did what he did every evening when Gunnar visited Walter's Station—shadowed the little man like a scout screening an army patrol.

Jay Eldon Blackenby visited the Nordic Summer twice more during the weeks following his first foray. In both instances he came alone, unaccompanied by the San Miguel County Sheriff who was happy to stay as far from the Fall Creek enclave as possible. Blackenby pumped Antonio Gutierrez for word from his wife's family. He did not, of course, tell the Spaniard that he had steamed the original letter open to see if Gutierrez was acting in good faith, then sealed it again before sending it via a special messenger into Mexico.

For his part, Antonio Gutierrez wept and apologized for any lack of haste on the part of his wife and family. What Antonio did not see fit to disclose was the fact that he'd never married and could, therefore, have no wife, nor a supposed family to invest in his ventures, nor advise him on same. The truth was, he'd written the letter to one of his cousins by his father's younger brother.

Gunnar's Mine

She was a Sister in the Convent of San Cristobol de la Concepcion in Durango, and by now would be puzzling over the strange letter from a cousin who must be going mad among the gringos.

Blackenby also brought an offer of twelve hundred dollars for Gunnar's claim. He privately confided this to Jethro, who told the Amalgamated man that he was certain Gunnar would refuse, but that he would convey the offer at a time when the Spaniard was not in earshot.

Just as Jethro expected, Gunnar refused the new offer which was immediately upped to fifteen hundred. Jethro shook his head at the latest figure, suggesting there was little he could do. He did, however, promise Blackenby that if Amalgamated would up the offer to three thousand, he would try very hard to persuade Mr. Einarssen to take it.

Blackenby threw up his hands at that, but when he returned, he offered two thousand to Gunnar and a formal contract for deed to Gutierrez.

For his part, Gunnar pondered long and hard before turning the offer down, while Antonio actually dripped huge tears on the proffered contract before shoving it back unsigned, with his heartfelt apology that when a matter of honor arose, his family must take priority.

Blackenby dispatched a telegram from end-of-track at Redvale to an agent in Guadalajara, asking if he could find means to bring pressure on Senora Gutierrez de Valdez y Mendoza and her family to release Antonio from his obligation to them. The agent wired back six days later to ask for further instructions.

Accompanied once more by Sheriff Barnabas Richards, Jay Eldon Blackenby visited Gunnar's mine the very next day.

"I now understand," Blackenby said, "that you gentlemen were having your fun at my expense. But the games are over."

Jethro and Antonio sat on rocks at the mine mouth, staring morosely down at their boot toes. Gunnar squatted between them, roughhousing with Puppy and staring up with an unreadable face at the Amalgamated barrister.

"If I had my way, I would not even be here. However, my employers insist I tender this one final offer. Gunnar Einarssen, you have been offered two thousand dollars for your discovery claim, placer claim, and cabin. Antonio Gutierrez, my principals offer one thousand dollars for your Placerville District claim. These offers are final and non-negotiable. Take them or leave them."

Jethro slapped both knees and the dust flew. "Well, boys, what do you think? Shall we get back to work?"

"Ya," Gunnar agreed, coming creakily to his feet. "Too long have we spend on dis t'ing anyway."

Gutierrez stood to follow his partners into the Nordic Summer. But before he did, he paused to stare malevolently at Amalgamated's lawyer. "Did you, senor, think you could get away with offering more for this perimeter mine than for the one I have in the center of the richest district?"

"Final offer, Mr. Gutierrez. Take it or leave it."

The thin moustache curled. "It has been most interesting, talking with you, senor. I will look forward to your next visit."

Though the last days of summer still blazed in the little valley of the San Miguel, the first smudges of yellow brushed the very highest mountainside aspens, and homesteaders' and miners' wives raced flocks of birds for the last, clinging berries. End-of-track took a breather at Redvale, then raced across the Redvale bench for the

Gunnar's Mine

final San Miguel crossing before laying up the valley's east side, for Placerville.

Grading crews, meanwhile, passed Placerville, then Fall Creek four days after. Bets were taken that the grade would be made into Telluride by mid-September, though privately, Jethro could not understand how a usable rail grade could be cut through the narrow canyon to climb nearly two thousand feet in such short distance.

Both Jethro and Gutierrez continued ceaselessly to patrol the Gunnar's mine/Walter's Station perimeter. Only the little Swede worked at extending the Nordic Summer's tunnel.

Jethro seldom slept in the cabin through the warm summer nights, choosing instead to bed down near where the wolf-dog was chained, half-way between mine and cabin. Antonio sometimes joined him, but always kept his own schedule, often slipping into the night to take up a station at another point.

Both Antonio Gutierrez and Jethro Spring expected another attempt would be made on them at any moment. And they waited.

The Rio Grande Southern crossed the San Miguel for the last time on the first day of September. September 1 was also the day Abigail Whittle brought news that a gunman was reported to be in Placerville, bragging that he was going to kill Jason Frost.

"What's his name?" Jethro asked, opening his clasp knife and whittling a toothpick.

"I'm told it's Benjamin Pack. Jason, he stopped by Walter's Station when he rode into the district a week ago. I thought he looked like a killer then; now I'm certain of it."

Jethro smiled. "What did he look like?"

"He had the coldest eyes. They were blue."

"Have you looked at mine?"

"Yes. They're gray. But they're not cold. Not at all like the eyes of a killer."

"Perhaps it depends on who they're focused on."

Puppy wanted into Gunnar's lap, but she was growing too big to hold, so the man scratched her ears.

"Mr. Frost," Abigail said, "you are not treating this with sufficient seriousness."

"What do you wish me to do?"

"Go away for a while, at least until this beast leaves the valley."

"Why do you suppose he came here?"

Abigail, hands on hips, looked very stern. "It's obvious. He was brought here to kill you."

"Well, that would be one way to make me leave, wouldn't it?"

"It certainly would!"

"And another way to make me leave would be to frighten me away, wouldn't it?"

"You would be alive, however."

"But I'd be away, wouldn't I? And that's what Amalgamated's after, isn't it?"

"What, then, will you do?" she asked.

He snapped the clasp knife shut and sighed, staring at his feet. "I suppose the thing to do would be to go and talk with this Benjamin Pack fellow; maybe find out how determined he is to kill me. Who knows? I might be able to reason with him." He met Abigail's look of horror with a twinkle in his eyes.

"Jason Frost, you're incorrigible!"

"Ay t'ink Abbie right," Gunnar said. "Is no good t'ing will come out of yew to die."

Jethro smiled at his friend's use of 'Abbie'; it was the first time he'd heard Gunnar refer to her in that manner. He smiled at the woman before returning his gaze to the little man. "Gunnar, you wouldn't last a month if they got rid of me."

Gunnar's Mine

"Den here you should stay. Let dis gunshooter come to yew. Others have comed here and dey didn't do a t'ing."

Jethro shook his head. "I should've guessed it. Of course they would bring in a slickhand to take care of me."

"Jason," the woman said, "you cannot be thinking what I think you are. You cannot employ their methods. You cannot shoot this Benjamin Pack from hiding. Andrew and his people would have the law on you in a moment."

His hearty laughter surprised her, and the little Swede, too. When he subsided, it was abrupt. "Fear not, ma'am. If it comes to it, Benjamin Pack won't die from a dry-gulch in the back."

While they watched, Jethro untied the holster thong from around his thigh and unbuckled his gun belt. Then he laid holster and belt on the ground, slid out the Colt, spun its cylinder, flipped it out, and dropped its loads into his palm. He then stripped the weapon, carefully wiping it clean with a handkerchief before reassembling it, flipping the cylinder in place and snapping the loading gate in place. Finally he eared the hammer back and studied the cylinder's spin. So concentrated on pulling the trigger was he that he actually jumped when the hammer snapped shut without a flaw. Five more times he eared back the hammer and dry fired the weapon, oblivious to his surroundings and his companions.

Satisfied at last, Jethro loaded the Colt, then turned his attention to the holster. He wiped it out with his handkerchief. The handkerchief came out stained, so recently oiled had the holster been. Then he slid the Colt in and out several times, and was obviously pleased at the fluid slide. At last he stood, belted the weapon back around his waist, wriggled it into place on his thigh, tied it down and suddenly the Colt was in his hand!

"I guess I'm ready to talk to Mr. Pack," he said.

"I believe you are, Mr. Frost," Abigail murmured.

"To approach him in a saloon in Placerville—this, senor, is the height of folly."

Jethro shrugged. "It's smarter than letting him pick the time and place."

Antonio stamped his foot. "But it is the lion's den, senor. He will have henchmen there. You will face many guns. You cannot win against many guns."

"It'll be quick, Anton. If I can get in and make it quick, I can get out before anybody else wakes up."

"But what makes you think you can beat this Benjamin Pack?"

Jethro smiled. "I'm betting my life on it."

"But the people at Amalgamated are not fools. They would contract with only the best."

"No, my friend—for they did not first get in touch with me."

"You make like a fool."

Jethro placed a hand on the Spaniard's shoulder. "You and Gunnar should remain together until I return. If I had my choice, I'd want you in the mine. Stay away from the cabin. They won't come in the dark the next time, so you won't have that for an advantage."

Antonio seemed to be thinking. "Maybe we stay at Walter's. Or maybe we take Gunnar to Walter's and I go with you, yes?"

"No, Anton. You can't leave the mine so they can occupy it. And I hope you won't leave Gunnar alone. He's game, but he's no fighting man. Not like you."

"Nor you, senor. Go with God."

Gunnar's Mine

Now that it was in God's hands, however, Jethro Spring had second thoughts. Not about whether he was pursuing a just course, but whether he was as fast with a gun as he was during his New Mexico days.

He approached Placerville from the mountains towering across the San Miguel—the way he should be expected to approach the town. But coming through the thick, north-slope forest was an approach with which he was most comfortable and the one someone waiting in ambush might be expected to fear tbe most.

Tough men who were fast and deadly with guns were plentiful in southeastern New Mexico's Lincoln County. Though he was respected by many and feared by some, Jethro Spring, known then as Jack Winter, was neither deadliest nor fastest. Billy the Kid might've filled that role, but there were dozens of others in the running: Doc Scurlock, Charlie Bowdre, and the Coe boys on one side; John Selman, Tom Hill, Frank Baker, and Buck Morton on the other. All were deadly. At least half of them, though, were dead. Along with Jesse Evans, Morton, Hill, and Baker were the four who actually killed Jethro's friend and employer, John Tunstall, precipitating the blood feud that became known as the 'Lincoln County War'.

At the thought of Jesse Evans, Jethro paused, then grinned. Of Tunstall's four killers, Evans was the only one still alive. *But that's not for lack of trying on my part,* Jethro thought, recalling the long chase through the White Sands after Jethro caught Evans and Tom Hill robbing a sheep camp.

He'd taken a bullet from Evans at that time, but returned the favor. Then ensued the two-week chase between cripples, ending when Evans took shelter with a cavalry patrol that was in the field chasing renegade Apaches.

A door slammed below and Jethro went to ground.

Evans had him dead to rights when Jethro spent a couple of days and nights in a Lincoln Jail while Jesse Evans, despite having warrants out against him, served as a guard at the facility. But the townspeople of Lincoln had saved him, throwing up a citizen guard around the jail, and sending other citizens to join him in his cell.

He sighed, putting the past behind him just as he had for so much of his life. Now he must concentrate.

It was after midnight when he waded the San Miguel and approached the backroom door of the San Miguell Emporium, jimmied it open, and slipped inside. Hasty repairs to the jimmied door took only a few moments. Then Jethro moved very carefully in a room whose only light came from cracks around the door into the main saloon. He felt around, took inventory, and finally settled behind a full, fifty-gallon whiskey barrel that stood on end in one corner.

Finally the saloon noise dimmed and he heard Chalkie stacking chairs. Then the door to the storage room opened and the saloon owner came in carrying a candle and rolling an empty beer keg. Shoving the empty near Jethro's hiding place, the barkeep rolled a full one into the saloon and apparently set it up. Then Jethro heard him climb the stairs that led to his sleeping quarters.

Jethro Spring was awake long before Chalkie and, also, long before most of Placerville. He stood and carefully began exercising, wincing when a floorboard squeaked. Afterward, he avoided the spot. Finally Chalkie began moving upstairs and when the intruder heard the saloon owner coming down, he crept back into hiding.

Gunnar's Mine

The saloon master came into his storeroom twice more before opening the Emporium, both times for full cases of whiskey in bottles. Each time he carried a candle into the dimly lit room. Finally Chalkie opened his doors to a visiting public who could wait no longer for a morning fix.

The walls were thin and, as it turned out, Jethro could hear much of what the patrons said. He tried putting an eye to a crack of light at the ill-fitting door, but could see nothing. Once he chanced opening the door to a slit, but recognized no one, nor did he see anyone he thought might look like a dangerous newcomer. At last he retreated to his corner.

All day Jethro waited. All day he fretted, but he came from patient stock—mountain man father and Blackfeet mother. As the day grew dark, daylight ceased to creep in from the outside door. Still he waited, listening for the shout of invitation that would mean someone of importance had entered, the tell-tale words that would identify the man he sought.

Again he exercised. Chalkie came for another keg of beer, nearly catching Jethro in the open. Another hour passed, and another. Then he heard it—the shout!

"Hey, Ben, when you gonna get that Frost?"

The reply was muffled, but still audible: "When he walks down the street." *The voice was coming nearer.* "And if he ain't got enough guts to do that, then I'll go down to that rat haven and kick him out."

Jethro exercised vigorously for several more minutes, then jimmied the outside door to expedite his retreat. He returned to the saloon's backroom door, slipped his Colt in and out of its holster several times, then swung the door wide. "Benjamin Pack," he called into the sudden hush, "I'm told you're looking for me!"

A figure whirled from the bar. "Winter!" Jesse Evans hissed as he clawed for his gun.

⇒ Chapter Nineteen ⇐

The San Miguell Emporium was packed that Saturday evening, the 8th day of September, year of our Lord, 1883. Except for two, all figures might have been cast in wax. The wax ones were caught with drinks half-way to their lips, or dealing cards, or bent over with laughter, or spitting in a cuspidor; a mustachioed one was caught with a half-chewed cigar and wiping the bar with a rag. But all those motionless figures weren't made of wax— they just seemed that way. When the man known as Jason Frost jerked open the backroom door and called to the gunfighter known as Benjamin Pack, every other person in the low-ceilinged room caught his breath and froze.

When Jesse Evans went for his gun, Jethro Spring followed suit. For ever after, it was sworn by those present that all they saw was a blip, a blur, a sleight of hand. Suddenly both men held guns and both guns were roaring.

Gunnar's Mine

Even during that split second of blurred action, Jethro had to beat down a powerful urge for haste. Though he'd seen it before, he could hardly believe Evans' speed. Later, he was unsure who fired first—but the one thing he was certain of, was who fired last. Still later, he wondered if it was Jesse's surprise that caused the last of John Tunstall's killers to hurry his aim. This, in turn, made Jethro wonder if he'd been the one surprised that day, whether his own aim would've been as careful and calculated.

As it was, he felt the white-hot slash of a bullet in his lower left side at the same time he saw Jesse Evans slammed backwards against the bar. He also watched Jesse jerk three more times before sliding to a rest with his head propped against the brass rail at its feet.

With the roar of gunfire still ringing in the room, Jethro Spring, in an uncharacteristic show of bravado, blew smoke from the Colt's barrel and said to the frozen crowd, "Tell Andrew Whittle to hire better gunslingers next time."

Then he melted into the night.

Despite his best efforts to focus on the subject at hand, all Jethro Spring could think about as he trotted down the wagon road to Fall Creek was John Tunstall, and how the last of his former employer's killers was dead. *I got two, John,* he thought, *and Billy got the other two.* But Jethro shook his head when remembering Morton and Baker were shot down from behind, while his two—Evans and Hill—were downed with guns in hand, shooting at him.

He crossed the footbridge at Walter's Station in the darkness, noting a light still gleaming from the kitchen at the rear.

Gunnar's cabin was dark and forbidding when he stopped to knock. It wasn't until then that the wolf-dog announced his presence to the world. But when he walked over to the dog's chain, the big beast stopped barking and wagged its tail. He scratched the animal's ear as it licked his wrist and strained to smell his bloody side.

"We knew it was you when the dog stopped barking," Antonio said, looming from the darkness.

"Almost as good as new, too," Jethro replied.

Gunnar's white faced flashed as he struck a match. "Look so good, yew do not," he said.

"Fact is, pard, you don't look much better," Jethro countered. "If you feel bad enough to need a shot of whiskey, don't let me stop you."

"I, too," the Spaniard muttered, striking another match and holding it close to Jethro's side.

Back at the cabin, with his shirt off and Gunnar dabbing at his wound with a rag steeped in boiling, soapy water, Jethro raised his glass and said simply, "He missed and I didn't."

Antonio raised his glass and toasted, "To his miss."

But Gunnar was more introspective as he sipped. "Miss by much, he didn't."

"How bad is it?" Jethro asked. "Went all the way through, didn't it?"

"Ya, it did."

"And it's not bleeding now?"

"It seeps only a little," Antonio said, bending to examine the wound more carefully. "Certainly it hit no organ. If it does not become infected, you will soon have only another scar to impress the ladies."

"It'll hurt, though. Right?"

"Possibly a little. But it should not keep you from working."

"Come on," Jethro said, "I won't be able to swing a

hammer for a month."

"On your left side it is," the Swede said, as he placed a folded and sterilized cloth over the wounds, then began wrapping long strips of cloth around Jethro's torso. "Yew swing from the right."

"But swinging with any strength requires twisting, Gunnar. You know that."

"Okay," the little man said. "Ay give yew tomorrow off."

"Tomorrow's Sunday!" Jethro laughed, wincing from the pain.

It was Abigail Whittle who provided details of the gun battle at the San Miguell Emporium to Gunnar Einarssen and Antonio Gutierrez. She arrived breathless, at mid-morning. "Where is he?" she asked. "Was he wounded? What did he tell you?" When she spotted a bloody rag still hanging from the wash basin, she cried, "He's been hurt! Is it serious? Where is he? Answer me!"

Gunnar held a forefinger to his lips until the woman subsided. he said, "Ay don't know. He left."

"Left?" she wailed.

"Dat's what ay said; he left."

"I see. He's at the mine. With Antonio?"

"Ay t'ink dey left on patrol."

"Oh thank God!" she cried, collapsing onto a block of wood. "Then he's all right."

"Ay t'ink all right he is, if dey don't shoot no better."

"So he was wounded. Tell me where, Gunnar."

The little Swede pulled up his shirt and pinched his left side, just above his hip. "Right dere is where. It went in and out wit'out hurting much. Anton say is all right if it don' get in … in …"

"Infected?"

"Ya."

"When can I see him?"

"Ay don' know. Here is Anton now."

She turned on her block of wood with a grand welcoming smile. "Where's the hero?"

He shrugged. "If neither I nor Gunnar will suffice, senora, I fear you will have to wait until Gunnar's 'mans' conquers other continents."

"I want to hear what he's told the both of you about his meeting with the hired killer." She waited. Finally, exasperated, she asked, "Well?"

"Yew wanted to know what my mans told us?"

"Yes-s-s."

"Dat was it."

"You mean he told you nothing?"

"Nothing," Gutierrez said, "except that his enemy missed and he didn't. So now it is for you to share with us the tale of his valor, senora. For you to come up here so soon in the day means you must have heard something. And that is…?"

So Abigail told them some of the dozen-odd stories that had emerged early at Walter's Station, many of which were blown all out of proportion by people who weren't even there. But from Stanford Briggs and Allen Whitethorne—who *were* there—she told of the back door flying open and Jason Frost standing there like an avenger from God. How Benjamin Pack had fired first, then was pinned to the bar by a barrage of lead coming in staccato thunder from the avenger's weapon.

"I never knowed a revolver could be fired so fast," a dumbfounded Briggs had said. "Sounded like a Gatling gun, it did. And that blowhard gunslinger didn't have no more chance than a snowball in hell after his first one."

"And you could cover the four holes in his chest

Gunnar's Mine

with the ace of spades," Allen Whitethorne added. "I reckon he was dead from the minute he crossed Lizard Head Pass, to ride down into the San Miguel."

"Senora, did you ask what all the others in the emporium did at that time?"

"I did. But Mr. Briggs said it all happened so quickly, no one thought to do anything. One moment the door slammed open, the next, guns were firing. Then Jason Frost was gone."

"Was there pursuit?"

"Now *that* I didn't ask."

Gutierrez's smile was chilly. "That is what our friend fears most. It is why he moves like a wraith between Fall Creek and Placerville. And it is why I must join him. *Buenos dias,* senora."

Abigail Whittle left Gunnar's fort shortly after Antonio returned to perimeter patrol. Even so, she was back within the hour to report to Gunnar that her cook, Juanita, and the handyman, Juan, told her Sheriff Richards passed through Fall Creek, riding north. They said he passed shortly after Abigail left for Gunnar's fort the first time. "Obviously he's gone to investigate the shooting."

When the little man said nor did nothing except puff on his old pipe, she added, "We should tell Jason, shouldn't we?"

"Ay will do that."

Abigail Whittle would've been even more alarmed had she known that her stepson, Andrew Whittle, was trying to convince the sheriff to bring a murder charge against the man both knew as Jason Frost. But the sheriff, although in Whittle's pocket, was dubious.

Despite the fact that Andrew produced a dozen men

to swear Jason Frost appeared in the doorway with his gun already in hand, there were twice that many who'd already sworn Frost's hands were empty when he loomed in the doorway.

Then there was the evidence of the spent bullet still lodged in the door. First of all, the torn wood was fresh. Secondly, it was waist level, *and* on a trajectory to have come from Benjamin Pack's weapon. Thirdly, Pack's gun had been once-fired. And lastly, several of the closest observers to the shoot-out testified that Frost had been hit in the exchange.

But—and for the sheriff, it was a big 'but'—any of the four holes in Benjamin Pack's chest would've certainly killed him, which indicated to Barnabas Richards that a dead man would've had a difficult time shooting an assailant if that particular assailant had fired first.

"My people will view this as unsatisfactory, Richards," an angry Andrew Whittle snarled, waving the sheriff's report. "We want Frost put away where he can do no more harm."

"I'm sorry that the evidence doesn't support your goals, Mr. Whittle," Richards said, "but if I went to the court with any other conclusion, I'd be laughed out of the county. And what good would I be to you then?"

A telegraph line followed grading crews into Telluride by mid-September and the first Rio Grande Southern engine puffed into Placerville on September 20. That first engine pushed flatcars loaded with rails, creosoted crossties, bedding plates, and spikes. There was a gondola with ballast gravel directly ahead of the engine, and an office car directly behind the coal tender. All were trailed by a dining car and four bunkhouse cars.

Tracklayers spent an entire day in Placerville, laying

Gunnar's Mine

switches and sidings, then they moved on for Fall Creek and points beyond. The following day, a supply train puffed into Placerville, pulling six flatcars loaded with machinery and two boxcars containing God knows what. The railcars were switched to two of the new sidings, then the supply train backed away, headed for Redvale and its normal supply run. But when it reappeared the following day, it trailed a swank private car that was also switched into a Placerville siding.

With hats removed, Andrew Whittle and two of his most trusted lieutenants met the private car. Also on hand was Jay Eldon Blackenby.

Three men eventually descended the ornate steps. Two wore topcoats. One also sported a tophat, the other a derby. The third man from the car was hatless, dressed in green corduroy trousers and a white, open at the throat, cotton shirt. He carried rolled-up maps in one hand and a two-foot slide rule in the other.

Jay Eldon Blackenby met the newcomers as equals. Andrew Whittle and his lieutenants lay somewhere in stratas beneath. The group strolled to the sidings and the laden flatcars they contained, moved to the graded plots where buildings were planned, and examined two or three near-to-hand mines. Then two of the newcomers, accompanied by Whittle and Blackenby, repaired to the private car while Whittle's lieutenants and the engineer went over his maps in detail.

"So you have yet to consolidate the district, Mr. Whittle?" the taller of the two topcoated gentlemen said, pulling off his coat and throwing it at a hovering servant. "That was our foremost directive."

Whittle hung his head, meekly submitting to the implied criticism.

"And you, Blackenby," Douglas Garrity continued, turning his attention to the attorney. "What about you?"

"They are recalcitrant, Douglas," Blackenby smoothly replied. "They're ensconced in their little enclave and it seems they feed off each other for strength."

Garrity switched back to Andrew Whittle. "You are our man on the ground, Whittle. It seems we misplaced our trust."

Whittle took heart from Blackenby's response and said, "We've tied up easily ninety percent of the district already, sir, with every prospect of acquiring the final ten percent before actual operations begin."

"And just how do you intend to accomplish that?"

Whittle's eyes darted to the attorney, then to the car's exit door. "We're working on it, sir."

"You certainly are. One notable example recently died in a tawdry display of the power and reach of Amalgamated Minerals and Mining."

Whittle licked his lips. "We underestimated this man Frost. Obviously, Einarssen and Gutierrez have employed a professional of the highest order."

"Then why, pray tell, are we employing professionals of a lower order?" Garrity shot back.

"It won't happen again, sir."

"Tell me, Mr. Whittle, what will happen again."

"All right," Trenton Ledbetter said. "That's enough. I'm less interested in recriminations than I am in results." He was short and pudgy, with jet black hair parted in the middle.

Garrity strode the length of the car, then returned to poke a finger at Andrew Whittle's chest. "Ledbetter is in operations, Whittle, but I'm in accounting. And I'll want to have analyzed your ledgers by this time tomorrow."

"Certainly, sir."

"I'll also expect to see a comprehensive plan—with timelines and costs for acquiring the remaining mining claims in the Upper San Miguel mining district."

"Yes sir."

Garrity turned to Ledbetter and said, "Your witness."

Trenton Ledbetter chuckled. "You must excuse Douglas. He gives the impression of being restless for results, but he never acquired the wherewithal to achieve them." Ledbetter waved to comfortable leather chairs around a low table. "Cigars, anyone? Steward, you may take drink orders."

When everyone was seated, Trenton Ledbetter leaned back and said, "Mr. Whittle, I believe it would be fair to say we're very pleased with the quality of ore samples you've produced. I believe our engineers have found effective means of reduction and we're anticipating a very profitable enterprise in this district—perhaps one that will rival Telluride in profitability and reliability."

Andrew Whittle beamed as Trenton Ledbetter continued.

"We will, of course, bring in an operations manager—a man with considerable hardrock and production experience, as well as crushing and amalgamated knowledge. As a reward for your tireless efforts, you will be his direct assistant, with responsibilities for local conditions, labor relations, and local political management."

Whittle had, of course, hoped for an even greater role in the southwestern Colorado operations of Amalgamated Minerals and Mining. However, given his limited mining and manufacturing knowledge, being Assistant Manager for an operation as extensive as this was certain to be, was indeed a plum position.

"There are a few loose threads that need to be tied up, however, for you to reap such a generous reward." Whittle's blood ran cold. "The first of these, of course, is rounding out the acquisition of the remaining claims within the district. After all, our commitment to the necessary investment in the area was contingent on that requisite."

Trenton Ledbetter paused, raised an eyebrow and allowed just enough time for Andrew Whittle to nod. "And the second is the matter of your mother. What shall we do with her, hmm?"

Whittle rearrangeded his feet beneath the coffee table and stammered to Trenton Ledbetter, Vice President in charge of Western Rocky Mountain Operations for Amalgamated Mineral and Mining Company that he would also resolve that issue to Mr. Ledbetter's satisfaction.

With that assurance, Ledbetter motioned to the servant to usher Mr. Whittle out, then turned his attention to Jay Eldon Blackenby. Just as Whittle stepped from the doorway of the coach, he heard Trenton Ledbetter ask in a mocking tone, "And now, Blackenby, what do you have to say for *your* failure?"

The private coach left Placerville on the 25th of September, ushered to Grand Junction by a special Rio Grande Southern engine sent for that sole purpose. That evening, shortly after closing time, six masked and drunken toughs arrived at Walter's Station and kicked open the door. They drove out Juanita and Juan, who cleaned the kitchen, trussed Abigail Whittle and proceeded to wreck the place.

Sheriff Richards' investigation disclosed nothing. However, an interesting development ensued when, much to the consternation of Rio Grande Southern's management, tracklaying crews, only a mile and a half south of the station and especially fond of Abigail and her food, shut down work for a day in order to help her

Gunnar's Mine

and the Zapapas clean up the damage and rebuild the kitchen and dining room. In addition, there were enough threats issued against the unknown perpetrators of the attack that only a fool would've admitted to having had a role in the original destruction.

Four nights later, an arsonist burned the stable at Walter's Station to the ground. Two horses and a milk cow died in the fire. Subsequently, only a mile downstream from Walter's Station, a miner from Placerville was found floating in the San Miguel, his throat cut. And a couple of days later, the body of another miner from Placerville was dumped unceremoniously on the porch of Andrew Whittle's office. Stuffed in the dead man's mouth were broken shards from a crockery coffee mug like those used by patrons of Walter's Place and broken during the night of destruction and vandalism.

The following Sunday, half the tracklaying crew struck for a day of rest and religious contemplation—during which they helped Abigail Whittle with a barn-raising. The affair was complete with a whole, barbecued beef, lots of spiked punch, and sufficient conviviality to bring the men back to dine at Walter's Station as long as they were anywhere within traveling distance.

An angry storm of telegrams from Rio Grande Southern to Amalgamated Minerals and Mining's Denver office followed the second tracklaying interruption. Coinciding with the telegram flurry came a visit from a delegation of leading Telluride citizens to Placerville. The delegation delivered a clear warning that any future move against Walter's Station by anyone, known or unknown, would be taken as an attack on Telluride by the minions of Placerville, upon whom retaliation would be visited with dispatch.

Sheriff Barnabas Richards stayed behind to offer counsel. "They're pretty wrought up, Andrew," Richards told Whittle. "They want that railroad and they'll brook no more delays by man or beast."

"Are you inferring I had something to do with those attacks?" Whittle demanded.

The sheriff stuck a toe in the stirrup, swung on his horse, and said, "If you can't stop it, Whittle, then I expect there'll be war between Telluride and Placerville. Be interested to see what's left o' your town then."

During the following week, Andrew Whittle brought in an old buffalo hunter who specialized in long-distance shooting. His telescope, shooting tripod, and Sharps rifle were found on a ledge directly across the San Miguel from the mouth of Fall Creek, but the man himself was never seen again.

Meanwhile, October inched toward the halfway point, the railroad inched toward Telluride, and the yellowing aspens dropped into the valley bottoms.

Chapter Twenty

The manager for Amalgamated Minerals and Mining Company's new complex at Placerville arrived during the second week of October. Alexander Coen was a no-nonsense Welshman with practical knowledge gleaned from mining operations over much of North America and the British Isles. The first thing Alexander Coen did was scald and skin Andrew Whittle to within an inch of his Amalgamated life.

"Ledbetter told me about you," Coen said. "Told me you were becoming an embarrassment to the company. Said to tell you to stop any further operations against your mother or you'll turn the whole damned district against us, if not all Colorado, including its Governor. Ledbetter said tongues are wagging in Telluride and Grand Junction. He said I'm to be the judge as to whether you'll remain my assistant. Said if you can't handle the local conditions any better than you've shown since he and Mr. Garrity were here, how can he expect you to handle labor management and political considerations?

"Welll answer me, dammit! Don't just stand there!"

"I'll try to do better, Mr. Coen," Andrew Whittle mumbled.

"You'll do no such thing. You'll do no more of anything concerning Walter's Station or the people of Nordic Summer without my express orders. Is that clear?"

"It is."

"All right. Now that we understand each other, you may show me the progress of our building construction. After that I want to review maps of the mining district; see how each mining claim relates to the whole. And after that, the records of your assessments of samples from each claim."

After the mining engineer had shuffled meticulously through the assay reports while Andrew Whittle sat across the desk from his glowering superior, Coen looked up and said, "These reports from Einarssen's claim on Fall Creek are inadequate."

"Yes sir, but you see we didn't even *start* obtaining samples from perimeter claims until after that man Frost came to the valley. After he arrived, acquiring samples from the Swede's claim proved dicey."

"All I can see is that reports on these samples are inconclusive."

"Yes sir. But we do know the man is taking some gold from the claim."

"How do you know that?"

"One of our agents was a confidant of the Nordic Summer people."

"And that person is...?"

"Benbrooke. Unfortunately he's no longer available. Frost ran him from the district; perhaps killed him. Benbrooke saw the gold, mostly in placer form."

Gunnar's Mine

Coen dropped the sheaf of papers onto the desk. "This is a hardrock district. Placer gold has been picked over long ago."

"That's true. But we suspect Einarssen pursues a buried stream with his tunnel. It can't yield much, but it's how he keeps both his placer claim and his discovery hardrock claim."

Coen stared at his assistant while drawing circles on his desktop with a forefinger. The new manager shuffled though the reports, until finding the one he wanted. He thumped it and said, "The Spaniard's claim is crucial."

"Yes sir. That's what I think, too. But the man is crafty and very determined. He kills easily, is quick to take offense, and is known to be deadly with several types of weapons. Word is out that the man was a high-ranking military officer in Mexico. Certainly he's a knowledgeable mining man. Our problem is complicated by the fact that he's taken refuge at Fall Creek. The combination of Frost and Gutierrez makes them largely impregnable there."

The manager sneered, "Especially would a man who cannot eject a single woman old enough to be his mother, find a combination of two competent fighting men impossible."

It was a week to the day after Alexander Coen's arrival as Amalgamated Minerals and Mining's District Manager, that he sent word by a messenger almost too terrified to deliver it that he and Jay Eldon Blackenby would arrive at Gunnar Einarssen's cabin at precisely ten a.m. the following day for an important peacemaking conference.

Antonio Gutierrez received the message, consulted with the Swede, then sent the messenger away with instructions to tell Mr. Coen they would listen to what he had to say.

When he returned from patrol, Jethro Spring listened skeptically to Alexander Coen's initiative. "Peace?" he said. "If it's peace they want, all they've got to do is stop attacking us."

"You must not be opposed to listening, my friend," Gutierrez said.

"I should have a good feeling about this, is what you mean, isn't it? Well I don't. It might be a trick."

"That we must guard against. Naturally Senor Gunnar will receive the envoy while you and I ensure there is no trickery involved."

Alexander Coen and Jay Eldon Blackenby ate a hearty breakfast at Walter's Station. Halfway through their meal, the man Blackenby knew as Jason Frost took a stool a few feet from their table. Abigail flashed the newcomer a smile and said, "Coffee, Jason?"

He nodded, then said, "That'll be all though, ma'am." Then he swiveled on his stool to take in the two Amalgamated men. "Very good to see you again, Mr. Frost," Jay Eldon Blackenby said. "Are you here to accompany us to our meeting?"

Abigail Whittle, in the process of delivering Jethro's coffee, dropped it, the cup shattering on the counter edge.

"No, Mr. Blackenby," the dark-faced man said while Abigail brought a rag to sop the mess. "Not to 'accompany' you, but to follow and make sure everything is on the square."

Blackenby chuckled. "It is, my boy. It is." He caught Alexander Coen's eye before asking, "Why don't you join us? Meet Mr. Coen."

Gunnar's Mine

"I reckon I'll meet him soon enough," Jethro said, swiveling back to the counter and his replacement cup of coffee.

Blackenby and Coen paid for their breakfast at precisely fifteen minutes of ten, leaving a generous tip and praising both the service and the food's quality.

As Jethro spun on his stool to follow, Abigail whispered, "Be careful, Jason."

When he emerged into the brisk fall air, Jethro saw that Coen and Blackenby were studying the new barn, talking quietly. Blackenby waved an arm, as if to take in Walter Hopkins' original Deeded Land Claim. Then the Amalgamated men noticed Jethro, walked to the San Miguel footbridge, and started up the trail to Gunnar's fort. The young man kept them in sight every step of the way.

Gunnar met them. Gutierrez came from across the creek. No invitation was extended to visit inside the cabin and Blackenby defused the slight by lightheartedly saying, "It's such a splendid day, why don't we talk out here?"

Introductions were made. Gunnar and Antonio exchanged handshakes with Coen and Blackenby. Jethro remained outside their range of conviviality, but sufficiently near to hear what was said. Blackenby was apparently in charge of the meeting, but despite his stoic expression, Jethro could see that it was Alexander Coen's agenda that was in effect.

Coen, listening, but not paying attention, turned his attention to Jethro. There was not a trace of emotion in either man. Coen found his eyes, Coen studied his eyes, Coen moved on to examine their backtrail, then swung to take in the cabin, the trail to the mine, the creek, and the hillside above. Then he returned to study Jethro.

Antonio cut off Blackenby's drone by asking, "If the senor manager does not wish to engage in this discussion, then why are we here?"

The 'senor' manager leisurely broke off his gaze at Jethro to focus on the Spaniard. "It is in the interest of peace that we are here, Senor Gutierrez."

"Ahh, peace! I, too, am in favor of peace. But we did not break it so why do you wish to talk with us? Why do you not speak with the warmongers?"

"I have," Coen replied without varying the level of his monotone. "It is my company's policy to pursue a neighborly policy with all other interested individuals within the district. We regret any overt action that might have been applied mistakenly toward you people, and give our solemn word that it won't happen again."

"And where is the proof, senor."

"We could begin by telling you of Andrew Whittle's dismissal. We've also dismissed any of our people who had prior involvement in what you call 'warmongering'. We are here. We are willing to give you any other assurance you need if you will but tell us what it is. Is that not enough?"

Grudgingly, Jethro gave the manager credit for promptness and delivery. But he was troubled by the man's lack of passion, causing the younger man to edge nearer.

Blackenby said, "Of course, if either of you gentlemen has changed his mind about selling his claim for a very large profit, we're ..."

Gutierrez interrupted to continue his dialogue with Alexander Coen. "If I understand you, Senor Coen, I am free to return to my own mine without trouble from any of Whittle's men?"

"Senor Gutierrez,"—the proper Spanish address did not go unnoticed by either Antonio or Jethro—"Andrew Whittle has no men. In fact, Mr. Whittle is no longer in this valley."

"How long has he been gone?" Jethro asked.

"Welcome to the discussion, Mr. Frost," Blackenby said.

"He was discharged three days ago," Coen continued, "and left on the supply train within an hour."

"I can return to my mine?" Antonio asked again.

"Senor Gutierrez, you can do anything you wish, as long as it does not negatively affect my company."

Antonio's teeth flashed.

Gunnar said, "And us, yew will leave alone?"

Coen threw up his hands as if in dismay. "Mr. Einarssen, I'm trying desperately to repair Amalgamated Mineral's tarnished image, brought about by that knave Whittle. What must I do to assure you that my company and I are sincere?"

Jethro said, "It is your company's policy to be neighborly?"

"It is," Alexander Coen said, glancing the younger man's way.

"When was that policy adopted?"

"When my principals discovered the activities in which Andrew Whittle had been engaged."

"And when was that?"

Coen's eyes flashed and there was a note of anger in his reply. "When they arrived here; when the tracks arrived in Placerville."

"Then check me if I'm wrong, Mr. Coen, but wasn't it after they'd departed that the first attack on Abigail Whittle's establishment occurred? And didn't the second occur less than a week later? And let's not forget the arsonist, either. His body was found floating in the San Miguel. Wasn't he an employee at one of your mines? And the man who was found dead on Andrew Whittle's porch, with broken crockery in his mouth—the same bastard found deep inside the borders of Gunnar's claim—wasn't he an Amalgamated man? Didn't every single one of these events occur after your *principals* had already met with Andrew Whittle and supposedly cautioned him against 'tarnishing' the company's image?"

"But that was before I arrived, Mr. Frost," Alexander Coen responded without missing a beat. "Those incidents were the very reasons for Whittle's dismissal."

Solemn-faced, Jethro nodded. "So these two men here are free to engage in the same freedoms belonging to other Americans: life, liberty, and the pursuit of happiness?"

"No, all *three* of you are free to engage in those freedoms. Not just Mr. Einarssen and Mr. Gutierrez."

Jethro acknowledged the point with a further nod, then changed topics. "But if they now wished to sell, they would find you a ready buyer."

"Not me personally, Mr. Frost, but Amalgamated. My company would be interested in purchasing Mr. Einarssen's and Mr. Gutierrez's holdings, yes."

"And if they aren't interested in selling, you'll not hold it against them?"

Coen sighed. "That is the purpose of this meeting, Mr. Frost. To assure them of the sincerity of our position."

"I am also the bearer of good news," Jay Eldon Blackenby interjected. "Out of deference to the inconveniences erroneously visited upon you in the past, Amalgamated Minerals and Mining has agreed to pay three thousand dollars for each of your claims." The attorney nodded to Antonio, explaining, "That reflects the value of the strategic location of your claim, Mr. Gutierrez." With a nod to Gunnar, he added, "And the offer matches Mr. Einarssen's counter-proposal."

Jethro turned and strolled away. He could feel Alexander Coen's eyes following him to the cabin, where he picked up his Winchester and telescope. Outside again, he trotted up-creek. Well out of sight of prying eyes at Gunnar's fort, he crossed the creek to climb the mountainside above. Finally reaching his desired level, he contoured at a trot to an outcrop that afforded him a view of Placerville and much of its mining district.

He arrived back at the cabin an hour after dark. Both Antonio and Gunnar were sitting at the table, a candle and an uncorked bottle between them. Puppy was the only one who seemed genuinely happy to see him— Puppy and the wolf-dog chained outside.

"What you see?" Gunnar asked, getting up to fetch Jethro a cup.

"Nothing," he admitted. "Maybe they're playing straight and maybe they aren't. They're getting far along on a couple of the big buildings. And they're moving machinery up to Benbrooke's old claim, and maybe to Snowcroft's and Davis's as well."

"Whittle? Did yew see him?"

"No. I thought about going into Placerville and bringing back a prisoner, but changed my mind when I considered an ordinary townsman or miner might not know a hell of a lot more than we do."

"Yew think Abbie might know? If her wort'less son left, ay mean."

"I stopped by to talk to her. She knows nothing. Hasn't seen Andrew since their confrontation; the one that happened just after she moved in at Walter's Station."

Jethro poured a liberal slug, set the bottle down, threw off half and said, "Well, how about you? Are you thinking of selling?"

Gunnar slammed the table with his fist. "Ay will not

sell, by Yupiter! No!"

"Neither will I," the Spaniard agreed. "But what I might do is go back and look at my mine."

"It might be the last thing you do, Anton."

"Who will live forever, senor?"

Jethro shook his head. "They're splitting us up. Three straws together is more than three times as strong as one alone."

"Ah, but Senor Jason, what if they speak the truth? You do not understand people like these. If they jump their offer three times, they do this for reasons beyond a well-intentioned attempt to make amends. Isn't it possible they offer a fair price?"

Jethro nodded. "They did assay work on your claim—quite a bit, I think."

Gutierrez chuckled. "You are not the only one who visits Placerville's mining claims in the dark, senor. What if I ask them for their reports on my claim? Those reports might be instructive, do you not think?"

Jethro threw off the rest of his whiskey, took a blanket and a tarp from his bed and said, "Well, Anton, you can trust him if you want, but I won't."

The following day, Jose Antonio Gutierrez de Valencia y Mendoza returned to his mining claim outside Placerville. First, however, he visited the Amalgamated Minerals and Mining Company office of Alexander Coen, where he badgered the clerk until he was admitted into Coen's presence. There he demanded the assay reports of his claim, was surprisingly given them, then ushered from the premises.

From Coen's office, Antonio climbed the hill to his claim and checked his mine. Then the Spaniard made his way to the cabin.

Gunnar's Mine

Presumedly, Coen's clerk was the last person to see Jose Antonio Gutierrez de Valencia y Mendoza alive.

Chapter Twenty One

When Antonio Gutierrez pushed open the unlocked door to his cabin, he expected to find it ransacked. To his surprise, it seemed intact—at least as much as packrats and field mice had allowed. Prudently, he closed the door, then began opening rifle ports and window shutters to allow more light. It was while doing so that he heard a noise at his door. Picking up his shotgun, he slipped to the door, turned the latch and jerked. The door didn't open!

Antonio jerked again, then realized it was padlocked from the outside. He smelled smoke at the same time a steady drumbeat of rifle fire drove him from the door and the windows. He was proud of those windows, and cursed to see them disappearing in tinkling shards. He braved a couple of rifle slits, but could see nothing. Then flames began licking up from beneath the floor in one corner.

The Spaniard smiled grimly as he pulled his bed

Gunnar's Mine

from the wall and lifted the concealed trap door. With practiced skill, he dropped into the hole beneath, reached up for the shotgun and his rifle, then began crawling along the hidden tunnel in the dark. It was the shotgun muzzles that collided first with the rock and concrete wall.

Antonio dropped the shotgun and pushed forward to feel the wall. *Trapped,* he thought, sitting back against the wall. *Oxygen,* was the next thing to cross his mind. *Will there be enough oxygen left in the stub of this tunnel when the fire eats the cabin?* He scrambled into the burning cabin, planning to pull the mattress from his bed to plug the tunnel. It was then that the two hundred pounds of dynamite placed beneath the cabin exploded!

As usual, it was Abigail who brought news of the tragedy to Gunnar's fort. "I've telegraphed the attorney, Thomas Oglesby, of our plight," she said, "and requested an audience with Governor Grant. I'm expecting a reply soon."

The younger man wasn't at the cabin and, as a matter of fact, if Abigail had waited only a little longer to deliver her news, Jethro might have beaten her to Fall Creek.

He'd waited a day for the Spaniard's return, then trotted to his mountain view-spot over Placerville, saw through his telescope what had happened to Antonio's cabin and knew in an instant that he and Gunnar were the only ones left of the holdouts on the San Miguel.

It was snowing softly when he knocked on the cabin door. Gunnar lit a candle, let him in, then shuffled slowly to his bunk. "Whiskey is on table," he said, looking up at Jethro. Tears filled his eyes. Puppy pawed at his knee

233

in sympathy.

"Ay believed dem. Like Anton, ay believed dem." When Jethro stood rooted, saying nothing, Gunnar asked, "W'at we do? The Nordic Summer is everyt'ing to me. Ay don' want to lose her."

Jethro shook his head as if to clear it. He reached for the bottle, pulled the cork and took a deep swallow, coughed, then swiped the back of his hand over his lips. "They had the dynamite under the cabin—must have. When he went inside—blooey! The poor sonofabitch never had a chance!" He whirled to throw the bottle against the door, wrestled with himself, then instead, took another swig.

He strode to his bunk and sat upon it, knees almost touching those of Gunnar. He took yet another pull, then handed the bottle to Gunnar who, Adams apple bobbing, drained it. Thus, it was Gunnar who threw the bottle against the door. The empty bottle bounced away to hit the floor, then roll to the stove and stopped.

"What are we going to do?" Jethro mused, studying his hands. When Gunnar failed to reply, he decided, "We can't stay here, that's for sure. They're playing for keeps now, and this cabin can't be defended." His hands failed to give him answers so he came to his feet, striding the five steps to the end of the cabin and back again. "I don't much like the idea of getting trapped in the mine, either. Too easy for'em to starve us out up there ... or worse."

"Abbie, would she...?"

"No, Gunnar. They've moved way beyond caring about her or any other living creature. The only thing they care about is getting hold of every goddamn piece of ground from Fall Creek to Placerville. If she tries to help, they'll run right over her like she was dirt. You can't risk it."

"Ya, is so. Ay don' want her hurt."

Gunnar's Mine

Again Jethro strode the length of the cabin, this time kicking the empty bottle as he passed. On his return, he detoured to the door, slammed it with his fist, then came back to stand in front of Gunnar. "We have to leave," he said abruptly. "We must go away for the winter, then come back in the spring."

"No!" Gunnar cried. "Ay won't leave my Nordic Summer."

Jethro either failed to hear him, or ignored him. "We must hide from them because they'll after you like maggots after meat."

"Ay won't."

Jethro dropped to his knees before Gunnar, pushing away Puppy, who wanted to play. "Gunnar, look at me. It's the only way. Your assessment work is done for this year, way more than you need to maintain your rights. We'll come back next spring and do enough to prove up for that year. The thing to do is stay alive. As long as you are alive, they can't legally touch the Nordic Summer—as long as you're alive and the assessment work is done. It's our only chance. You *must* do it!"

There were more tears in the man's eyes, but he put his hands on his knees and softly asked, "Dis t'ing; how do we do it?"

Jethro gave a sigh of relief. "We'll need bedrolls and food; clothes, too. We're going to be far from here for a long time. I don't know how much money you have in reserve, but however much it is, you don't want to leave it here."

Gunnar pushed to his feet and went to his cupboards of dynamite boxes. "Ay must take Anton's dishes."

Jethro smiled. "We'll need paper to wrap them in, and a dynamite box with a lid to protect them."

"Leave on the railroad, is dat it?"

"No, Gunnar. They'd nail us in a heartbeat on the railroad. We've got to get away from towns, telegraphs, and Amalgamateds. That means horses. I'll trot down to Vidkun's for my two. Maybe if you'd write him a note, he could see his way free to sell us a couple more."

"How long gone will yew?"

"It'll take a couple of days to get there, shoe the horses, and get back. You've got to stay alive until then. Can you do it, pard?"

"In mine?"

"I'd rather you didn't. They'll surely have a watch on this place by the time I get back." He sat down on the table, head in hands, thinking. At last he raised his head and said, "I'd rather carry our stuff away from here and hide it. That way, maybe we can get back with horses without'em knowing, then get the hell away from here."

"What about Walter's Station?" Gunnar wondered. "Ay could hide there and Amalgamateds could look here all dey want."

Jethro slammed the table. "That's it! We can talk to Abigail and explain to her what must be done. If she can tuck you and our stuff away in the barn for a day or two, then I can come back in the dead of the night to load up."

"When to go?"

Jethro smiled. "Well, little man, there's no time like the present to start."

Abigail Whittle readily became complicit in the preparation for her friends' flight. She even, during the dark of night, helped carry their equipment from cabin and mine to a hiding place in her new barn.

An already weary Jethro Spring, wanting to be past Placerville before daylight, trotted away from Walter's Station upon completion of their last trip. "Keep

Gunnar's Mine

Gunnar out of sight," he told the woman. "And that includes Puppy."

"It will be done," the woman promised. "His own mother wouldn't be able to find him." Then she added, "Go with God."

Vidkun Bloomquist accepted Gunnar's note without question. He offered Jethro a pallet in his barn and while the younger man slept, caught up four horses—Jethro's two, and two of his best, light-work animals. Then Vidkun fired his forge and shod the animals his friend Gunnar needed for his escape.

Bloomquist finished shoeing the animals two hours after dark. Jethro was in the saddle, heading for Fall Creek an hour after that, trailing Baldy and Vidkun's horses down a road icy from freezing rain. He pulled up in front of Walter's Station during the wee hours, and soon a little cavalcade clattered from the station while faint pink was tingeing the eastern sky.

Abigail hugged all three—the two men and Puppy. "I'm sorry you missed Mr. Oglesby," she said. "Had I known he was coming, I might have arranged a meeting. But he had to catch the midnight coach or remain another day."

Jethro smiled, reaching out to grasp her shoulder. "It's all right, Abigail. I can do without another lawyer in my life anyway. Let's just hope he can do some good."

She had tears in her eyes as she squeezed Gunnar's boot. The little man sat astride Baldy, legs outthrust, boots barely reaching halfway down the big pony's belly. "Go with God," she whispered.

Gunnar reached down and placed a gloved hand over hers. "Ay t'ink ay will go wit' Jason. Him ay trust more."

She smiled through her tears, saying, "Ay t'ink you're right, my little man."

The cavalcade of exiles crossed the wagon road, the new railroad tracks, and the San Miguel River as night turned to day, fleeing up Fall Creek, heading west. Before the sun was an hour high, they'd reached into the foothills. There, in a hidden little hollow, they holed up for the day while Jethro studied Walter's Station and what he could see of Fall Creek from a high point. Just as another night began to fall, the dark-faced man spotted the first plume of smoke rising from Gunnar's cabin.

They ate a cold supper, then saddled and were on their way deeper into the mountains forming the Dolores-San Miguel Divide, riding throughout the night.

Again, they holed up. Again Jethro studied their backtrail. He returned at noon, sliding down from his snow-covered observation point. "Let's go, little man," he said, pointing to the mountain peaks ahead. "We'll want to cross up there before any more weather comes in."

They made it over the top during a run-up to a big storm, then down the other side into a little tributary valley of the Dolores River. Finally an exhausted Gunnar said, "The horses, a rest ay t'ink dey need."

Jethro nodded. Snow continued to fall, but at least they'd worked down out of the wind. He'd hoped to find some forage for the jaded animals, but with night falling and a foot of snow lying across the land, that hope seemed distant. So he reined Tanglefoot into a grove of aspens and unsaddled the horses. Each was grained and loosed to graze as best it could before Jethro built their first fire since leaving Walter's Station.

Later, fed and rested, the men lazed by the cheering

blaze. "Are yew not afraid the horses, they will leave?" Gunnar asked.

Jethro's teeth flashed in the firelight. "Well, they sure as hell won't go back the way we just came. Not through two, maybe three feet of snow by now. And they've never been here, so they haven't got any idea where they might find something better."

Gunnar said, "Baldy, he would not leave me."

Again Jethro grinned. "Not while you've got his grain." Both men were silent for a long time, then Jethro leaned forward to take their coffee pot from the coals. After he'd poured for both Gunnar and himself, he said, "Besides, there's always grass within an aspen grove. You might want to remember that. It might not be as sweet as that growing in a meadow, but it's usually taller and horses can paw for it better."

Curious, Gunnar asked, "How yew learn dis?"

Jethro took a moment to answer. Finally he said, "My pa."

"'Bout him, yew tell?"

Again, the younger man's teeth flashed in the firelight. "He was the best there ever was; a real mountain man. My ma was wonderful, too. She was a Blackfeet princess, or so Pa said." Then he turned grim. "They were gunned down like dogs, trapped like we might have been in the Nordic Summer."

"To know the papa, yew are ... how you say?"

"Lucky?"

"Ya. Lucky. Ay don' know my papa, but my mama was a good woman. Bootiful. Like Abbie."

Jethro looked quickly at his little friend, but Gunnar stared into the fire, seemingly lost in memories. "They burned your cabin, Gunnar."

When the little Swede looked up from the flames, he continued, "I saw the smoke during our first day away, when I watched to see if anybody followed. I didn't tell you because I was afraid you'd want to go back. And that would've meant certain death."

The face Gunnar presented looked decidedly gray ... and old. "Dey ruin everyt'ing dey touch. Why dey do it?"

The younger man shrugged. "I don't know, Gunnar. I only know you're right."

Jethro was first out of his soogan the following morning, knocking snow from the canvas. Gunnar heard him stirring, and poked a head out. "Get up little man," Jethro called. "Somebody's gotta go look for horses." Just then, Baldy stamped from a few feet beyond Gunnar's head, and one of Vidkun's draft horses nickered softly from another direction. Jethro laughed.

"I'll build a fire and fix breakfast," the younger man said, "while you grain the ponies. That all right?"

They ran into their first elk shortly after continuing down-canyon, heading for the Dolores River Valley. First a cow snorted and it seemed as though an entire mountainside erupted above them.

"Pity," Jethro said as the herd banded together and fled into the distance. "If there wasn't so much snow, and there was a little more horsefeed, we'd stop here until we ate one of them critters."

"Dey are bootiful."

"Like Abigail?"

"Ha, ha. No, not like Abbie."

The exiles saw their first sign of civilization in the Dolores country in the form of an old dilapidated trapper cabin shortly after encountering the elk. Not long thereafter, they descended below the snow line and Jethro led the way into a side canyon. They found a tiny flat along an unnamed creek with intermittent flow and scummy pools, and decided to camp.

"Stop so soon?" Gunnar asked, looking up at a sun that had hours to reach the western skyline.

Gunnar's Mine

Jethro slipped the headstall from his saddlehorse, then turned to Baldy. "Yeah, I think so. From here on out, it makes less difference where we go, than that we stay out of sight. There isn't enough feed to stay here long, but the horses need a good bait of grass, before we move along."

"Where den we go?"

The younger man shook his head as he stripped Baldy's saddle. "I don't rightly know, little man, but as soon as they figure out we didn't go north to Grand Junction, or south over Lizard Head Pass, the Dolores River country seems like the next place they'd look." After pulling Tangle's saddle, he turned to the two packhorses, loosening the diamond on each, throwing off the packropes and hitches, then removing the packcovers. Before pulling loads from the patient draft horses, Jethro said, "What we need is a couple of days to rest and catch our breath. After that, we'll see."

Before evening, Jethro caught Tanglefoot and one of the draft horses. When Gunnar asked him why he'd chosen those two to tie for the night, he explained, "We're out of the snow now and if we give'em a chance, they might wander. By breaking up the partners, we cut down on that risk."

"Ay don' see ..."

"When all of'em are out together, you've probably seen how Tangle and Baldy stick together, while Olaf and Sven team up. By tying Tangle and Olaf for the night, Baldy and Sven are more likely to be here in the morning. Then before we leave, we'll turn out the ones we kept in, and bring in the ones who had all night to graze. Get it?"

"Ya. I not so dumb."

Later, the two men discussed their options. "Across the Dolores is Mormon country," Jethro said. "It's not a place where many gentiles like you and me would ordinarily go. On the other hand, we might get lost in some remote place where agents from 'A Double M' would never find us. There's a bad side to hiding out in Mormon country. Most of their kind are way too curious about visitors who don't think much about Joseph Smith and his revelations about Moroni and a couple of tablets of silver."

"Ay don' know dis t'ing Moroni."

"No. Well, it ain't important. My pa didn't think much of'em for what they done to Ol' Gabe Bridger. But the point is, their country might be a good place for us to hide. They're basically good people, hard-working and honest. They just want to be left alone, and maybe they'll leave us be."

"From the Nordic Summer is far?"

"Well, little man, we're not trying to get away from the Nordic Summer, only from Amalgamated Minerals and Mining. And hiding in Mormon country might be just the way to do it."

Chapter Twenty Two

Crossing the Dolores River was easy, even at night, but finding a way to get their horses up the western escarpment to the Plateau above the Dolores Valley, was damned tough. Finally, with daylight coming on, Jethro called off the attempt, and they dropped back into the canyon. There, horses and men took refuge in a thick copse of ancient cottonwoods.

After they'd made a hurried camp, Jethro left Gunnar in charge of grazing one horse at a time, well out of sight of prying eyes, while he trotted off down-canyon, hoping to find a route over the escarpment during daylight hours.

They made it during their second attempt, but it was close. In desperation, the men unpacked the two draft animals in order to coax them through the narrow slot they were forced to clamber through to reach the top. After all their horses were atop the plateau, Jethro and Gunnar carried the packs up, then reloaded the animals.

"Is good we have horses to make it easy for us, ya?" an exhausted Gunnar Einarssen said as he sprawled against a tree while Jethro lashed the top pack in place on Olaf.

"Come and help me, little pard," Jethro grunted, taking up slack on the packrope. "It might be a one-man diamond, but two make it a helluva lot easier."

Jethro and Gunnar passed beyond the hamlet of Monticello just before their second day in Utah dawned across the land. Taking refuge in the foothills leading to Abajo Peak, Jethro decided to return to Monticello for a few final supplies.

"I don't know how long we'll be out, Gunnar, nor where we'll go. We might be out of reach of a town for a long time, so we'd better resupply while the getting is good."

"What yew use for money."

Jethro shrugged. "I don't have any money, do you?"

Gunnar nodded. "Ya, dat I have. But maybe dey better not know how much."

Jethro grinned. "Well, if we have some and they know it, they'll know more'n I do." His grin broadened. "Do you know how much we have?"

The Swede shook his head, but he pointed. "Is in dem saddlebags. Is heavy. Is gold coin yew brought from Grand Junction. Yew feel an' tell me if you t'ink is enough."

Jethro picked up Gunnar's saddlebags and said, "Enough to buy bacon and beans." Then he threw the saddlebags to the ground and muttered, "Poor Baldy."

It was near dusk when a sorrel mare trotted into Monticello, carrying a mean-looking, down and out cowboy. Once inside the general store, the dirty and

Gunnar's Mine

unshaven cowhand pulled off his boot, took two gold coins from inside and threw them on the counter, telling the proprietor he'd taken'em from a dead peddler down at Hovenweep. The proprietor rushed to fill what he thought was a bandit's order.

Not long afterwards, the cowboy jogged south out of Monticello. His supplies were lashed behind his saddle cantle and the remaining gold coin was tucked into one of his trousers pockets. Word had traveled quickly, so most people in the remote community breathed a sigh of relief to see the cowboy go.

Coincidentally, however, when the supply train from Cortez came in, one of the teamsters demonstrated considerable interest in a stubble-faced stranger with a low-hanging gun; especially one who paid in gold. By the time the teamster arrived back in Cortez, sent a telegram, and Monticello was visited by Andrew Whittle and three other toughs from Placerville, the stranger's trail was twelve days old. By then, Gunnar Einarssen and Jethro Spring were riding up the San Rafael Swell.

The searchers spread out; one south to check throughout the new Mormon community of Blanding and down to Bluff on the San Juan River; one north through the hamlet of Moab, then following the Colorado River valley to Grand Junction; and the third, up the Green River as far as Desolation Canyon before giving up the search. Andrew Whittle chose east, to Cortez and on to Durango.

Actually the third searcher twice crossed the fugitives' trail during his Green River foray, but by the time he reached the ferry crossing at the mouth of the San Rafael it was coming on Thanksgiving and the weather was souring. When the ferry operator claimed to have seen nothing of two men, one of whom was a runt, and the other astride a sorrel mare, the Amalgamated man tucked his neck deeper into his mackinaw coat and rode

245

back to the plateau, following it up the Green to the crossing at Price River.

The reason the San Rafael ferryman hadn't spotted the fugitives was because Jethro insisted on moving only at night or off beaten paths. Besides, a November crossing of the Green was far from difficult, even without ferry passage. With snow falling in the high country and the rainy season gone throughout most of the Green River lowlands the stream was, by mid-November, at its lowest ebb. Choosing a place to ford the Green at that time was largely a matter of selecting how one would drop into its canyon, then climb out the other side.

"They tell me this is called the 'Angel Trail', Gunnar," Jethro said, twisting in the saddle to call back over the backs of their scrambling packhorses. "Reason, so I get it, is that it's so steep that anybody traveling it needs a guardian angel perched on his shoulder."

He grinned when he received no answer from a companion who had both eyes squeezed shut and a death grip on his saddle's horn. "They say it's all part of the 'Outlaw Trail' down from Canada, where rustlers run horses both ways—from Mexico to Canada and back again."

"If we gets to the top, ay hope yew will tell me."

Jethro and Gunnar spent most of December in the San Rafael country, first on the plateau north of the river, then when it turned to bitter winter, dropping to the river bottom. Most of the time, the men took shelter under south- and west-facing overhangs that had been much used by ancient Indians referred to in the Southwest as 'the Anasazi' or 'Ancient Ones'.

"Why they goned?" Gunnar asked, staring above their heads at a wall that held a row of ocher handprints.

Gunnar's Mine

"Some of'em looks like they were painted on and some looks like they've been picked out," the younger man mused, stroking his growing beard. "That one looks like a man with broad shoulders. And that one looks like a mountain sheep."

It began raining softly, so Jethro moved their gear beneath a rock overhang while Gunnar started a fire. Soon the little man sat down on the remains of a low rock wall, stretching one hand to the flame and the other to Puppy's ruff. Then he reached into the sand at his feet and picked up a tiny corncob. "Dey were farmers?" he asked.

"Had to be, Gunnar. Too many corncobs around everywhere we go. But there are bones, too, so I suppose they done some hunting."

Later Gunnar called the younger man to a remote crevice within the overhang and pointed to a human skull. "What yew t'ink dey hunted?"

Jethro picked up the skull and showed Gunnar how it'd been stoved in by a blow from behind. "Maybe they ate each other."

Desert bighorns roamed the canyons and cliffs of the San Rafael and Jethro downed one to augment their sowbelly and beans for Christmas dinner. He also pulled out a bottle of whiskey he'd squirreled away since Monticello.

"Mormons don' drink, yew said." The little man stood holding the precious bottle in both hands, his voice accusatory.

"That's right, little man. But I didn't say they're above selling it to a thirsty gentile."

Later in the evening, Gunnar laid a bag of gold nuggets in Jethro's lap. "Merry Christ's Mass," he said.

Jethro hefted the bag, then juggled it from hand to hand. "I can't take this," he said.

"Paid, yew have not been for long time. Now yew have."

"Gunnar, there might be as much as a thousand dollars worth here."

The little man perched on a small boulder worn smooth from the butts of countless humans over thousands of years. "What does gold mean to me?" he said. "Ay don' want it if the Nordic Summer ay can't have."

"You'll get her back, Gunnar," Jethro said, extending the sack to his friend. "In fact, you haven't lost her and you won't ... if we can keep you alive."

The little Swede ignored the gold. "Maybe being alive is not so goot."

"Now you're talking crazy," Jethro growled, pitching the bag atop Gunnar's soogan. "That's the kind of muddled thinking that got Anton killed."

Gunnar retrieved the gold and pitched it onto Jethro's bedroll. Then he kicked off his boots. "Ay go to bed."

Later, as the fire flickered its last, Jethro whispered, "Merry Christmas," into the darkness.

"Ya," Gunnar replied.

They moved from the San Rafael in the middle of January to a hide-out camp on the bank of the Green River. Denver and Rio Grande train whistles occasionally echoed into their canyon, interrupting their sleep. One morning, Jethro said, "I have to go into town to re-supply, Gunnar. I'll take Baldy for a packhorse. You stay here and watch Olaf and Sven and take care of camp."

"Ay go with yew."

"No, Gunnar, I don't think so. They're looking for two people who fit our descriptions, so let's not make it easy for 'em."

"Ay go, and yew stay."

Gunnar's Mine

Jethro chuckled, counting off on his fingers: "I'd agree to that if it wasn't so easy to spot you for size, if you could talk without a Swedish accent, and if you could sling heavy packbags on a tall horse."

Jethro was gone the full day, riding back into camp and swinging from his saddle at dusk. "I got what we needed, pardner, but we got to get a move on. There was too many curious people in Green River wondering how a drifter came by a bag of gold coins."

He jerked the loaded panniers from Baldy and threw the gray's packsaddle on Sven. "First off, the guy at the mercantile bit each of the coins. I guess they don't trade much in gold." Jethro added, "I suppose it's mostly Mormon script. Anyway, he had to call the banker to show him the coins."

After Jethro made adjustments to the packsaddle's straps, he continued, "Then the town constable wandered in and the banker showed him the gold, and the storekeep called to the railroad agent to come look at a real, twenty-dollar gold piece."

Gunnar, helped by Puppy, began breaking camp, rolling their bedrolls, gathering up pots and pans, and packing the fine china dishes once belonging to the family of Jose Antonio Gutierrez de Valdez y Mendoza.

"They kept asking questions. 'Where'd I come from? Where had I been? Ain't much gold coins passed around here, stranger,' the constable said. I told him there wasn't likely to be much more, either, if he kept sticking his nose into other people's business."

Gunnar brought him Olaf's packsaddle.

"He wanted to know my name and when I told him 'Haaken Nordstrom', he said I didn't look like a Swede to him. So I told him I wasn't, that I was black Norwegian. That made him mad, but he stopped asking questions. Only thing is, he disappeared and I'll be surprised if he's not out trying to unravel my tracks."

"Yew hide dem?" Gunnar asked. "How?"

"I headed north and west, then circled into the desert and rode up a dry wash until I hit the railroad. Then I followed the tracks to another wash, went through a big herd of cattle, then came as hard and fast as I could back to camp. It won't be good enough if the constable is any kind of tracker, but it might buy us enough time to get into hard, mountain country."

They crossed the Green River at midnight on the Denver and Rio Grande Railway bridge. Three days later, Jethro led them into the foothills north of Grand Valley and made camp. During the following week, the two men and their horses retreated further and further into the Book Cliffs.

Finally one day, Gunnar said, "Sven has a loose shoe, sounds if."

Jethro nodded. "Time to clench'em. I was hoping they'd last until we got to Grand Junction. Then we could find to a blacksmith and get'em some new boots."

The following morning Gunnar squatted on his heels, morosely petting Puppy. "When we go to Grand Junction?" he asked.

Jethro looked up from where he held Sven's big hoof between his knees. "Hand me that axe, will you little man?" With the blunt side of the single bit held tight against the curled nail end, Jethro pounded the nail head with a rock. When he'd completed the circuit of that shoe's eight nails, he dropped the hoof, straightened and said, "Probably a month, or maybe two." He picked up Sven's left hind, pulling the hoof out across his thigh and began clenching the nails in its shoe. "Should be two months if we do it right."

"Ay want to go back now."

The younger man dropped the big horse's hoof and straightened to look at his employer. "Gunnar, be reasonable. They've burned your cabin. You don't know

Gunnar's Mine

what shape the mine is in. Even if we could stay in the mine, it's still winter and it'd be tough."

Gunnar said, "A tent, ay could buy."

"Then it's important that we're able to do a certain amount of assessment work to keep up your claim. Be hard to do in the winter—and I expect it's still winter up there." He moved around to pick up Sven's right hind. "Be better to wait until the weather turns warmer, then camp out, do enough assessment work to qualify, and be ready to run again if need be."

But after only two weeks of hiding out in the Book Cliffs, Jethro gave in to the older man's entreaties and moved to a camp on the East Fork of Salt River, within an easy day's ride of Grand Junction.

It was during the second week of March that Jethro took their horses to a Grand Junction blacksmith for new shoes. "It'll take all day, Gunnar, but I should be back in time for supper. If not, don't wait for me."

The older man said, "Ay want to go back to my Nordic Summer."

"Three more weeks, little man. Then we'll head for Vidkun's and leave the horses."

Dusk descended as the younger man returned from Grand Junction on his sorrel mare, trailed by Baldy and the two draft horses. He thought for a moment that he'd missed camp and reined Tangle in. He stared around into the night, hearing the East Fork of the Salt gurgling to his right. The mare kept fighting her head and pulling on her bit until the rider let her have her way. Only a moment later they pulled up at the camp ... a cold one. It was also a camp without a black and white mutt trotting out to greet them.

"Hello the camp!" Jethro called. "Gunnar!"

Both his and Gunnar's soogans were unrolled, just as they'd been when he'd ridden out. Jethro swung from his saddle, knelt, and felt the ashes from their morning fire. They were cold. "Puppy!" he cried, knowing it was futile. Wherever Gunnar was, that, too, was where he'd find Puppy."

With darkness descending, Jethro moved the horses back into the tamarisk brush and grained them. Then he built a fire. When it was burning well, he pulled out a flaming brand and went over the immediate camp area as well as he could in the darkness. There were no signs of a scuffle; no other horse prints in the sand.

With a sinking heart, Jethro fried a few slices of bacon, then bedded down for the remainder of the night. He was up at daylight, breaking camp and saddling horses. While the horses polished off their grain, he unraveled Gunnar's tracks.

What he found was that the little man had probably followed him from camp, the morning before. When Jethro trotted back to his horses an hour later, he knew positively that Gunnar had headed for Grand Junction. He also knew the little Swede had deliberately stayed fifty feet to the side of the wagon road, apparently so Jethro wouldn't be likely to spot his tracks while returning from the blacksmith.

At the Rio Grande Southern ticket office in Grand Junction, Jethro discovered what he'd expected—that a little man speaking broken English had purchased a ticket to Fall Creek almost twenty-four hours before. Accompanying that little man had been a small, black and white dog.

CHAPTER TWENTY THREE

Jethro Spring stood outside the Grand Junction ticket office cursing under his breath and weighing his options. One thing for certain was that Gunnar was back within Amalgamated's grasp and it was probable that his enemies knew it. Jethro shook his head. If his friend had avoided the railroad's brakemen and hopped an empty ore train, he might have gone undetected. But he hadn't. The damned fool had bought a ticket with a twenty-dollar gold piece!

"What should I do?" Jethro asked himself aloud. If he caught the next train out, he'd be a full day behind his friend. His gaze wandered over the horses. What about them? He'd have to stable them. That'd take an hour or two. On the other hand, traveling to Fall Creek by horse would take two full days, even without the two draft horses. Could Gunnar stay alive so long? A day behind the little man now, plus two days on the trail. Hell, three days! Three days behind the little Swede.

He knew Gunnar would go directly to Walter's Station. Could Abigail Whittle protect him for three days?

But didn't Abigail tell them last fall that a Denver lawyer was looking into their case, presenting it to the Colorado Governor? Might the all-powerful Amalgamated Minerals and Mining Company be reined in by now? Or might they have been satisfied with driving away a fringe claimholder like Gunnar, while taking over Antonio Gutierrez's claim that lay in the heart of their operations?

He shook his head. Hell no! An outfit like Amalgamated would never be satisfied; they'd want it all. But had there been an investigation? Is it possible they've been checked—at least temporarily? Have they been reined in long enough to allow Gunnar to stay alive for one day? Two? Three?

Again his gaze wandered over the patient horses. He strode down the station steps, jerked the mare's hitchrope loose from the rail and swung into the saddle. "Hell with it," he muttered. "I'll figure it out on the way to the San Miguel."

Gunnar had been recognized by no fewer than three Amalgamated men within minutes of his boarding the Rio Grande Southern coach. Each passenger avoided the little man's eye, but two detrained at Placerville while the third made sure Gunnar exited at Fall Creek.

The wolf-dog announced him, even before he hammered on the door.

"Gunnar!" Abigail cried, responding to his midnight pounding. "This is wonderful!"

But the flames of her jubilation were banked when she discovered her little friend was alone. "You mean

Gunnar's Mine

Jason isn't with you? Why not? Where is he?"
"Ay left him at Grand Junction. To come alone was only way ay could get to Nordic Summer."
She pulled him into the station, lit a candle, then sat down across a table from him. "I'm not sure I understand," she began, tugging at her flannel nightgown and the knitted, woolen overwrap. "Why did you have to leave Jason in order to return to your mine?"
Gunnar shrugged. "Ay ask him, but he say, 'No'. He say 'nother mont' we should wait. Ay wait for five mont's and ay don' want to wait no more. But he won't listen."
She took his rough hands in hers. "Gunnar, how did you come here? Did anyone see you?"
"Ay rode railroad. Ya, in coach was others."
"Were you recognized?"
He shook his sad face. "Ay don' know. Me, who would know?"
She bit her lip. "Gunnar, you dear man, what if they still want to kill you?"
"Den with shovel, ay hit dem."
"Quit this nonsense!" she suddenly spat. "These men are killers. My own son is one of them. You don't even have a shovel, Gunnar, don't you see? They burned your cabin; looted your mine." She began crying. He withdrew his hands and shrank back into his chair, unable to deal with her tears.
"Yew say Andrew Whittle, he is one of dem?" he asked.
"Yes, you little fool! Everything Amalgamated Minerals and Mining ever told you was a lie. Andrew never left. In fact, I'm certain he was the one behind the Antonio's death."
Gunnar stared down at the hands he'd taken from her grip. She asked, "Will Jason Frost come?"
"Ay don' know. Ay t'ink so. But ay don' know."
"But he knows you are gone?"

"Ya. But maybe he not find out where 'til in morning."

She jumped up to pace the dining room, finally stopping by his side. "Did anyone else get off the train with you, Gunnar?"

"Ay don' know. Ay didn't see dem."

"But they could have?"

"Ya. Was five or six udders. To Telluride ay t'ink dey go."

"And you didn't even look." She bit her lower lip while staring through him. At last she nodded. Placing a hand on his shoulder, she said, "Gunnar, it will be at least a day, perhaps more, before Jason Frost can get here and hopefully save us. We must concentrate on keeping you alive until then."

He placed a hand over hers, turning his long, lined face upwards. "If ay die, in my Nordic Summer ay want it to be."

She placed her other hand over his and said, "We'll both go there first thing in the morning."

The necessity of gathering food and supplies, and the woman's need to give instructions to Juanita and Juan, kept Abigail and Gunnar from reaching the Nordic Summer as early as they wished. They were ready by mid-morning, however, about the time Jethro Spring had puzzled out Gunnar's tracks and was well on his way to Grand Junction.

While Jethro jogged to Grand Junction, Gunnar packed bedding and a Spencer carbine up the trail to the Nordic Summer. Meanwhile, Abigail Whittle carried a basket filled with foodstuffs from Walter's Station. Behind them trotted Puppy. Gunnar paused at the cabin site to stare with his sad, hound-dog look at its ruin. But

Gunnar's Mine

they were soon on their way again. Both of them stopped at the creek, laughing at the thought that this was where Abigail had first surprised Gunnar and Jethro in the bathing pool.

"You looked like a plucked chicken," she giggled.

"And an angel yew looked."

She blushed. "You know how to turn a lady's heart as well as her head."

They hesitated at the tunnel mouth while he studied the tailings heaps. "No more samples did dey take," he said, plainly puzzled.

"Well," she said, "they were certainly busy up here for the first months after you left."

He shook his head. "Ay will never leave again."

She said, "I'll bring the wolf-dog up here tomorrow so you can tie him outside."

They ducked inside, located Antonio's old bed-chamber and left Gunnar's food and bedding before heading for the tunnel's far end in order to examine the extent of Amalgamated's exploratory work. It grew dim as they advanced farther into the tunnel. Gunnar paused to light a candle. "Is yust around bend," he said. Guided by the flickering light, they rounded the last bend.

"Well, well," Andrew Whittle drawled, leaning indolently against the headwall. "To find you here, mother, is something of a surprise." Whittle held a revolver. He eared back the hammer as they watched in shock.

Puppy leaped forward, fangs bared, growling. Whittle shot the dog.

Gunnar cried out, dropping the candle and swinging the Spencer up, jacking a shell into the chamber.

Whittle actually laughed aloud in the darkness as he brought his revolver to bear for the second time. He should've paid more attention to the white of his teeth because his mother shot him between molars with a .32 over and under derringer that she jerked from the folds of her skirt. It might have been more difficult for Abigail Whittle to aim the second barrel within the tunnel's sudden blackness had she not knelt and placed the muzzle at her gurgling son's temple. At that distance, her aim was perfect.

Jethro Spring left the two draft horses at a farm on the Gunnison, then began a dash around the end of the Uncompahgre Plateau. He alternated often between Baldy and Tanglefoot, keeping the two saddlehorses moving at a steady trot. With fifty miles behind him and a hundred still ahead, Jethro rested his two ponies for an hour at Gateway, purchasing grain and a couple of forkfuls of hay from the stable owner there. Then man and horses pounded on into the night.

Abigail pushed wearily to her feet, while Gunnar's carbine clattered to the stone floor as he fumbled with the candle. As soon as he struck a match, she knocked it from his hand. "You mustn't make a light," she whispered fiercely.

"Ya," he said, sobbing. "Ay wanted to see Puppy is all." He dropped to his knees and picked up the dog. Death had been mercifully swift.

Abigail grasped him by the collar and pulled him to his feet. "We must get to the tunnel mouth!" she whispered in his ear. "If they command the mouth, we have no hope."

"Puppy?" he sobbed.

"Gunnar, if we get out of this alive, you can take care of your dog and I'll take care of mine. Until then, we

Gunnar's Mine

must try to save ourselves."

Both of them knelt to feel around the floor; he for his Spencer, she for her son's revolver, and whatever other weapons the dead man might've possessed.

They were driven back from the tunnel mouth by gunfire. Abigail was struck in the neck by ricocheting rock fragments. Back in Antonio's bedchamber, Gunnar cut strips from a blanket to bind the wound. A line of tears spilled down the little man's cheek. "Is my fault," he wailed. "Is my fault yew are hurt. Ay should have listened to my mans." He took her in his arms, but she pushed him away.

"There's no time for recriminations, Gunnar. We must cover the tunnel mouth. At the very least, we must not let them get into the mine."

The little man nodded, tears still coursing. He picked up the Spencer and said, "Here yew must stay." Then he dashed from the sleeping chamber out into the tunnel. It was only moments later when she heard him shout, "HEY, YEW OUT DERE! IS WOMAN HERE. SHE COMES OUT!"

"No, Gunnar!" she cried, leaping to her feet. But her cry was lost in the roar of at least a dozen rifles aimed into the tunnel.

The Swede was hit in the leg by a ricocheting bullet and stung all over by flying rock fragments before he could find his way back to Abigail. "What we do?" he wailed. "Dey kill yew, too!"

She shook him. "Gunnar! Gunnar, get a grip on yourself. Are we safe here if they throw dynamite into the tunnel?"

They both slid down, backs to the wall, to sit on the blankets. She helped him pull off his boot, wiped the wound clean with a piece from her petticoat, then wrapped it in a blanket strip. After she'd finished, she repeated her question. "Well? What about their trying to blast us out with dynamite?"

He shook his head. "Was one t'ing Anton said; why he wanted dis room away from outside."

Bullets still ricocheted down the tunnel, but Abigail edged to the corner of the sleeping nook and fired once in return. The Swede raised his eyebrows at her. "Keep them honest," she said, raising her voice to the rising drumbeat of rifle fire that answered her random shot. When the drumbeat subsided, she continued as if she'd not been interrupted "So far we've not fired back since Andrew—that...that bastard son of a...a she-devil slaver who ..."

Gunnar leaned toward her to place an index finger over her lips until she subsided. Then both man and woman again leaned back against the stone wall as gunfire rattled in from outside, bullets whining and bouncing down the tunnel.

"Ay am sorry," he said at last. "Ay am sorry yew must die, too."

She sighed and covered one of his hands. "Whether one dies is not so important, Gunnar. It's how one *lives* that counts. We can both be proud that we've lived lives of which we're in no way ashamed." When he said nothing, she continued. "And we can be assured that someday, we'll be avenged. If not by Jason Frost, then by God and all his angels."

Gunnar stared out the cubbyhole opening, across the tunnel, seemingly lost in thought. Then he shook his head and said, "Dey not kill him. Dey not kill him because he won't let dem."

"Then you think he will get here in time to save us?"

Gunnar turned to stare sadly at her. Again tears welled in his eyes as he shook his head. "Is my fault dat he won't. Is my fault dat yew will die, too."

She squeezed his hand. "Don't, Gunnar."

"Is my fault dat we will both die."

Gunnar's Mine

Again she squeezed his hand. "Please don't."

"Is my fault dat we both will die today."

The eyes she focused on his sad, drooping ones, widened. "What do you mean?"

Daylight caught Jethro Spring five miles short of the forks of the Dolores and the San Miguel. He slumped in the saddle, but smiled grimly when recollecting another long ride, this time from the ranch of his friend, John Tunstall, to the New Mexico town of Las Vegas. "Two hundred miles that one was," he told his sorrel mare as they jogged along. "You were along for part of the way on it, too."

Jethro had ridden from the ranch against the advice of all his friends. He said he was going to provide support for Alexander McSween and John Chisum who, it was thought, had been unfairly jailed. In truth, he rode those long miles in wet snow and driving rain to help Susan McSween, the vivacious and—he had to admit—naughty wife of the Lincoln attorney.

Three days and two nights he'd spent in the saddle on that journey, straddling three different horses. Though this was but a hundred and fifty miles instead of two hundred, and the weather was bluebird instead of rain and snow, changing mounts meant merely leaping from the back of one tired horse into the saddle of another tired one.

Thus the weary man and his two tiring steeds paused during this second mercy ride, at the first crossing of the San Miguel. Here he again grained Tangle and Baldy and turned them loose to graze while, propped against a cottonwood log, he dozed.

He passed Vidkun Bloomquist's place at Redvale in mid-afternoon, thought for a moment about obtaining a fresh horse, then remembered that Vidkun had only draft animals on his farm. Jethro judged the sun to be an hour away from sinking behind the western hills as Jethro's two horses plodded across the San Miguel for the last time. *Eighteen more miles,* the exhausted man thought. *Be there around nine, maybe ten. Goddamn you, Gunnar, you better be okay.*

"What did you mean," Abigail asked, squeezing the little man's hands, "when you said we will die today?"

His gentle smile was wistful. He looked away from her, then took a deep breath and returned to gaze resignedly into the woman's light eyes. "When yew say dey work up here at the Nordic Summer, is dat true?"

"Yes. Of course it's true."

"But ay saw no work in the tunnel."

"What about behind Andrew?"

"No, not'ing."

Her brow wrinkled. "I don't understand what you are trying to say, Gunnar."

"Ay t'ink all dere work was above."

She shook her head as if to clear it. "All right. Didn't Antonio tell you that he believed the real wealth of this district lay in the rocks above?"

"Ya."

"So they were exploring up there. I don't see …"

"Ya. Dey worked right over the Nordic Summer tunnel."

"All right, they worked over …" Her eyes widened as she realized the implications of what he was saying. "You think they will blow up the mine!"

The little man's head slowly ratcheted up and down.

Chapter Twenty Four

Two weary horses plodded to a halt in front of the hitchrack at Walter's Station. The door jerked opened, and there, framed in lantern light, was a man Jethro had never seen before. A star winked from the stranger's shirtpocket. "This place is closed."

Jethro tilted back his hat so the light reflected from his face. "I'll need some oats and hay for my horses."

"You just hard of hearing, or are you uncommon dumb? I said this place is closed."

"Is Abigail Whittle around?"

The law officer, whoever he was, barked, "Y'all git, hear? Y'all git or y'all will git got!"

Jethro rubbed his two-month beard, stared at the ground, and ventured a step nearer. He then lifted his face so the lantern picked up the coldest gray eyes the deputy had ever seen, causing him to take an involuntary step backward. "A few answers is all I need," the nighttime visitor said. "What's going on here? Where's

Abigail Whittle? Why can't I get feed for my horses where I've got feed for them before? Tell me something. Please."

The deputy took a single-fire shotgun with a Damascus barrel from behind the door. "If anybody asks questions around here, mister, that anybody'll be me. Who are you?"

Jethro smiled. "Just a friend of the Whittle family. I told my Uncle Walter I'd check on Aunt Abigail is all. Is she all right?"

The deputy seemed to ponder the question, so Jethro asked, "How about cousin Andrew? How about him?"

The man leaned the shotgun back inside the door. "You all'd better come back in the morning and talk to Sheriff Richards. He's in the middle of his investigation and he says he wants this place sealed off." The man spread his palms helplessly. "I'm only following orders, stranger, and I'm sorry as hell."

As an afterthought, the deputy asked, "What did you say your name was?"

"Didn't say," Jethro replied.

The deputy reached back for the shotgun, but by the time he'd readied it, Jethro Spring was gone.

After leaving Walter's Station, he reined the tired horse to a halt in the road, wondering what he should do next. It was Tanglefoot that alerted Jethro to the woman's presence by her ears going up and staring to the side.

"Senor Frost!" The voice was low and urgent.

"Juanita?"

"Shh. *Yo quiero hablar con usted.*"

He swung from his saddle and, leading Tanglefoot

trailed by the light-colored packhorse, followed the frail old woman through riverbank willows to the junction of Fall Creek and the San Miguel River. There she turned and, brushing back silver-flecked hair escaping from beneath her shawl, said, "*Esa senora esta muerta.*"

Jethro sighed. "How did she die, Juanita? And where?"

"*Un companero muerto tambien.*"

Jethro's exhaustion washed over him. *Gunnar's gone!* He lashed the two horses to streamside brush, then threw down a coat and motioned Juanita to sit down. Then he knelt before her, and took her hands in his. "Tell me what happened, Juanita. Please."

The old woman, sobbing intermittently, told in broken Spanish and English of the nighttime arrival of Senor Gunnar, and how the Senora Abigail had become alarmed that Senor Frost did not also arrive. Juanita said both Abigail and Gunnar had left for the mine during mid-morning, and that soon shooting began and continued all afternoon. Then, slapping her palms over her ears, she sobbed, "*Mucho estampido un la Montana!*"

"So there was an explosion?"

"*Si i una explosion.*"

Still holding the old woman's hands, he asked, "Have you or Juan been to the mine?"

She shook her head. "*No, senor. No entro ni un hombre a de clarar.*"

He gently pulled the aged woman to her feet and said, "Thank you, senora. You've helped me. I don't know what I can do, but you go with God."

She nodded, then was gone.

Jethro slipped like a shadow across the road to Walter's Station, entered the barn, and under the watchful eyes of the deputy's docile bay, stole a half-sack of oats for his own tired and hungry horses. When daylight came, Baldy and Tanglefoot contentedly grazed in a hillside glade, north of Fall Creek.

Their master lay atop the same hill, peering through his telescope at the place that had once been the tunnel to Gunnar's mine—but was now a mass of rubble. He was surprised there appeared to be no rescue efforts underway. Instead, a dismal warming fire smoked near the rubble heaps, away from a tent so poorly pegged into place that its sides flapped in the breeze. Their hands outstretched, two men squatted near the fire. Two saddled horses nervously pawed the roots from aspen trees near Gunnar's old cabin site.

A few minutes later, the men saw a dirty, bearded stranger approach. "Off limits," one of them shouted. "Go away!"

Jethro continued on. The men stood, and when Jethro was within twenty feet, the one on the right—the one Jethro knew as 'Lon'—exclaimed, "It's him!" Bright metal stars winked on the left breast of both men's coats.

"Don't do anything foolish, boys," the newcomer advised. "I just came to see how the rescue effort is going and to ask a few questions."

Both men gripped rifles, but their muzzles were down and it seemed mutually understood the guns should remain that way for peace to prevail.

"Ain't no rescue effort goin' on," Lon said. "Figure it ain't no use."

"Besides, the sheriff ain't here," said the moon-faced one.

"Okay, tell me what happened."

"Won't do that," Lon said. "You want answers, you talk to the sheriff."

"Where is he?"

"Us, we hear no evil, see no evil, speak no evil," Moon-face said.

Gunnar's Mine

Jethro flashed a smile. "Friend, I'm willing to do just that, but where should I go to look for him?"

"Wait long enough and he'll be right here," Lon replied.

"I'm willing to wait, right enough. But are you boys willing to let me?"

"We got orders to keep everybody away," Moon-face said, "and I don't see Jason Frost's name excepted."

Jethro nodded. "You boys are just doing your jobs, I guess." He began backing down the trail. "But you're making me do things the hard way. You might want to remember that." He turned at a hundred yards and trotted away.

"What did he mean there, at the last?" Moon-face asked his partner.

"I don't know. But one of us better get word to the sheriff that he's here."

"You do it," Moon-face said.

"Oh no, you're the one in charge."

Moon-face laughed. "Aw, go ahead and follow him down that trail. He can't touch you; you're a deputy now. He touches you and he's outside the law."

Lon smiled grimly. "And for what went on here, we're inside it? Besides, I get the feeling he'd have as much respect for the law as a schoolmarm has for a fart. Naw, I think you ought to go."

So the two men stood by the sputtering campfire arguing about who should ride to Placerville to inform the sheriff that Jason Frost had returned. They argued so long and forcefully that the subject of their debate slithered through the rubble to within thirty feet of their campfire. Finally, Moon-face threw up his hands and headed for his horse.

Not two minutes had passed after Moon-face disappeared when Lon was knocked forward into the fire. He rolled away, fighting sparks, while the man he knew as

Jason Frost kicked his rifle from the fire, jerked the six gun from the prone man's holster, then focused a pair of gray eyes on the camp tender. Jethro pulled his boot knife and stood flipping it over and over in his hand. "Lon," he said, "what am I going to do with you?"

Five minutes later, Jethro Spring had the entire tale. He knew the holes had been drilled into the mountainside months prior to their actually being packed with powder and fuses lit. He knew those charges had already been placed by the time he'd left the Gunnison, riding pell-mell for the Dolores. He also knew Andrew Whittle had died in the mine with Gunnar and Abigail, and that Gunnar had tried to get their attackers to let the woman go free. More importantly, he knew the plan's architect had been Andrew Whittle, but that Alexander Coen had been present and issued the orders to set off the dynamite.

Jethro learned that Sheriff Richards had been notified the following morning, probably reaching the mine about the time Jethro dozed at the forks of the Dolores and San Miguel Rivers. In addition, he learned that Sheriff Richards had deputized several miners who were standing nearby, then gone on to Placerville to investigate further. That the sheriff had not returned for a full twenty-four hours was bewildering to both the guard and the man who continually flipped the throwing knife before his face.

Jethro let Lon scoot up with his back against a boulder. He caught and pointed the knife at his prisoner. "You know what happened to Drogue don't you?"

"Yessir."

"And how about the gunslick, Benjamin Pack? Were you there?"

"Y-yessir."

"Now I'm going to leave you. I'm going to carry your rifle and your revolver down by your saddlehorse

Gunnar's Mine

and leave them against a tree. But before I go, I want to leave you with this thought: If you ever tell another soul that I've been here, I'll look you up and either do unto you as happened to Drogue, or I'll leave you like Pack, with so many holes in you that rainwater will pick up speed when it seeps through your worthless corpse."

Lon stared at his feet, shaking helplessly.

When Jethro Spring had ridden through Placerville during the blackness of the previous night, he could tell great changes had been made during his absence. Huge buildings had been constructed. Many clanked with operating machinery, even late into the night. There were men still coming and going in the streets. Vague shapes staggered in the blackness. Honky-tonk music spilled from the San Miguell Emporium, while at least two additional saloons spewed out music and drunks. But visiting in the daylight gave an even more sordid impression as the lone man sauntered up the main street, heading for Andrew Whittle's former home.

New buildings on this street spread so haphazardly and dilapidatedly it seemed almost as if a capricious God had broadcast their seed by hand. The reduction plant up the hill toward Billy Benbrooke's old claim was belching smoke and he could hear, even at that distance, the clanging of its machinery. Walking to town, he'd passed hordes of hovels where slack-jawed women sat on porch stoops and snot-nosed kids played in the road dust. A switch engine was at work at the sidings, moving loaded ore cars and placing empties.

Jethro Spring shook his head. He was here for a reason and that reason would need a quick hand and a clear mind. He'd considered the risk and dismissed it. With Gunnar dead, he was nothing more than a weed without roots. He knew, as did Amalgamated, that without Gunnar he could only be a nuisance and not a thorn. True, they might suspect him of seeking vengeance, but those responsible for the deaths of Gunnar Einarssen and Abigail Whittle, had only to take certain precautions to avoid danger to themselves until the man they knew as Jason Frost tired of waiting and vacated the country. Certainly they'd never suspect that very same man would stroll up the main street of Placerville with the object of an eye for an eye so shortly after the cause for anger occurred—not right in front of God and everybody.

When Jethro approached Whittle's place which, as the frightened mine guard had told him, was now Amalgamated's main office, he found a crowd gathered around tarps of white duck that covered three mounds. When the crowd parted to let him through, he saw a leg ending in a patent leather shoe extending from beneath one tarp.

The sheriff waited for him, sitting hands on knees on the office steps. "The Mick said you'd be along."

"The Mick?"

"Yeah, Miklewski. The deputy down at the mine cave-in."

Jethro's smile never reached his eyes. "Is that your story, sheriff?"

"What story?"

"That it was a mine cave-in."

"That's what it is until I get a chance to investigate it further. That investigation got sidetracked by this."

Jethro wheeled slowly, eyes sweeping the crowd of miners behind him. Curiosity, not fear, not anger, seemed their sole expression.

"By the way, Frost, where was you day before yesterday?"

"The day before yesterday," Jethro mused, so quiet-

Gunnar's Mine

ly only those nearest to him heard. "Well, I talked to the ticket agent in Grand Junction in the morning. Somewhere around noon I made arrangements to leave a couple of horses with a farmer on the Gunnison River. And come nightfall, I was at Gateway buying grain for the horses I rode. Why?"

"What about yesterday?"

"What about yesterday?" Jethro chuckled. "Well, I was at the mouth of the San Miguel shortly after sun-up, and nooned at the first crossing. Then last night about ten, I talked to your deputy at Fall Creek. Again, why?"

"You have anything to do with this?"

Jethro's eyes followed the sweep of his hand to take in the bodies. "To tell you the truth, sheriff, I haven't got the foggiest idea what the hell you're talking about, but if that's who I think it is, I heartily approve."

The sheriff stood and strode to the tarps. "These two," he said, pointing to the one with the patent leather shoe thrust out, and the one next to it, "are Coen and Blackenby. I suppose you're up here to talk to 'em about Einarssen's mine."

"It's possible that thought crossed my mind, sheriff."

"Well," Sheriff Richards said, kicking the third tarp, "this one beat you to it."

"Who's he?"

"Nobody now. But he was somebody you knew, Frost." With that, Richards curled back the tarp flap from the face belonging to the third body.

Jethro grinned. "Welcome back, Billy. You didn't quite redeem yourself, but you died trying."

Chapter Twenty Five

The story, as Jethro put it together, first from the sheriff, then from surrounding onlookers, was that Benbrooke had stormed into the office after dark, the evening before, shouting for Andrew Whittle. Apparently he was shot and wounded by a guard on the way in and, though he'd probably never previously laid eyes on Alexander Coen and Jay Eldon Blackenby, shotgunned them both as the only worthy recipients of his blazing hatred for Amalgamated.

Billy's fumbled efforts to reload were swiftly ended by guards bursting belatedly into the office.

Jethro assumed Benbrooke had been out to the mine, seen the devastation, and hadn't learned that Andrew Whittle had died within the tunnel with Gunnar Einarssen and Abigail Whittle. That he actually had, through chance, killed the man most responsible, might, Jethro thought, ease Billy's passage across the River Styx.

Gunnar's Mine

"What do you figure to do, Frost?" the sheriff asked for the second time.

Slowly his mind came back to the present. "What can I do, sheriff? Gunnar's dead; Gutierrez is dead; Krajcyk is dead. Every honest, independent miner on the San Miguel is either dead or gone. What can I do about it? Nothing that I can see. But I'm damned sure that's something you'll have to live with for the rest of your life."

"I don't want no trouble from you."

Jethro sighed. "You won't get it, sheriff."

"You promise me that, and I won't take you in."

The younger man's eyebrows shot up. "For what?" he said. Then he grinned and said, "What the hell! You have my promise."

Three minutes later, Jethro walked into Chalkie's San Miguell Emporium and slapped a silver dollar on the counter. "One of your tepid beers, my good man."

Chalkie drew a mug, scraped off the foam before topping it off, slid it across the counter and said, "No charge, my equally good man."

Jethro drained the mug in one lift, left the dollar on the counter, and strode to the batwings. Just before leaving, however, he turned and said, "I still think you need to take that extra 'L' out of Miguell."

Chalkie smiled.

Jethro spent a leisurely week drifting up and over the Uncompahgre Plateau, traveling it just as spring began up there. He picked up Vidkun Bloomquist's two draft horses at the Gunnison Valley farm of Oscar Crelar and spent another week trailing them home to their owner.

"Stay here, Jason," Vidkun said. "I can use a good man. I know Gunnar thought you was good, and that's enough for me."

Jethro shook his head. "Thanks, Vidkun, but I'll be moseying on. Where, I don't know. There's got to be a place somewhere on this earth where a man can go and be himself without the threat of a bullet from the dark."

"You might find that place here," Gunnar's Swedish friend said, "if you only look."

"And you don't think I'd see the little man's face in every sagebrush bush?"

Vidkun hung his head. "That is what I will see, too."

Jethro spent another restful week letting his horses graze the lush, spring grass of the San Miguel, building their strength against the days or months ahead—whichever they might be, wherever he might go. Finally he rode into Placerville to pick up supplies for his coming journey.

While in town, he stripped the saddles from both horses and carried them into a leather shop for a couple of minor repairs—reinforcing the packsaddle's harness and getting new rigging straps for his Visalia. While the saddles were being repaired, he led Baldy and Tangle to the blacksmith's shop to make sure their shoes were properly set. The smithy convinced him the ponies should have new shoes. "These'll do if you're gonna ride around a pasture a couple of times a week. But if you plan on any tough-country travel, these ones you've got on'em will let you down."

It was dusk by the time Jethro was ready to travel. First, he saddled Tanglefoot. Then, leaving her at the hitchrack, he led Baldy between the two laden packbags and spilled some grain on the ground beneath the big gray horse's nose. After that, he picked up the worn sawbuck and the Navaho blanket, deftly flipping the blanket across the big pony's back, then settling the packsaddle in place. His next effort was to pull the britching down over the horse's rump and lift the heavy tail free. He trailed idle fingers along the Baldy's side as he moved to the front, by habit, checking the loose-hanging cinch and breast strap for wear spots or flaws. He saw the man approaching as he buckled the breast strap in place.

"Are you Jason Frost?"

Jethro eyed the newcomer from beneath lowered lids. The man was nattily dressed and Jethro didn't trust the type. "Could be," he muttered, pulling the latigo strap tight.

"Well, are you or aren't you?"

Jethro grunted as he picked up one of the loaded panniers and hooked it in place. Then he brushed past the stranger, saying, "I got better things to do." He picked up the second pannier.

"I doubt it, sir. If you are indeed Jason Frost, then you are the beneficiary of Gunnar Einarssen's estate. You could be a wealthy man, Mr. Frost—if you are Jason Frost."

Jethro dropped the second pannier, lifted the first from the puzzled horse, jerked the latigo loose, and unbuckled the packsaddle's breast strap....

Don't "hang around" wondering about Roland's work—go to his website ...

www.rolandcheek.com

... and read sample chapters from any of his books

It's the website of the guy recognized as an expert on those wild creatures & wild features found amid the West's best places.

Sign up at no cost for Roland's weekly newspaper column via e-mail: www.rolandcheek.com

Historical Westerns
Grizzly Bears
Elk
Rocky Mountain Adventure
Humor

No need to remain confined by lack of knowledge or understanding about God's favorite places, times, features, and creatures

www.rolandcheek.com

Other Books by Roland Cheek

Fiction

Echoes of Vengeance 256 pgs. 5½ x 8½ $14.95 (postpaid)

A military outpost situated in an isolated region of the Department of the Upper Missouri. An embittered commandant who believes unkind fate kept him from fame and glory during the recent War of Secession. A band of starving Blackfeet too riddled with smallpox to withdraw to their reservation. A young mixed-breed army interpreter whose aging parents are with the Blackfeet tries to prevent a massacre-in-the-making; he's beaten and dragged to the guardhouse for the attempt.

Thus the stage is set and principal characters in place for the opening pages of Echoes of Vengeance. It's a tangled tale of daring and adventure as the youth flees echoes from his revenge. From Mississippi dock to Modesto prize ring, from Cherokee Strip to Colorado end-of-track, Jethro Spring treads the line between death and survival, merit and rascality, growth and degeneration.

Bloody Merchants' War 288 pgs. 5½ x 8½ $14.95 (postpaid)

Poor farmers and ranchers gripped in bondage by an iron triangle of crooked merchants, an oppressive military, and a corrupt Territorial government. Thus, the town of Lincoln, New Mexico Territory, was not a good place to be ambushed by events that spiral an unwilling fugitive into a conflict without clear distinctions between good and evil, right and wrong, friend and foe. Eventually Jethro Spring chooses, but did he make the right choice? With Billy the Kid? For John Chisum?

Book two in the Valediction For Revenge series features the adventures of Jethro Spring, wanted for killing a U.S. Army Major responsible for brutally murdering the young man's parents.

Lincoln County Crucible 288 pgs. 5½ x 8½ $14.95 (postpaid)

Third novel in the Valediction For Revenge series continues the life of Jethro Spring, a man torn between cultures.

The story opens after the terrible gunbattle where Alexander McSween and many of his partisans perish and with the "Santa Fe Ring," a crooked triumvirate of the United States Army, Territorial government, and merchant-stranglers in near-total economic control of southeastern New Mexico. Young Jethro is undecided about remaining, or riding into the sunset. His head tells him a man with a price on his own head should drift on. But what of the widowed Susan McSween? Or of his friend, Billy the Kid? Or the starving Mescalero Apaches? Or the poor Anglo farmers and Mexican peons strangling from "the ring's" bloody yoke?

And what of this new, incoming Territorial Governor, Lew Wallace? Might there be hope?

Gunnar's Mine 288 pgs. 5½ x 8½ $14.95 (postpaid)

Fourth in the Valediction For Revenge series chronicling the adventures of mixed-race fugitive Jethro Spring. Set in southwestern Colorado miining country.

Non-Fiction on next page

Nonfiction

Learning To Talk Bear 320 pgs. 5½ x 8½ $19.95 (postpaid)

An important book for a God's music is wind soughing through treetops, dove wings whispering at waterholes, the mournful cry of a lost-in-the-fog honker. It's a harmony that became addictive, and carries even into my dotage. Elk music took me to the dance. Bears—particularly grizzly bears—keep me dancing. Grizzlies, you see, are the Marine Band of the animal world. They swagger with the calm indifference of an animal who knows he has nothing left to prove. So why does this John Philip Sousa of wildlife resonance—an animal who not only fears not, but cares not—receive such a bum rap from the planet's most fearsome other creatures—us?

Good question. Not all grizzly bears are Jeffrey Dahmers in fur coats. That's the why for this book.nyone wishing to understand what makes bears tick. Humorous high adventure and spine-tingling suspense, seasoned with understanding through a lifetime of walking where bears walk.

The Phantom Ghost of Harriet Lou 352 pgs. 5½ x 8½ $19.95 (postpaid)

In the beginning there was heaven and earth; and the earth was without form and void and little tow-headed boys wandered around barefoot with hands in pockets because there was nothing upon the land to catch their imagination. And God looked upon His work and saw it was not yet good that no thing existed to challenge those boys. And so an autumn came to pass when eerie whistlings drifted into the valleys from distant mountainsides and the by-then lanky teenage boys threw away their toys and accepted the wapiti challenge that would make them men! And God and girls saw that it was good.

If you've heard a different version of this story, that's your problem. I heard it but once—this way. And so I became an elk hunter. Then I became infatuated with all creatures, and eventually a believer that God's handiwork is composed of such intracacies that a quest to understand has taken the rest of my life. The Phantom Ghost of Harriet Lou is about that quest.

Dance on the Wild Side 352 pgs. 5½ x 8½ $19.95 (postpaid) by Roland *and* Jane Cheek

It was her idea to compete in a man's world. "Competing in a man's world" is the way Jane referred to her growing enchantment with outdoors adventure. That upsets me. I understand that people must struggle with relationships. I realize love must be learned and earned, and that it can be lost through choices made. Some might applaud the thought of a lady determined to become her "own woman" in a man's world. Not me. What bothers me is not that my petite wife of more than four decades wants to compete in outdoors proficiency, but where in the hell does she—or anyone else—get the idea that all in nature belongs to men?

This book, then, is about two people in love sharing a life of exciting adventure and growing in the process. In reality it's about everyone over forty who has lived and loved and struggled together toward a common dream. What makes this particular book's storyline remarkable is how many times these people fell on their butts while doing it.

My Best Work is Done at the Office 320 pgs. 5½ x 8½ $19.95 (postpaid)
 Roland Cheek's popular stories of low chuckles and high adventure got their start far from bierstube and beltway, around wilderness campfires. The best of those riveting tales of wild people, wild places, and wild things eventually made their way into the guy's newspaper columns and radio scripts. As a result, Roland's audience exploded from a handful of campfire gatherers to a coast-to-coast mushroom cloud numbering in the hundreds of thousands.
 Now there's a book composed of the choicest of those stories. You can see for yourself why Roland is widely known as America's Rocky Mountain Sage; why his tongue-in-cheek wit is so irreverent, but so relevant; why fans re-read old newspapers for his columns and pause in their work or sleep to listen to him on the radio.

Chocolate Legs 320 pgs. 5½ x 8½ $19.95 (postpaid)
 Her story begins as an ursid Shirley Temple, a cute blond phenom amid the real-life Shangri-la of Glacier National Park's most scenic mountain valleys. In time, however, the curtsying knockout zoomed to Princess Diana-sized celebrity, demanding more than admiring glances and the flashing bulbs of paparazzi cameras. It was those outsized demands and an ever-growing haughtiness that attracted official attention.
 Chocolate Legs is an investigative journey into the controversial life and death of one of the best-known grizzly bears in the world; by a long-time journalist who has lived (and sometimes brushed near death) with the great beasts.

Montana's Bob Marshall Wilderness 80 pgs. 9 x 12 (coffee table size) $15.95 hardcover, $10.95 softcover (postpaid)
 97 full-color photos, over 10,000 words of where-to, how-to text about America's favorite wilderness.

See order form on reverse side

Order form for Roland Cheek's Books
See list of books on page 278

Telephone orders: 1-800-821-6784. *Visa, MasterCard or Discover only.*

Website orders: www.rolandcheek.com

Postal orders: Skyline Publishing
P.O. Box 1118 • Columbia Falls, MT 59912
Telephone: (406) 892-5560   Fax (406) 892-1922

Please send the following books:
(I understand I may return any Skyline Publishing book for a full refund—no questions asked.)

Title	Qty.	Cost Ea.	Total
_____	____	$ _____	$ _____
_____	____	$ _____	$ _____
_____	____	$ _____	$ _____
		Total Order:	$ _____

We pay cost of shipping and handling inside U.S.

Ship to: Name _____
          Address _____
          City _____ State _____ Zip _____
          Daytime phone number (_____) _____-_____
Payment: ☐ Check or Money Order
          Credit card: ☐ Visa ☐ MasterCard ☐ Discover
Card number _____
Name on card _____ Exp. date ___/___
Signature: _____